KATE MASCARENHAS is a part-Irish,
part-Seychellois midlander. Since 2017,
Kate has been a chartered psychologist.
Before that she worked as a copywriter,
a dolls' house maker, and a bookbinder.
She lives with her husband in a small
terraced house which she is slowly
filling with Sindy dolls. Her first novel,
The Psychology of Time Travel, was
published in 2018 to wide acclaim.

Also by Kate Mascarenhas

The Psychology of Time Travel

The Thief
ON THE
Winged Horse

KATE
MASCARENHAS

HEAD
of
ZEUS

Typeset by Divaddict Publishing Solutions Ltd

Printed and bound in Great Britain by
CPI Group (UK) Ltd, Croydon CRO 4YY

Head of Zeus Ltd
First Floor East
5–8 Hardwick Street
London EC1R 4RG

WWW.HEADOFZEUS.COM

Dedicated to Peter Flynn

Since 1820, Kendricks Workshop has made and sold magic dolls. The firm was founded by four sisters:

Lucy Kendrick, née Peyton (1798–1898)

Rebecca Jackson, née Peyton (1800–1864)

Sally Botham, née Peyton (1804–1884)

Jemima Ramsay, née Peyton (1802–1821)

In 2019 the workshop continues to trade as a family business. It is staffed by:

Fifty-one descendants of Lucy Kendrick, including:

Conrad Kendrick (1955–),
current owner of Kendricks Workshop

His twin brother Briar (1955–),
retired dolls' house maker

Briar's daughter Persephone (1998–),
the workshop sales assistant

Seventeen descendants of Rebecca Jackson, including:

Alastair Jackson (1984–),
Head Sorcerer at the workshop, and husband to
Rieko Kitegawa (1980–), furnisher of dolls' houses

Eighty descendants of Sally Botham, including:

Hedwig Mayhew (2000–),
housekeeper to Conrad Kendrick

Her mother Margot (1981–),
landlady of the workers' pub

Their cousin Dennis Botham (1946–),
Deputy Sorcerer

And no descendants of Jemima Ramsay.

1

In Oxford there lies a small river island called Paxton's Eyot. It is secluded from the nearby colleges, partly because of the dense trees growing at the perimeter. The Thames flows to the west, the Cherwell to the north, and a narrow ditch curves round the south-easterly side. It was here that, last September, a young stranger crossed the footbridge. He had paint-flecked fingers, and dark hair that fell into his eyes no matter how frequently he pushed it back. His name was Larkin. Larkin had come to the eyot in search of two things. The first was Magic. The second was A Job.

Almost as soon as he stepped onto the eyot he lost his mobile signal. But he had no desire to phone, or be phoned by, anyone he knew. The sun was low and bright in the sky and starlings were weaving in a murmuration above the trees. Larkin explored an orchard. The bark of one tree was engraved with the image of a man on a winged horse, and beneath it, a single word: THIEF. Undeterred, Larkin scrumped four quince and hid them in his bag.

Shortly the orchard gave way to a row of cottages. The eyot was less than a mile long, but that was sufficient to house a hundred families. And there, at the end of the terrace, Larkin came to his destination: the Kendricks' famous workrooms, the only source of magic dolls in this country or any other.

The stone façade resembled the Euston Arch, for the building was Roman in style, with tall pillars upholding a portico. The great doors to the shop were arsenic green and topped with a leaded fanlight. Larkin skipped up the central steps and lightly pushed the door open, into a compact hallway. On the walls were three wooden plaques painted with two centuries of names: the descendants of Kendrick, of Botham and of Jackson, together with relations by marriage. A fourth plaque was headed *Ramsay*, but was otherwise blank. Larkin spent some time reading the lists and of course he recognised the names. They were the same names available in the public records; the same lineage that Larkin had traced, in his teens, after his mother had disclosed that their own, official, family tree contained a falsehood.

Larkin stepped through the second set of doors, to where the Kendricks' dolls were on sale.

A young woman stood behind the counter, next to a brass till. She didn't acknowledge Larkin's entrance, apparently because she was engrossed in a ledger. Her black hair was artfully piled upon her head, Gibson-girl style. She was somewhat fat, had a complexion like bisque, and was scowling deeply – from concentration or bad mood Larkin couldn't yet say.

He turned his attention to the wares. The magic dolls lined every wall. They were shielded by iron bars. Each doll extended her right hand between the rails, as though beseeching the customer. Larkin placed his finger on the nearest tiny palm. Instantly he felt a rush of Heady Optimism. He removed his finger, and the Heady Optimism vanished as quickly. The doll was dimpled; she wore a taffeta dress and white lace cap. Her neighbour was dressed as a shepherdess, complete with crook, and stiff bow beneath her bonnet. At the touch of her hand, Bucolic Bliss swirled through Larkin with sweetness and intensity. He let her go, bringing the Bliss to an end.

There were many dozens more dolls. He caressed all of them, drawing a new feeling from each one. A china doll, with a cracked face, was the last of them. Despite the fracture her powers were intact. Her cold touch left him Gloriously Exultant. The sentiment thrashed inside him, against his ribs, in every pulse, and he savoured its depth and novelty. The doll watched him with blue glass eyes. Damaged, yet inspiring Exultation; how could Larkin resist purchasing her? He hadn't come to buy, but he now had no intention of leaving without the doll.

He approached the sales assistant. A name tag was pinned to her dress. *Persephone*. Romantic parents, seemingly.

"Yes?" she said. Her tone was so surly Larkin laughed. She made a poor ambassador.

"I'd like to buy the broken doll," he answered.

Persephone raised an eyebrow. Clearly, his laughter hadn't endeared her. But she said: "Good. I'll be glad to see the back of that one."

Larkin took a fat roll of bank notes from his inner pocket, in accordance with the price, and placed them on the table. Persephone gave them a perfunctory rifle, which showed either surprising faith in his honesty, or a disregard for Kendricks' bottom line. A trill marked the stowing of his cash in the till.

Persephone then slipped from behind the counter. She heaved back the iron railings and picked up the doll with the cracked face. She shoved the railings back into place with a clang.

"What caused the crack?" Larkin asked, when she'd returned to her station.

"I don't know." She placed the doll in a silk-lined box, which she slid across the counter before returning to her ledger. Larkin watched her write several entries in precise, lower case letters.

Evidently she thought their business was complete. But Larkin made no move to leave.

"I also wish to speak to Conrad Kendrick," he said, smiling.

"Why?" She didn't lift her head.

"I want to work here."

"Are you descended from Sally Botham?" she asked. "Or Rebecca Jackson?"

"No."

"You can't be a Kendrick!" Incredulous, she met his eye at last.

"No, I'm—"

"This is a family business. You must be descended from Botham, Jackson, or Kendrick to work here – or marry in. Conrad Kendrick won't consider anybody else."

"What if I said I'm descended from Jemima Ramsay?"

"I'd call you a liar." She spoke coolly, without condemnation, as if he bored her. "Jemima Ramsay died with her unborn child, in 1821, and left no other offspring."

"The child didn't die. Jemima Ramsay ran away with a French man, and her husband announced her death to avert gossip."

"That's not true." Persephone narrowed her gaze at him, perhaps weighing whether he was deluded or deceitful. "Jemima Ramsay is buried in St Ignatius's church."

"Will you allow Conrad Kendrick to judge the story for himself?" Larkin asked.

"I'd be in trouble if I allowed any Tom, Dick, or Harry to see him."

"What would make it worth your while?" Once more Larkin took a roll of money from his pocket, and she shook her head.

"Not that."

"Then what?" There must be something.

Her cheeks flushed. It was rather becoming. He waited.

Almost crossly, she demanded: "Give me your buttons."

"My buttons?" he repeated, sure he must have misheard.

"That's what would make it worth my while. Or don't bother, if you value your buttons more than meeting Conrad. Leave without seeing him, it makes no difference to me."

Larkin looked down at his coat buttons. They comprised half a dozen ebony ovals, and were of good vintage quality, but were otherwise unremarkable. Each was secured via two central holes apiece, which flanked a shallow ridge – as though someone had pinched the button between thumb and forefinger, and the wood had unexpectedly yielded.

"Very well," Larkin agreed, the buttons holding no particular value for him.

Persephone beckoned him, peremptorily. He crossed the boundary that separated customer from worker. She reached beneath the counter for a pair of gold scissors – they were around three inches long, and shaped like a stork. For the time it took to sever the buttons they stood toe to toe, close enough for him to detect the scent of apple soap on her person. He listened to the croak of scissors cutting thread, and felt a thrill of nerves, that a stranger held a blade to his chest. Particularly a stranger who demonstrated, in their short acquaintance, eccentricity and ill-temper.

"When will Conrad Kendrick expect me?" Larkin checked.

"Not till tomorrow morning. He accepts selected visitors between half eleven and half twelve, at his house. I'll tell him you requested an audience. He might even let you in, for a laugh. But he won't give you a job. Jemima Ramsay had no offspring. And Conrad will never hire an outsider."

"Too set in his ways?"

"If you like. He's nearly sixty-five." She bowed her head to cut the last button. Larkin observed a bee alight in the whorl of her hair. He was about to alert her, but it looked so at home there he said nothing.

When he left the shop he was satisfied. The meeting with Conrad Kendrick would take place; despite Persephone's warnings, Larkin was still sure that, face-to-face, he could secure himself an apprenticeship. Wouldn't that be wonderful, Larkin daydreamed? To sculpt those dolls? To command the emotion of whoever touched them? He deserved that chance, and it was in his grasp.

2

Outside Conrad Kendrick's house, the leaves were turning gold and russet. Hedwig Mayhew – tanned from summer, ochre plait twisted round her crown – was cutting yellow roses. She'd worked for Conrad since leaving school a year ago. Despite her youth she relished domestic management. The house – an early Georgian residence – had fallen into poor repair, so Hedwig had spent that year scheduling plasterers and chimney sweeps and plumbers. Builders fixed the failing lintels; masons repointed bricks. Then Hedwig paid them, as she was Conrad's representative, from Kendricks' bank account. Her favourite responsibility was settling bills, because she liked imagining that she, instead of Conrad, was immensely rich.

Today, as roses fell in Hedwig's creel, an ageing painter brushed the door with indigo gloss. Hedwig had just cut the final flower, when she saw a second man approach the gate. A young man, this time, smoking a cigarette. Presumably the stranger that Persephone, the Kendricks shop assistant, met the day before. He wore a faded t-shirt with Russian lettering, and black jeans. Though his coat was cut with expertise it was uncared for: all the buttons were missing, and the threads remained. His cheeks were hollow. Hedwig guessed he needed a good meal. And yet he was, to Hedwig's thinking, pretty, albeit in a disreputable way. Byronic curls, and startling blue eyes... Some people liked that kind of thing.

"My name's Larkin," he said. "Conrad Kendrick should be expecting me. I'm ten minutes early – they were cleaning my room at the Eyot Tavern, so I set out—"

"It's fine," she reassured him, smiling. Margot Mayhew, Hedwig's mother, ran the Tavern without much sensitivity for guests' requirements. "Conrad won't admit you yet... You'll have to wait until he's ready. I can take care of you till then."

She winked at him, cheerfully, and dropped her shears into the basket. Larkin followed her along the path. When they reached the door, the painter stood aside to let them pass and they crossed a crumpled stream of linen till their feet met chequered tile.

She gestured at the wooden pew, positioned by a coat of armour. "Take a seat."

He didn't move. She saw him looking at the marble stairs – or rather, looking at the spandrel, which had always been enclosed by iron bars. They caged the most important doll Conrad owned: the Paid Mourner.

In 1821, to mark the passing of her sister Jemima, Lucy Kendrick had made the Paid Mourner. The head was carved from wax; the limbs and chest from elm. No ordinary elmwood, either. Lucy broke a single bough from a tree Jemima planted as a girl. The tree was felled a century later. Kendricks Workshop used pieces for parquet flooring.

"That doll," Larkin said. "I've read about her, many times. May I take a closer look?"

"You can try."

He stepped towards the bars, and peered in. Hedwig joined him. By the half light, the doll was just discernible. Her face was painted cream and pink. A pair of crescents represented lowered eyes. She wore a feathered hat – the plumes as black as guillemots – which matched her velvet gown. The cage's single door was fourteen inches high, at shoulder level. Sitting on the latch were two iron figures, guarding the Paid Mourner as if they were her jailers.

"She's beautiful," Larkin whispered.

Hedwig shrugged, because exquisite detail, the very craft of miniatures, did not seem wondrous to her. Only financial worth inspired her interest. Growing up on Paxton's Eyot ensured her grasp of trade information. The most important thing about the Paid Mourner was the market value. Pride in Kendricks' wealth made Hedwig boast; she whispered, gleefully: "She's worth two million pounds."

Larkin's eyes widened. "Two million?"

Hedwig nodded.

"But there's no lock on the cage," Larkin muttered.

"Open it. I dare you." Mischief lay ahead.

The first step of lifting the latch on the cage door was gripping the iron jailers. No other way to move the latch was possible. With reverence, Larkin touched them both – and recoiled with a small cry.

"What happened?" Hedwig queried.

"The figures," said Larkin. "They feel like Consuming Paranoia!"

"Most effective, aren't they? And gloves don't protect you."

"But surely, if you were determined to—"

"The only living people who've opened that door are Conrad, and his brother Briar. No one else. The Paranoia always proves too much to bear."

"We'll see." He gripped the iron guards again; again he let them go.

"Don't feel bad about it," Hedwig said. "The sorcery's *very* strong... As strong as sorcery gets. Efficacy depends on good materials. Any enchantment grows more potent if it's laid on iron."

"I didn't see any iron dolls in the shop."

"The Sorcerers usually make them on request, for connoisseurs. The average buyer likes more ornamental, mobile dolls, and finds iron enchantments too intense. In general, iron's outsold by bisque and porcelain."

"Hm. I bought a china doll yesterday."

"Oh, did you?" Hedwig had assumed, from first impressions, *all* the dolls were dearer than he could afford. She suspected he may prioritise his hobby over food and clothing, even if his funds were meagre. Or perhaps – like Conrad, letting houses run to ruin – this man was rich and needed help to spend his money well. To gauge his cash flow, Hedwig asked: "Which china doll was that?"

"As far as I'm aware she didn't have a name. Her face was cracked. She made me feel Glorious Exultation."

"Ah... I know the one." Persephone's father, Briar, had kicked the doll in a drunken rage one afternoon, when he still worked at Kendricks. Following the incident he was persuaded to retire. The doll remained on the market, albeit at a reduced rate to reflect the damage. She still wasn't cheap.

"Did I make a good purchase?" Larkin's eyes were smiling.

"Yes, you did; I'm sure Persephone explained that *all* of Kendricks' dolls are good investments." Hedwig checked her watch. Eleven thirty on the dot. "Time to show you in."

They entered Conrad's drawing room where, as his years advanced, he spent the bulk of his time. Today he sat before the fire, besuited in olive green, embroidering cloth in petit point for miniature upholstery.

Conrad's basalt eyes appraised their visitor as Hedwig introduced him, but the stitching didn't cease.

He said: "My dear, the purple silk is missing."

"Should I find it now?"

"It isn't lost, it's stolen. The culprit's long flown. Remember, leave a bowl of milk outside this evening; he'll take that as ransom, and will return the thread tomorrow." Conrad held the old beliefs about appeasing the fae folk. Having given his instructions, he deigned to speak to Larkin. "My niece, Persephone, described you. And she said you have a tall tale to tell us."

The creel of roses hung from Hedwig's arm. She took it to the table, where a vacant vase awaited, and she would still be in earshot.

Larkin leant an elbow on the mantelpiece. *Presumptious*, Hedwig thought.

"I'm here as a distant relative," he began. "With a desire to reconcile."

"This doesn't have the ring of truth. Your speech is wrong. We speak a specific way in this family."

Larkin looked bemused; and Hedwig didn't blame him. All her relatives shared spoken cadences – a rhythm – but Larkin could fairly point out such things were learnt, not genetic.

After pausing, Larkin tried again. "The story of Jemima Ramsay's flight has passed down six generations of my family. I'm her descendant."

"No. She died in 1821 and left no issue," Conrad said firmly.

"She fled to Occitania with her lover; I've checked the church records there myself. The very month of her supposed funeral, she gave birth to a child who was baptised Philippe Jehan. She lived the rest of her life in France."

"She didn't; Oxford's parish records mark her passing here. She's buried up the road, at St Ignatius."

"The coffin's empty, I guarantee it. I've brought proof."

"Mr Larkin, I have no desire to see your fake papers *en français*."

"They're not fake; but in any case, I also have one of Jemima's possessions. It's been passed down – my father gave it to me, as his gave it to him." Larkin searched his inner pocket, then withdrew a small paper package, tied with twine.

Conrad stopped his sewing, finally, to watch Larkin pull the paper free. The twine unravelled – Hedwig shifted slightly for a better view – and Larkin triumphantly revealed

12

a threadbare book. Without its packaging the book emitted a mildew scent that filled the room.

Larkin passed the book to Conrad.

"Look," Larkin said. "She wrote her name on the flyleaf, and dated it."

"Anyone could write that. *You* could have written it."

"But I didn't."

Conrad turned the pages. "The rest is illegible. Just what's this book meant to be?"

"I don't know. It's been ruined by damp. One of the pages can be read; there's a diagram of a doll, all the limbs and joints labelled. Have you seen any of her other drawings? Does it resemble them?"

Hedwig knew that Conrad owned a safe for family documents. If pictures still existed, they were there. And Conrad seemed to recognise the diagram, because he took a lengthy look. She saw a subtle change in his expression. Conrad closed the book.

"Why d'you want to work for us, Mr Larkin?"

"To make people feel joy – and awe – and every other emotion that your magic brings. No other doll maker can teach me that. The Kendricks Workshop is unique."

"So it's sorcery that attracts you, not the craft of miniatures. But only the most gifted of our craftsmen are permitted to learn sorcery. I take it you lack craft?"

"Not quite. I studied Fine Art at Central Saint Martins, then spent a further two years training myself in the making of automata."

"Have you ever worked for a firm that specialises in dolls?"

"No. I only want to work for you."

A canny answer, Hedwig thought. Admitting prior allegiances, brief or otherwise, would rule Larkin out in Conrad's view. The Kendricks hoarded their knowledge jealously.

"Let's say I asked you to make a doll," suggested Conrad. "One that caught my likeness—"

"I'd make a grodnertal," Larkin interrupted.

Conrad chuckled. "Surely not! A wooden peg, sold for pennies? Do I look cheap to you?"

"No. Grodnertals are durable. They're hard to break."

"And what enchantment would be laid upon it?" Conrad pressed. "What feeling would it call to mind?"

The visitor dropped his gaze in deference. "Self-respect."

Another laugh from Conrad. Hedwig noted he was charmed. He wasn't, however, fully taken in.

"I believe your passion's genuine," said Conrad. "And the book is credible. Regrettably, that's not enough to work here. You see, I don't have arbitrary faith in birthright. What matters, over everything, is loyalty. Rewards for kin aren't automatic. I must *know* their past – and *know* how they will act in future – and *know* they'll never give our secrets to competitors. That's of utmost consequence. If we must have new blood, I permit the hiring of a suitably vetted spouse – for marriage is a solemn, and legally binding commitment to the interests of this family, not easily undone. *You* have made no such commitment; I don't know you; and I have no reason to believe you will be loyal."

"Let me convince you," Larkin pleaded, but Conrad merely handed him back the book.

Hedwig was unsurprised by Conrad's decision. Twice in the months since she'd held the housekeeping position, men had made eager applications to join their firm, undeterred by the knowledge Kendricks was a family business. On both occasions, Hedwig's own perspicacity had uncovered they were sent as corporate spies. Didn't it make sense, then, to be suspicious by default of Larkin – no matter how charming he was? Hedwig only differed from Conrad in her belief a talented enemy could be turned, with the right incentive, into an asset. But outwardly she must show support for his actions.

"I'll see you out," Hedwig said to Larkin.

He stared as if, till then, he'd forgotten she was there. "Do you believe I have a right to be here?"

"That isn't up to me."

"Why not? Which branch of the family are *you* from?"

"Botham." Hedwig said again: "I'll see you out."

"No need." He left the room, the door clicking softly shut behind him.

Conrad resumed his sewing. Hedwig took the vase to the bay, because the window overlooked the garden and she wished to see their visitor depart. She saw him walking down the path, towards the river. Angrily, it seemed; he kicked a stone. It was a shame he would be leaving. She again considered Larkin's readiness to buy the cracked doll, and what that signified of his finances. Paxton's Eyot was short of wealthy men. Oh, half a dozen Sorcerers had money saved, but they were all old and married.

"Has he gone?" asked Conrad.

"Yes. He said he stayed at my mama's last night

– presumably he's walking back there. Now you've turned him down he'll pack his bags and vanish, I expect."

"He didn't say where he came from. Only mentioned where he studied, and – which part of France did he sojourn in?"

"Occitania." She paused. "I wonder if Jemima Ramsay *did* elope there."

"Either way, he couldn't work for Kendricks."

"No... Except..." She chose her words with care. "That book looked genuine. And if it is, he might have *other* things she owned. Like books that aren't illegible. Or secret records, of her hexes, and..."

"Her enchantments!"

"Yes. Things worth a pretty penny, if he sold them. And even if he wasn't a spy, he might be tempted to take them where they're wanted. What other option would he have now?"

"You think I turned him down too rashly?"

"Not at all. You're so perceptive, Conrad, when it comes to character, and you're exactly right to value loyalty. I simply think this chap requires a watchful eye. That's easier if he works for you."

As he reflected, Conrad cupped his chin. "I *could* employ him, but in a reduced capacity. He'd only be permitted to craft the dolls; not lay enchantments, or be present when the Sorcerers do so. I'd inform the family he can't be privy to details of how enchantments work."

"Until he'd earned your trust."

"Understand, he may never deserve it. But if we hold the magic out as a reward, he'll stay, and we'll have him where we can see him. Quickly, catch him up – he can't have got too far."

She ran until she'd cleared the bend in the path, then slowed her pace despite her orders. Let Larkin reach the pub, and stew a little; maybe feel the disappointment of his hopes. She wanted him to be grateful for any offer; then he wouldn't challenge Conrad's conditions. She strategised this way in Conrad's interest, anticipating factors he often overlooked. Wealth had made him a poor judge of other people's motivations and reactions. So often, money had allowed him not to care how other people felt at all.

3

When Persephone Kendrick was six years old, her father built her a dolls' house. At Kendricks Workshop this was the old, unquestioned way of things; the making of dolls' houses is always about fathers and daughters.

Persephone had provided him with the rudiments of what she wanted. Two bedrooms – one for a parent; one for a child. A bathroom painted citrine. Real electric lights. He had drawn a sketch, of how the house would look, holding his pencil slightly crooked. His thumbs were misshapen, because he had broken them in fights many times over, and he always endured the fractures without getting them set. Each line on the page had a measurement attached. The shell of the house required seven pieces of wood, and the internal walls would need eight. He cut them from pine, with a hand saw, while Persephone watched, one plait end in her mouth. When the house was assembled he made the stairs, joining the treads and attaching spent matchsticks for balusters. Then he hung doors, swearing at the tiny hinges as he did so.

"Fucking things."

"It doesn't matter, Daddy, I don't need the doors to open," Persephone said hurriedly.

"If they stand ajar, they look more real." He persisted, so that every room had a glimpse of the next.

The first thing Persephone did when the house was finished was put her head inside. Her ear rested on the floor of the living room, and her nose was level with the carved mantelpiece. The house smelt of sawdust. Her father always smelt of sawdust, mingled with beer and sweat. She liked the smell, but it made her feel sad in a way she couldn't name.

"I've not got any dolls," she said. "The house is empty."

"You can buy some, if you like. I'll take you."

She'd never been inside her father's workplace before. Certainly she'd seen it from the outside; nearly every grown-up on the eyot worked there, and she had witnessed one conversation after another about its goings on. The dolls displayed in the shop were intriguing but her father pulled her swiftly past them, to the door at the back marked *Staff Only*. On the other side was a strange lift that her father said was called a paternoster. They jumped in, and watched two floors drop past before getting out again.

The sign hanging from the ceiling read *Sorcerers*. Six men, including Persephone's cousin Alastair, were seated at small tables, painting dolls' faces under bright spotlights. The centre of the floor was made from glass. When Persephone looked down she could see right through the building. On the level below, there were men making dolls' houses – that must be where her father usually did his job – and another window beneath them revealed the women on the first

20

floor, papering small walls and painting furniture. Their movements were busy, reminding Persephone of the ants in the formicarium at school.

Alastair stood up, wiping his hands on his coverall. He had a thick neck and slightly protuberant dark eyes which always put Persephone in mind of a frog.

"Briar," he greeted Persephone's father. "Good to see you – and with a visitor, too."

"She wants some dolls to play with. Nothing fragile, nothing like you make for sale – a strong maquette would do."

"Let's see what fits the bill."

Alastair led them to a windowless storeroom. A single, naked light bulb swung above their heads. Crates of unpainted wooden dolls, more rough hewn than the ones on sale, were piled upon the shelves.

"What kind d'you want?" Alastair asked.

"A little girl," Persephone said.

Alastair rummaged through one of the crates. He looked at one, shook his head, and put it back.

"A little girl, a little girl," he muttered, passing over this doll or that. "Here's a nice one, Sephone. *Endearing Candour.*"

He placed it in Persephone's hands. She searched its face, which was marked a dozen times by the whittling knife. The maker had carved large eyes and a sweet mouth. Persephone could feel the Candour welling in her. It was a peculiar sensation.

"She'll need a mum and dad," Alastair said, moving his attention to another crate.

"She doesn't," Persephone cried out. "Just a mummy, not a daddy doll."

Alastair looked at her father, a touch embarrassed. But her father only took off his glasses, and rubbed at the lenses with a cuff, as if he hadn't heard Persephone's outburst.

"I'll fetch a daddy anyway," Alastair said. "In case you change your mind."

More cursorily than before, he picked a pair of dolls from the nearest box, and handed them to her. Now she had three feelings jostling inside her. The Candour; Desire to Appease; and Cool Detachment. She followed Alastair and her father out of the storeroom, back to where the men were painting faces and looking down on all the other workers, and her cousin said he would wrap the dolls in paper for her. She let go of them with relief. As the foisted emotions ebbed, there was room for resentment to flourish. Alastair, and the men who made these dolls, had put these feelings in her. She wished she could make dolls – and work magic on them – so that the only feelings she felt were of her own making. She tried to imagine herself at one of the tiny tables, painting a porcelain face.

"Why aren't there any women up here?" she asked.

Her father and Alastair and the other men laughed.

"The candour's worked," said Dennis Botham, a stocky man with greying mutton chops, who was also Persephone's godfather.

"The women do interiors," her father said. "They've a knack for that, because they tidy homes in real life, too. Compared to men they're more emotional, so working sorcery on dolls would stir them up a lot."

"But you said Lucy Kendrick worked sorcery, you said she taught her sisters, who taught their sons—"

"They're dead," Dennis cut in. "And they had help."

"From who?"

"The Thief on the Winged Horse!"

"But—"

"I'm sorry," said her father to Alastair. "We'll be getting on now."

"It's all right, Briar." Alastair crouched, to Persephone's level. "When you're thirteen, Daddy will teach you how to lay an enchantment. Just the one, and it will be yours, forever. That's traditional on the eyot. If someone turns out to be good at dollcraft – if they're better than everyone else – we apprentice them as a Sorcerer, and they can learn *all* the other enchantments. Do you see? Only the very best people at craft get to do it as a job. Only they get to learn all the enchantments."

Persephone sensed there was some insult in this explanation, though she couldn't put it into words beyond asking, high-voiced with indignation: "How are *all* the best people men?"

"Let it go, now, girl," her father said, frowning.

The change in his expression silenced her. Alastair handed him the wrapped dolls, and they left.

Now, she was an adult. She wasn't making dolls on the top floor as she'd once imagined, despite repeatedly requesting an apprenticeship. She was out front, making sales, getting into trouble for being insufficiently cheerful with the customers. Two days after that stranger with the thin face had bought the Glorious Exultation doll, Persephone and the other workers were gathered on the ground floor for an announcement from Alastair. The stranger was at his side. He carried a doctor's bag.

"Settle down," Alastair began. "I know you've heard the rumours. Meet our new apprentice; this is Mr Larkin, who'll be training with the Sorcerers, subject to probationary restrictions."

"Welcome, Mr Larkin," said Galleren Kendrick – another of Persephone's cousins, from the architects' floor. Pointedly, he asked, "Are you a man of Kendrick, Botham or Jackson?"

"Ramsay," the stranger replied. "And just Larkin is fine."

A murmur rippled through the group. Persephone caught the eye of Rieko, Alastair's wife, a dark-bobbed Japanese woman with her hands in her dungaree pockets. She was twice Persephone's relative, because she was a distant cousin of Persephone's mother. Rieko ran the Interior Design department, and presumably discussed work matters with Alastair at home. But she shrugged her slight shoulders and shook her head at Persephone, as if to signal: *this is all news to me*.

Alastair coughed for attention. "Conrad Kendrick has been persuaded that our information on Jemima Ramsay was incomplete. It seems there's evidence that she lived, as did her offspring, giving rise to a line we weren't aware of. Larkin's keen to start a reconciliation."

Persephone thought of her own long-held desire to be a Sorcerer; no one in the workshop ever entertained her ambitions. This Larkin had arrived with a preposterous tale and less than a week later was given a job.

She walked to the front of the group.

"Does he have any skills?" she asked Alastair.

"We take apprentices with *promise*—" Alastair began, but Larkin raised a hand to halt him.

"I've brought a sample of my work," Larkin said, lifting his doctor's bag onto the nearest table. He opened it, and took out an intricate toy. The workers craned forward to look.

The toy comprised two figures: a young man in the tricorn hat of a highwayman, and at his side, a bonneted woman with a choker. Larkin twisted a key in the toy's base. The dolls shifted into motion. Swooping, the young man kissed the woman, and with his free arm, stole an even smaller doll – no bigger than an inch – from the woman's pocket.

The crowd sighed with pleasure. Persephone fell in love alongside them. The Kendricks did not make wind-up dolls as a rule; the mechanics distracted from the magic. But this had a fluidity of motion that was charming and, more importantly, showed Larkin's talent was genuine. With this proof of his ability, Persephone wished still more intensely that she were in his place. No, more than that; she wanted to *be* him. To have a vision, and to be permitted to realise it, was so enviable – and unimaginable to Persephone in her own form.

She reached out, to brush her fingertips against the thief. She felt nothing but cold tin.

"There's no enchantment," she whispered.

"No," Alastair said. "And until further notice, you

mustn't discuss how enchantments are laid in his presence. Larkin's familial tie, along with his obvious craft, make him more than eligible for the job. But by Conrad's orders he must serve a probationary period. If we're satisfied with his attitude and progress in post then he'll learn all the enchantments in due course. In the meantime, *I'll* work sorcery on Larkin's dolls."

That was interesting. Larkin hadn't wholly got his own way yet, then. Still he was smiling as he returned the highwayman to the doctor's bag. Why shouldn't he smile? When Persephone first met him, she thought his confidence was misplaced; he had no justification to state so boldly that Conrad would believe him. But he *had* been believed. Now he would be taught by the best crafts people in the world, and would be further rewarded in time. He would be one of the men on the top floor, like Alastair and Dennis, who decided how other people should feel.

The workers drifted back to their benches, and Persephone returned to her till. Dennis took some paint and a brush to the foyer, where he would add Larkin's name to the lists on the wall. Persephone kept thinking of Larkin's smile. In the solitude of the shop, she tried to smile that way at the dolls. It hurt almost immediately, and for once she was glad to hear the ring of the bell as a customer entered.

4

On the morning Larkin started his apprenticeship, Hedwig was fulfilling routine duties, which included checks on their supplies for autumn, starting with a visit to the cellar. But she paused at the open doorway. A light had been left on below. As Conrad rarely ventured into this part of the house, and she'd not been below ground either, the glow aroused suspicion.

She looked down from the highest stair, which let her see a narrow sliver of the cellar, and it seemed empty. But she heard the shuffle of feet.

"Who's there?" demanded Hedwig.

A dishevelled figure shambled from an alcove. Briar; Conrad's twin.

"Good heavens, Briar!" Hedwig took the steps two at a time. "Whenever did you get here? And *how* did you get in?"

"I let myself through the back last night." Briar paused to clear the rattle from his throat. "I didn't mean to stay this long, or fall asleep... Just thought I'd borrow a few things we ran out of at home."

A door connected the cellar to the lower garden; Hedwig glanced at it, concerned he'd forced an entry, but there wasn't any broken glass or splintered wood. Perhaps the house painter had left it unlocked. She'd have stern words with him for that.

"Briar, you only have to ask us if you need essentials." Hedwig knew he didn't need essentials. Conrad's stocks of alcohol were in the cellar, and Briar reeked of whisky fumes.

He scoffed. "Ask you! By rights the house and everything in it ought to be mine."

This was an established grievance: Briar was the oldest son, which should have given him the strongest claim to the house, however his father's will excluded him. For years he'd harped on it, exhausting everybody.

"Briar, if you've been here hours then Sephy must be terribly worried."

"Serves her right." He sucked his teeth. "The little madam poured my scotch down the sink. She's disrespectful."

"Good for her. Now come on, out with you. I'm busy."

"Yes, yes."

She nudged him closer to the door. He placed a hand on the jamb, and searched his pocket, which produced a key. He shoved it in the lock.

"Is that key *ours*?!" exclaimed Hedwig.

Briar must have had it since his father's death. How many times had they been raided without knowing?

"I own this key," he said thickly.

"Be a pet and hand it over? I don't want to change the locks."

He swore, but passed the key to her.

"And the front door, too?" she prompted.

He relinquished a second key with equal grace before departure. Possibly he'd cut duplicates; on reflection, changing locks would still be prudent. Briar was quite out of control. Seph should keep him on a tighter rein.

Hedwig was at her desk by half past ten. She telephoned Saint Martins and enquired if a reference was available for Larkin. The administrator confirmed that Larkin graduated with a first, in Fine Art, two years previously. They connected her to his old tutor – an avuncular academic by the name of Emlyn Madoc.

"How delightful that Larkin should be working for you," he said. "I'm a Kendricks enthusiast myself. I own several of your magic dolls."

"Is that how Larkin heard of us originally? Through you?"

"I don't believe so. We talked of dollcraft often but he was already well informed. He said something of being a distant relation to the Kendricks dynasty."

In which case Larkin's lie about Jemima Ramsay's child – if lie it was – had been maintained since Larkin's student days.

"If I may say," Madoc continued, "you're lucky to have him. He specialised in sculpture and installation, where he excelled. His focus was remarkable."

"We feel very fortunate. So lucky to have snagged him from his last employers—" Hedwig rustled her notebook for effect. "Oh, *what* was their name again?"

"I'm sure he'd tell you himself of any relevant positions; to my knowledge he wasn't working at all. It was always his intention to travel for a while after his degree – in Europe if not further."

"Satisfy my curiosity; not many people get to travel for two years without employment. Does he have an independent income?"

"I believe he's financially supported by a family member, yes, but I'd rather not be drawn on that if you don't mind. We're straying far afield of his academic record."

As Madoc would supply no further information, Hedwig gave her thanks and said goodbye. Soon it would be time for elevenses. She fetched the tea and biscuits from the kitchen then called on Conrad in the drawing room to update him.

He occupied, as usual, the mustard velvet chair by the hearth. His shoeless feet were on the pouffe and his mouth was twisted with discomfort.

"Put aside those fripperies," he said of her refreshments. "I couldn't touch a morsel. I arose with throbbing pains between my shoulder blades, and they are yet to abate."

Hedwig placed the tea upon the table, sure he'd want some soon. Without waiting to be asked she stood behind him and massaged his neck and back. She took his grunt as thanks.

"I spoke to Larkin's college earlier. They said we're fortunate to have him."

"That remains to be seen. By his own account he left

there two years ago – and wouldn't a promising student have been snapped up, somewhere, in the meantime? We don't know his allegiance."

"You're right; we don't." She didn't say that Conrad was mistaken in his understanding of allegiances. He thought they were the product of enduring hierarchies, which depended on a natural longing for order. In his view, disloyal acts occurred when somebody misapprehended their place; the punishment must teach them their correct rank, and reassure everybody else in the tribe that order had been maintained. Whereas Hedwig knew that *any* person's allegiances could change, if you understood a person's motivations, and manipulated them accordingly. It was the only method by which she ever got her way.

Beneath her fingers, Conrad's shoulders gradually relaxed. She ventured a question. "Have you heard of Emlyn Madoc?"

"Gosh yes. Madoc's a collector, and a committed one. He even wrote a book about us recently." Conrad gestured at the bookcase by the window. "What brought him to mind?"

"He's the lecturer who gave me Larkin's reference."

"Hm. I expect Madoc would salivate at learning our secrets. He's spent enough money with us over the years. Maybe we were mistaken to think Larkin was tied to another firm. Perhaps he's working for an individual – an obsessive hobbyist."

"It might be nothing," Hedwig mused.

"My dear," Conrad said. "Would you pass me one of those shortbread fingers now?"

She served his tea in a china cup with biscuits balanced

31

on the saucer. While he sipped she scrutinised the bookcase, scanning spines until she spotted Madoc's hardback near the top. *Authenticity and Appropriation in Doll Making* was the name.

She thumbed the pages, pausing when she saw the Kendricks mentioned, which was often, though Conrad had exaggerated when he said the book was *about* them. She lingered on one particular paragraph:

How do Kendricks lay enchantments? It's the best-kept corporate secret in the world, and has been for two centuries. I find it quite extraordinary that, in a whole two hundred years, no employee has ever broken ranks by leaking the secret or setting up a rival firm. Theories abound as to why. The most popular concern Harold Kendrick, Lucy's eldest son, who managed the firm from the age of twenty-one and was known to be a cut-throat businessman. His correspondence contains veiled references to securing, through sorcery, the loyalty of his relatives by blood and marriage, for generations to come. But there are signs Harold's spell is wearing off. Recent years have seen the first divorces granted on the eyot, and a number of young people seeking employment outside Kendricks, reflecting a weakening of familial ties that would have been unthinkable even a generation earlier. How much longer can Kendricks keep their methods a secret? It is surely only a matter of time before a disgruntled ex-wife or a prodigal son spills the beans.

Hedwig tutted. Clearly Madoc *was* salivating at their secrets. She turned to the front matter to check which other books Madoc had written.

And her eye was caught by the dedication.

For Larkin.

Surely that couldn't be typical? Did lecturers often dedicate books to their students? Hedwig hadn't been to university, but it seemed inappropriate. Even in the kindest light it suggested favouritism, which lent credence to Conrad's theory Madoc and Larkin were collaborators.

"Hedwig, I feel abandoned," Conrad said. "As a companion you make a fine bookworm, I must say!"

"Just coming." Hedwig replaced the book on the shelf. She would keep watching Larkin.

5

Persephone sat alone in her bedroom, at the small dressing table that made do for a workbench. She dipped her slenderest paintbrush in a cup of chocolate acrylic. The buttons she'd cut from Larkin's coat lay before her in a row. Selecting one, she held the brush above it, poised, yet lacking the nerve to make a mark.

Focus, she scolded herself. Her attention was divided. She didn't worry, precisely, when Briar failed to return home for the night. She imagined him lying in a gutter, his head caved in by a mugger, or passed out on a bench as he succumbed to hypothermia. The images were persistent, but failed to raise her pulse or sicken her, because she had been picturing them since she was old enough to know he could come to harm. They were simply there in her mind, as an unfolding reel which she experienced passively.

She concentrated on circling the eyelet with her chosen paint, in a single, fluid line. *That doesn't look too bad*, she conceded.

Downstairs the front door banged. It could only be her father, because they lived by themselves in the little house; her mother had moved to Berwick nine years ago. Persephone felt commingled relief and irritation at her father's safe return. She listened to the familiar thwack against the wall as he discarded first one boot, then a second. The white noise of the pipes told her he had turned on a kitchen tap. Finally she heard the wheeze of the stairs as he ascended.

When he opened the door, he was odorous, but hale, as far as she could tell. He was holding a chipped mug of tea, and a roll of Jammy Dodgers was wedged between his side and his elbow. This must be his peace offering for his petulance over the scotch in the sink. Neither of them would mention that dispute now; nor would they discuss where he had been in the meantime. This was how they proceeded after any explosion of temper. A veil would be drawn down, and though they might refer to it in gestures, Persephone knew speaking out loud of prior arguments risked reignition.

"Just put the tea there," she said, nodding at the corner of her dresser.

He obliged. She attempted to circle the remaining eyelet. This time the line wobbled like a child on training wheels.

"Shit." She put down the brush in frustration. No; not only frustration, but temper. Why? Why would she get angry, at so small a thing as a crooked line of paint, but not at her father letting her think he lay injured on the streets of Oxford?

"You're very flushed," her father said, hesitantly.

"It's just warm in here."

He picked up the button. "What's this? Is it a little face you're making?"

"Kind of. The ridge in the button is the nose, the holes are the eyes. I saw them and thought they'd be a good shape for a doll's face, if I could paint them well enough."

Briar returned the button to her, and looked at his daughter fully.

"You're very flushed," he repeated.

"I'm *fine*."

"You know, Seph," he said, "sorcery's no job for a woman."

"So everyone says."

"It's just – all the energy you put into improving your craft – you're chasing something that's not meant for you."

"But serving in the shop *is* for me?"

"You have a point there," he said. "If you were like Cosima Botham, or Hedwig Mayhew – or if you were like… your mother… serving in the shop would be a better fit. They have the gift of persuasion. And they like it, talking people into things. But you're not like them. You're like me."

Jesus, she thought, *don't make me even crosser.*

He must have thought he'd said too much, because he beat a retreat to the hall. The added distance allowed him to finish, as if indulging an afterthought. "There has to be another option," he said. "Not just sorcery, or working in the shop. You're a bright girl. Don't waste your time over either of them."

Persephone swirled her paintbrush in the water jar. She heard her father walk to his own room, where she suspected he'd sleep till it was time for dinner.

*

Persephone spent most of her childhood trying to understand why there were no women Sorcerers. When she was around ten, an incident by the riverside increased her suspicion that her father, Alastair, and Dennis were in the wrong by saying it wasn't possible.

Her mother had bought her rollerskates, and she was experimenting with which areas near home provided the smoothest surface. So far, Jackdaw Lane – which was the closest tarmacked street – was the best for gliding cleanly. The lane was the very furthest Persephone was willing to stray; it was nearly at the main road, and well past the psychological barrier represented by the eyot's footbridge. When she felt she had skated enough, she returned to the grassy path that bordered the river. She traipsed through cornflowers, lifting her feet because the wheels wouldn't turn in the mud. The skates added unaccustomed weight and she grew breathless.

Before she reached the cottages she paused to rest by a wooden bench. An old woman was sitting on it. She was a stranger to Persephone, which was remarkable enough on the eyot, where everyone knew everyone.

"Hello," Persephone ventured.

The woman shot Persephone a look of indignation, and said nothing. She had the short chin of a person with no teeth in, but she was otherwise neat, with her white hair bobbed and combed, and a brightly coloured shawl about her shoulders. In her hand she held a paring knife.

The woman searched within the folds of her shawl. She

took out a cube of pale brown soap, which was about two inches long.

"Are you lost?" Persephone asked. She noticed the woman was wearing socks without shoes, and the mud was seeping into the white cotton. The old woman ignored Persephone's question. She took the knife to two corners of the soap, cutting a pair of tiny facets, top and bottom. The soap fragments dusted her lap.

Persephone sat on the end of the bench. She shuffled closer, keeping her eyes on the old woman as if she were a squirrel who might bolt if you came too near. Now the woman made a further incision, a third of the way down the cube corner. It formed a shallow *v*. On either side of it she cut two horizontal lines.

Finally, she spoke: "That is the bridge of the nose. Do you see? Between a pair of eyes."

Persephone nodded, although she didn't see, just yet, anything in the soap that resembled eyes or a nose.

Directly beneath the horizontal lines, the old woman made one downward cut, and one upward to meet it, creating a small pyramid. This, Persephone recognised, was more nose-shaped. To mark the nostrils the woman hollowed out two specks of soap.

"It is very important to leave in the septum," she said. Septum wasn't a word Persephone knew, but the woman tapped her knife on the narrow strip of soap dividing the nostrils. Persephone raised a hand to her own septum, to check its shape.

The old woman adjusted her grip on the knife. Instead of curling her fist around it, she now held it like a pencil. With the tip she cut two inverted pyramids on either side of the nose, far deeper than the other cuts she had made.

"You must put the knife in straight," she told Persephone. "No wiggling it around! The blade would break!"

"Are you a Sorcerer?" Persephone whispered, because the instructions suggested experience.

The old woman nodded.

"Once," she said. "In the past."

With her pencil-knife she continued. She made two swooping smile lines, again very deep, running from the sides of the nose. This addition gave the impression of cheeks. Of all the lines the woman had made, these were the first to be curved, not angular, and they brought a humanity to the face.

"I must add a mouth." The woman made a horizontal cut in a straight line. That interested Persephone, because when she drew a mouth on a piece of paper it was always *u*-shaped, and it occurred to her for the first time that nobody's mouth was shaped that way.

A second line, beneath the mouth, made a lower lip.

"Let's give her a little shave. Yes? Let's shave her little chin." The woman rolled the knife around the bottom corner of the soap, paring papery flakes away. Once she was satisfied with the chin she defined the nose more clearly and cut deeper into the eyes, to create shadows.

She took a second piece of soap from her shawl. This one had already been cut into a torso, arms, and legs. The torso did not look like any other doll Persephone had seen from the shop; the soap breasts were unmatched sizes. The stomach was marked with small, wriggling lines like the ones Persephone had seen on her own mother's belly, the marks she said came from growing Persephone inside her. Now the old woman licked the base of the soap head – Persephone shuddered in sympathy at how bitter it must taste – and sealed it to the neck.

Distantly, Persephone saw one of the Sorcerers, Barnaby Sabin, running across the muddy turf towards them.

"Oh no," groaned the old woman. She handed the knife and doll to Persephone. "Take these. Hide them in your pockets."

Barnaby's face was very red when he reached them.

"Hester," he scolded. "What are you doing wandering off?"

She said nothing.

"Augusta's been worried sick."

"Goodbye," Persephone said, sensing that the old woman was in trouble. Barnaby seemed to register she was there for the first time.

"Why didn't you let us know, Seph? We've been looking for her everywhere."

Persephone bristled. "I didn't know who she was."

At this Barnaby's face softened somewhat. "No. No, I don't imagine you would. She mostly has to stay indoors these days."

"How old is she?" Persephone asked.

"One hundred and eight," and then he was preoccupied with cajoling Hester from her seat, so Persephone left, half skating, half wading her way home through the mud. She sat on the front doorstep to remove her skates, and took the knife and doll surreptitiously from her pocket. The doll had the slightest undertone of an enchantment. Maybe soap didn't hold enchantments well. But it was definitely there. *Courage*, the doll evoked in a whisper. Persephone knew the Sorcerers had lied when they said it wasn't a woman's job.

6

In his first few weeks, Larkin made good progress in Kendricks Workshop. Each morning he arrived at seven for a twelve-hour day. Making dolls was hard on the eyes, the fingers and the spine; Larkin took solitary walks round the eyot at lunchtime, to allow his bones to decompress. But he was always eager to return to his workbench. The world outside, and the people that walked upon it, with their hidden thoughts and inclinations, seemed insubstantial compared to the small figures forming beneath his chisel. Most of the time he made wooden maquettes. These practice pieces, Dennis told him, were appropriate for an apprentice, as he could learn without the pressure of making dolls for sale until otherwise instructed. Larkin didn't protest that he was a practised, and nuanced, whittler. He obeyed; he perfected the exact angle of a doll's nose, the slenderness of her eyebrow, the curve of her ear. So absorbed was he in this work that when, one Friday afternoon, Dennis approached Larkin's workbench, Larkin twice failed to respond to his name.

He apologised for his inattention, and asked: "Am I needed?"

"The workshop's ahead of schedule. The other chaps are finishing early for the weekend. You can go with them if you like. But if you're tiring of maquettes, I can guide you in a new skill this afternoon, while things are quiet. Do you have a preference for what you learn next?"

Larkin sensed, in the offer, an implicit approval of his good work. He thought he could lose nothing by being bold.

"Enchantments," he said. "Teach me how to lay enchantments."

Dennis laughed uneasily. So far they'd adhered to Conrad's edict that the Sorcerers mustn't share their enchantments with Larkin. To maintain their secrecy, the six men carried out this aspect of their work after Larkin left the workshop each night.

"You can learn enchantments when you're more settled in," Dennis said. "For now, let's test your mettle in another material. Is there any medium besides wood that you'd like to try? Ceramics?"

Larkin brushed sawdust from the maquette, taking his time to reply because he feared his disappointment would show. He had applied himself these past weeks to show he *was* settling in. And Larkin was sure he'd told Alastair he already had some skill with porcelain; he was no more a novice with ceramics than he was with wood. But perhaps Dennis didn't know that – and in any case, he mustn't think Larkin was petulant.

"Might we try iron?" Larkin asked. Since seeing the Paid Mourner at close range – or rather, the guards that stood on the latch – Larkin had been intrigued by the possibilities of iron dolls, and particularly what Hedwig Mayhew said about the intensity of feeling they allowed. Larkin knew the basics of smithing, but so far hadn't been shown the forge. If Dennis agreed then Larkin would at least see some more of what Kendricks had to offer.

"Iron's a niche market," Dennis said, his eyebrows raised in surprise. "But if you'd like to learn more about it... I don't see why you shouldn't."

They went together to the small brick forge that stood behind the workshop. Dennis explained that the forge was run on coal. He demonstrated how the fire was lit and controlled, before urging Larkin to take a long rod of iron and heat the tip till it glowed white and amber. Silently Larkin accepted the instruction; a refresher did no harm.

"Now place it on the anvil," Dennis said. "You need a good strong surface to work upon."

He handed Larkin a hammer – more of a mallet, to Larkin's thinking – and encouraged him to strike the iron flat with repeated blows. Larkin weighed the hammer in his hand before beginning, judging it to be at least two pounds. He swung it with satisfaction.

"You need to work quickly," Dennis explained. "Quick blows, in succession, before the iron cools."

The heat from the dwindling forge and the exertion of striking made Larkin's skin itch beneath his cotton overalls. Dennis produced a series of additional tools, each secured through a hole in the anvil and designed variously to curl, pierce or twist the iron into the desired form. Eventually a flat, but undoubtedly human figure took shape upon the anvil.

"She has a truculent set to the shoulders," Dennis observed. "And her fists are up."

Satisfied with this appraisal, Larkin laughed.

"What enchantment would you like me to lay upon her?" Dennis asked.

Larkin had already been considering the matter while he worked.

"Determined Perseverance." He believed such an enchantment would suit her weight and rigidity as well as his own endeavours on the eyot. Still, with Dennis's question he no longer felt like laughing. It shouldn't be Dennis laying the enchantment. Larkin should be permitted to do so himself.

Shortly after seven that evening, Larkin finished work for the weekend. As usual he stepped into the paternoster alone; except, instead of travelling all the way down, he hopped out on the second floor. The lights were off there, as the architects had already left. But there was some illumination from the glass ceiling above. The half-constructed wooden houses, which lay all about, resembled a moonlit village.

Larkin could see, from below, the Sorcerers' workroom. He walked between the cottages and mansions, trying to find the best vantage, before standing on a drafting stool to gain height. This gave him a partial view of Dennis, at his small work table, handling the iron doll. Dennis dampened a cloth and swabbed the doll's back. He brought the doll close to his face – as if to sniff it, or kiss it.

At that moment, the door opened behind Larkin with a

rasp. He didn't stir – as if lack of movement could trick the onlooker into thinking he wasn't really there. Above him, Dennis shuffled his feet, scraped back his chair and made for the stockroom.

Only then did Larkin turn, to see his captor. Persephone was staring at him from the doorway. She wore a black coat with a plush collar. In her hand was a magnetic jig, which the men used during dolls' house making to hold small pieces in place. Swiftly she hid the jig behind her back. Her gaze flickered from him, to the glass ceiling above, and back again.

Larkin stepped down from the stool – boldly, to convey nothing in his behaviour was worth challenging. Neither of them spoke, and she didn't stop him when he made for the paternoster.

By the time Larkin reached the Eyot Tavern, he had persuaded himself he was in the clear. He would face no consequences for peeking when he shouldn't – for what had Persephone witnessed, after all? Merely Larkin on the wrong floor after closing, which there could be any number of reasonable explanations for, once he'd given it some thought.

The Tavern had an ornate interior, rather than the rustic aesthetic favoured by the pubs in central Oxford; red flock walls, gilt light fittings, and a ceiling heavy with Lincrusta. The building was very tall with rooms to let, including Larkin's own utilitarian lodgings, however the bar room was narrow, which quickly created the impression of a packed venue. That night it was busy with weekend celebrants. Yet Larkin sat alone for half an hour; which reflected, no doubt, his status as an outsider.

Just as he contemplated retiring to his room, Persephone entered the bar. Despite the lack of connectivity, Larkin took out his phone and scrolled through some old messages, as that seemed less suggestive of guilt than staring in Persephone's direction.

She approached the table a few minutes later with a half of stout. She placed it before Larkin and sat on the velour stool opposite. This was, for Persephone, remarkably conciliatory, though she didn't bother with any other niceties such as saying hello.

Instead, she stated: "You have to follow Conrad's rules."

"I'm sorry?" Larkin feigned incomprehension.

"Stop pretending. You know what I'm talking about. Conrad said you can't learn anything about enchantments yet. If you play spies, eventually you'll get into trouble."

A cheer rose on the opposite side of the room. Larkin looked across, to see a group of interior designers crowing over Jenga blocks. Persephone awaited his response.

"You're right," Larkin gave in, and it wasn't wholly appeasement. He intended to be obedient now; the risk of being expelled simply wasn't worth finding out the enchantments sooner. He'd win them by demonstrating his value to the company, even if it took longer. That was what he'd learnt from his scare – provided his superiors were lenient this time. "You know I didn't actually *see* anything?"

"Yes. I arrived in time."

"Have you told Alastair yet?"

"Alastair doesn't need to know. I'd land myself in it, too. So we're agreed? Neither of us says anything about it again, and you'll be more careful."

He didn't understand why Persephone would be punished for his misdemeanour. Then he recollected the way she had hidden the jig behind her back and realised that she wasn't meant to be on the second floor any more than he was. She didn't have permission to take the jig. Why she would want it was beyond him. She was a puzzle. He had thought so at their first meeting in the shop, since when they had barely exchanged words. She didn't really speak with anyone at Kendricks, though she occasionally growled at them.

"I should have thanked you," he said now. "For arranging the initial meeting with Conrad."

She rolled her eyes. "I don't have any influence over Conrad. He must have thought you were good, to give you a job."

"But I couldn't get to him without your say-so."

"No, all right – you couldn't, I suppose."

"I hope my coat buttons were useful." Larkin paused, to allow her to clarify her need of them, but she said nothing; so he prompted, "You sew, I take it?"

"What difference does it make?"

He laughed nervously. "I don't really have an answer to that."

"Sorry, I didn't mean to – I didn't want to be rude." A blush rose on her neck. "I just liked the buttons' shape and size. It made them suitable for a project I'm working on."

He sipped some of the stout. "You didn't buy yourself a drink. Shall I get you one?"

"No. I don't like alcohol."

"A soft drink, then. I feel bad; people can see you sitting there without one. They'll assume I'm ungallant."

"I see. I didn't think. I'm not thirsty at all. An orange juice is fine, if you really want to buy something, and don't mind me leaving it."

The queue at the bar was several people deep. He half expected Persephone to have left by the time he returned, due to her lack of social graces, but she was still where he had left her. She had taken off her coat, which indicated a willingness to stay for a while. He was glad of it. They shared a secret now, bound by their mutual desire not to get caught by Alastair. And that made them allies.

7

Three young women sat together in the snug, adjacent to the public bar: pink-haired Daisy Gilman; Imogen Strange, a freckled girl with chestnut curls who had been mute since infancy; and Hedwig, their implicit leader.

They'd gathered to make Venetian masks, in preparation for the yearly masquerade. The celebration, scheduled for the following weekend, took place in Conrad's house, and was an opportunity to bid the autumn farewell. Everyone approached by rowing boat, with lanterns aloft, if river levels permitted. Other than their masks, the guests dressed unfussily – the women wore dark gowns, the men vicuna frock coats – as the ground was often boggy in October. Games and bonfires were the evening's chief attractions.

Hedwig, Imogen, and Daisy held a plain mask apiece. Upon the tabletop were jewel-coloured paint pots, trays of sequins, glittering studs, and feathers, intended for embellishment. The snug was, in its smallness, fully occupied by their endeavour. Daisy briefly left her station to change the jam jar water. On returning, she announced: "Persephone and Larkin are drinking together."

Imogen forsook her mask at once, to spy with Daisy through the etched window, temples touching. Hedwig wasn't crass enough to join them, but awaited further details, regardless.

My word, they are together! Imogen signed. *Whatever's going on there?*

Hedwig guessed Persephone had noticed Larkin's good looks and deep pockets. Sitting one-to-one with such a new arrival was a risk. Most employees recognised that Conrad hadn't given Larkin full approval. Larkin was apprenticed to the Sorcerers, which indicated that – for now – he was a valued fixture; yet he was excluded from laying enchantments, rendering his status on the eyot ambiguous. Hadn't this occurred to Sephy? What would happen to her, if she fraternised with him, and Conrad ruled him too untrustworthy to take on permanently? Wouldn't Sephy's loyalty be questioned by default? She should have kept their meetings secret. Hedwig concealed her own affairs from Conrad, because he insisted on vetting any new partner unfamiliar to the eyot.

"I bet it's *not* romantic," Daisy said. "The Eyot Tavern isn't a romantic place to meet, is it? And have you ever heard of Sephy going out with *anyone*? She probably just saw an empty chair and took it. Do they *look* like they're on a date? Her face is looking very disagreeable."

That's how she always looks, signed Imogen. She laughed with Daisy.

"Girls," Hedwig said reproachfully.

I think it is *a date*, signed Imogen. *They're mirroring one another. What a sly cat Persephone is.*

Seph had never come across as calculating. Still, it didn't do to underestimate a person; maybe she intended to ensnare Larkin, and his income, while the other women showed excessive caution.

"Daisy, fetch him," Hedwig said. "We need assistance."

"With…?" asked Daisy scornfully.

"Masks, you goose! He graduated in Fine Art. That should help us considerably."

"And if he doesn't want to come?"

"He will – just say we need his insight." Flattery, in Hedwig's view, was always a persuasive strategy.

During Daisy's absence, Imogen divided up the diamante studs, and argued that her paintbrush was too stubby. Shortly, Daisy reappeared with Larkin, and instructed him to take a seat.

"I'm not sure what help I can be," he said.

"I heard you went to art school." Daisy sat upon the arm of Hedwig's chair.

"Yes – but you make masks every year," Larkin said. "By now, I'm sure you're all experts, degree or not."

"Daisy's just completed her own degree," said Hedwig. "In Italian!"

"*Ganzo! Essere in gamba*," Larkin said to Daisy.

Daisy shrugged. "*È il mio cavallo di battaglia.*"

"Do share," Hedwig urged.

"We exchanged pleasantries – that's all," explained Larkin.

"I expect you've worked in Italy," said Hedwig. Larkin

still had that mysterious lull in his employment history. Italy was just a hop, skip, and a jump away from Occitania.

"No," Larkin said. "My Italian is very basic. I learnt a few phrases to impress a girl."

"And was she impressed?" Daisy asked.

He laughed. "Initially."

"Was this a girl at university?" enquired Hedwig.

"Yes, actually."

"D'you get nostalgic, for your student days?"

"There's no point in missing university. I don't think I ever miss anything. When a time has gone, it's gone."

"That's never stopped me missing a time – or place, or person," Daisy cut in.

More fool Daisy; Hedwig agreed with Larkin, and never felt nostalgic. It was pointless loving something that was dead.

Imogen scanned the table, lifted paint pots, and nudged the bowl of sequins to one side. *Where did the tweezers go?* she signed. *I used them to position some sequins.*

Nobody knew what had happened to the tweezers.

"Leave your glass of wine out on the window ledge," suggested Daisy. "That should suffice."

Imogen swung the window wide, admitting an October draught. She balanced her unsipped grenache on the ledge before drawing the window back again with a shiver.

"Hang on," Larkin said. "What's wrong with Imogen's drink?"

"Nothing," answered Daisy. "It's an old eyot superstition. When we lose an object, we say it's been taken by the Thief; he's one of the fae folk, and he rides a winged horse. He only returns what we've lost when we offer something in exchange."

"What a racket," Larkin said. "There's an engraved tree, isn't there, in the quince orchard? The first day I arrived, I saw a man on a winged horse scratched on the bark."

"Imogen's grandmother did that, to warn people to leave those quince for the Thief," Hedwig explained, though she strongly suspected Imogen's grandmother of picking the quince herself.

"Will I run into him, this Thief?" Larkin said.

"He's tricksy and elusive," Hedwig said. She meant she'd never seen him. Only a few eyot residents claimed they had; even Conrad, who fervently believed the Thief must be obeyed, was yet to actually meet him. Hedwig trusted in the Thief's existence. She also knew that residents weren't above blaming him for their own light fingers. It was bad etiquette on the eyot to say as much out loud.

Daisy, spurning etiquette, said: "D'you remember when Dennis's hip flask went missing? He made an offering but the flask never showed up again. I always thought that Briar Kendrick took it."

"We don't know that." Hedwig saw a glint of metal in the bowl of feathers. She pulled out the tweezers, and returned them to their rightful owner. "Sometimes the Thief works invisibly, and sometimes he works through other people. Sometimes he decides the offering isn't good enough."

"He sounds an interesting fellow," Larkin said. "If rather creepy. I'm not at all sure I would want to meet him, after all."

"It's not the same for Hedwig," Daisy said archly. "A meeting with the Thief would just be like a family reunion."

Hedwig tutted.

"What am I missing?" Larkin asked.

"She's making jokes at my expense. I don't know who my father is, and on the eyot, traditionally the Thief is held responsible for single women's pregnancies. Daisy apparently suspects that my conception was a more banal affair."

"I didn't realise," Larkin said. "I'm sorry for prying – it's none of my business."

"Hush, I'm not offended. Just be careful how you speak of it round Conrad… He insists my mother calls herself *Mrs*, as a fae bride. Can't have people thinking she's a common or garden mum on her own. I expect you think we're old-fashioned, and I couldn't blame you… We *are* behind the times; who else cares about legitimacy, nowadays?"

"Not me. But some people do," Larkin said, with rare bitterness.

Hedwig looked at him, surprised by his vehemence. He swirled a brush in umber paint, and swept a line above the eye of Imogen's mask.

"Were you brought up by both your parents, Larkin?" Hedwig asked.

"After a fashion. We were all under the same roof." He changed the subject. "This masquerade. Am I invited, or not?"

Hedwig saw no reason to forbid it. Still she answered impishly.

"That depends!" she said.

"On what?"

"The masquerade's a special opportunity for match-making."

"It is?"

"I'll ask a question; if you answer, you can come. Who's the prettiest woman in this room? Reply without evasion."

Imogen and Daisy focused on their handicrafts, affecting lack of interest. Hedwig laid a dilemma at their feet, too – desire to be chosen by Larkin, wrested with fear of Conrad's censure. Expectation swelled; the snug was thick with it.

Larkin looked from one face to another.

"You're all delightful," he said.

"No, that answer's not acceptable. You must choose."

Larkin drew breath to speak again, and Mrs Mayhew swept into the snug to clear their glasses. She possessed a strong resemblance to her daughter, with great limpid eyes, hair as blonde as brass, and a perpetual Californian tan which took an effort to maintain in Oxford's autumn climate. Hedwig saw her as unambiguously middle-aged – for she was pushing forty – even if she were more youthful than the mums of Imogen or Daisy.

"My choice is Mrs Mayhew," Larkin said with relief.

Hedwig had sufficient grace to laugh. He was shrewd to take that opportunity; everyone would assume his selection of her mother was chivalric – a mark of respect for an older woman – whereas to choose a peer must snub the other two.

"My ears are burning," Mrs Mayhew said.

"You're the prettiest woman in the room, Mama," Hedwig explained. "According to Larkin."

Mrs Mayhew laughed. "For that he can have a free drink."

Larkin stood to pass her his empty glass. "Thank you. I think I'll take it up in my room."

At the doorway he verified with Hedwig: "Have I earned my invitation?"

"On a technicality," she said. Satisfied with this response, he left.

"Daisy," Hedwig said, "what did Larkin say in Italian?"

"He said my choice of degree was cool."

"That's all?"

"Pretty much. Although, I got the impression, that the girl he was trying to impress – she was probably from Florence. Or his teacher was."

"Oh? What makes you say that?"

"His pronunciation."

Hedwig made a mental note to check which doll makers were based in Florence. She was sure she'd find some. And she wouldn't be at all surprised if Larkin knew every one of them.

8

Persephone didn't linger, with her untouched orange juice, after Larkin had been summoned. She had viewed his departure with commingled disappointment and relief. Since seeing the kissing automatons she had been keenly aware of Larkin's presence whenever she caught sight of him. She'd had crushes on people before – for a while she'd harboured longings for the lissom woman who brought their post, and one spring fortnight staying with her mother she'd been smitten with the Scottish man in the downstairs flat. But they'd existed for her mainly in glimpses; they weren't walking round the shop all day, like Larkin. The nature of his appeal felt more complicated, as well. There was a blurred line between her longing to possess his advantages, and wanting to be near him. His talent acted like a halo, making every aspect of him of greater interest to her. She didn't know how to convey that interest. And churlishness was ingrained in her so deeply, she wasn't sure she was capable of acting differently. To have talked longer in the pub would have prolonged her conviction she was making a fool of herself.

It was almost pleasant to return to the night air, despite the chill, as the sky was clear and the moon full. Persephone's ears rang after the roar of the pub. Nearly everyone had been there that night, cheered by their weekend beginning early. More were coming – Alastair met her on the path.

"Not like you to be at the Tavern," he remarked.

The borrowed jig was in her coat pocket, pressing heavy and square against her thigh. She would return it on Monday – she always returned anything she borrowed over the weekend – but if she had asked outright for it, he would have refused her. She placed her hands in her pockets too, as if Alastair might otherwise see and reclaim his property.

"I was looking for Dad," she lied. "But he must be at the pub in town."

Alastair's bulbous eyes slid past her to the bright windows of the pub. She sensed his wish to be gone.

"Drink in town a lot, does he?" he asked, offhand.

"The beer's cheaper." She added pointedly: "And he's not earning any more."

"Probably better to cut the beer altogether then, isn't it? Have you ever suggested to him he should drink less?"

When, Persephone wondered, should she have begun parenting her father? When she was six? When she was thirteen? When Alastair had fired him – no, when he had *encouraged him to take retirement*? What stung her was not the letting go of her father, who she agreed had no place in the workshop if he was covertly drinking all day. The injustice was Alastair's smug certainty that Persephone was responsible for her father's behaviour, and thus responsible for her father losing his job. Not Briar himself; and not Alastair, who was surely the victim in this scenario, because he had to shoulder the unpleasant business of dismissing an ageing relative.

Persephone said none of this, because – after Conrad and Hedwig – Alastair had the most power over who worked where at Kendricks. If she were ever to escape the sales counter Alastair must agree. So she said, truthfully: "Dad doesn't listen to me."

"No? Pity. Maybe it's something about the approach you take. You'd best get on, see if he's reached home." Alastair swept past her into the pub.

His parting words would fester. Persephone concentrated on the jig in her pocket; she imagined telling Alastair that she had taken it, that she could take anything he had for herself, if she drove hard enough. But it was a consolatory daydream. She didn't really believe in it.

Persephone remembered first visiting the Eyot Tavern when she was around eight. Certainly it was some time after the dolls' house had been completed by Briar, and they had obtained her maquettes from the shop – the candid child; the detached father; and the appeasing mother. Akemi, Persephone's own mother, was spending a few days in hospital for an operation, the purpose of which had been left unexplained to Persephone. Briar was thus solely responsible for her. He was sober for the first two days. On the third, he announced they were going to the Eyot Tavern, as he'd promised Mrs Mayhew he would fix her rotten window sash. Mrs Mayhew, he explained, didn't have a man to do such things, like Persephone and her mother did. Anticipating complaints of boredom, he told Persephone that Hedwig would be there, too, for her to play with.

In this he was wrong. Hedwig was not there, and Mrs Mayhew admitted them by the side door because the bar was closed. She said Persephone could play with Hedwig's toys in the girl's absence. This suited Persephone very well. She was not overly fond of Hedwig, who had somehow mastered the art of persuading adults she was sweet and well behaved while always obtaining just what she wanted. Briar and Persephone were led up the stairs and she found it endlessly strange that a whole house should be positioned on top of the pub – a house starting at the wrong level, rather than on the ground – and it seemed to rearrange the world's order for her. Did every supermarket checkout girl, she wondered, sleep upstairs when the customers had gone for the day? The thought had never occurred to her.

"This is where Hedwig's things are," Mrs Mayhew announced, ushering Persephone into a lemon-hued room with a canopy bed and neat rows of toys on shelves. "Play with whatever you like."

Persephone heard the click of the door closing behind her, and turned in surprise. She hadn't expected to be fenced in. She heard Mrs Mayhew's and her father's voices, soft and getting softer on the other side of the wall. *A shame you couldn't find someone to watch her*, Mrs Mayhew said. Briar's reply was too indistinct for Persephone to understand.

The room was silent then. She turned her attention to the toys, some of which were unexpectedly intimidating. Hedwig had a mini video camera in primary colours for making real films, a hefty Play-Doh factory, an extensive collection of Night Garden soft toys – but no dolls' house, Persephone noted. No dolls with enchantments either. A selection of fashion dolls with vinyl heads and hard plastic bodies were stacked in a blue crate. Their wardrobe of frilled dresses and tiny heeled shoes was extensive. These plastic ladies were sophisticated, compared to Persephone's wooden family. She couldn't decide whether their lack of enchantment was preferable to being candid or detached or appeasing.

Replacing the dolls in the crate, Persephone reasoned that there must be magic dolls somewhere at the Tavern. Maybe Hedwig was too young for such a doll or even a sturdy maquette. Everyone went on about what a sensible girl Hedwig was for her age, but she was still two years younger than Persephone. So that at least explained why there weren't any magic dolls in Hedwig's room. Mrs Mayhew, as a grown-up lady, must have one. Alastair said everyone born on the eyot learnt an enchantment when they were thirteen. This idea immediately excited Persephone. Yes; Mrs Mayhew must have made her own doll, and given it her own enchantment.

Persephone bit her lip. She stared at the closed door. Mrs Mayhew hadn't said she must stay inside. If they met in the corridor, Persephone would say she was looking for the bathroom. She twisted the door handle and looked through the gap. A tune played from the living room, something soft sung by a lady. Persephone heard laughter and smelt cigarette smoke. It would be easy for her to tip-toe past without anyone knowing, and check the other rooms, to see where the magic dolls were stored.

There were a lot of rooms at the Tavern – and Persephone had not fully understood this was because it offered accommodation. She entered bedroom after bedroom, where the drawers were empty and the wardrobes bare. Never mind dolls; there were very few belongings of any kind. Over every bed was a framed picture: a print of a horse flying through the clouds. It was pretty, Persephone believed, if you saw it once. To see it over and over again quickly became boring, then sinister, because it made Persephone feel as if she were visiting the same spot repeatedly, no matter how much she wished to see something new and different.

Finding Mrs Mayhew's room broke the cycle conclusively. The door was open, and Persephone knew immediately this was where Mrs Mayhew slept, because it was a grown-up version of Hedwig's room. The walls were yellow, though not lemon this time – their shade was deeper, and murkier, like the end of Mrs Mayhew's fingers where cigarettes had stained the skin. An overflowing ashtray was next to the four-poster bed. A ginger cat, fat and twitching its tail, dozed on the bedspread. Instead of the print of the flying horse, Mrs Mayhew had hung an immense painting above the mantelpiece, in which that same horse bore a rider. Persephone thought the man was familiar, though the paint was grimy with age, obscuring the detail of his face.

Persephone remembered she could be caught by Mrs

Mayhew, and should search faster, not stare at the painting. No dolls were displayed, not on the window ledge or the shelves. She checked the wardrobe. Many garments were stored inside. Some were pooled across the base, having fallen from their hangers at some point and never been picked up. Persephone ran her hands along each dress, searching for a doll that Mrs Mayhew could have tied to a waistband. Nothing. And there was nothing on the vanity, or in the bedside cabinet. She looked under the pillows and found only wrinkled sheets. Finally she lay face-up on the floor, and wriggled beneath the bed. The dust made her sneeze. She blinked as she waited for her eyes to adjust to the dim light. And here, here she discovered what she'd been looking for. Trapped between the bed slats and the mattress was a doll, made from a clothes peg. A pipecleaner was twisted round the middle for arms. The face was painted on the top – glossy pink with cupid's bow lips. One of the legs had black writing on it. The letters were joined up, and Persephone sometimes struggled to understand joined-up writing. She puzzled out the words. *Visionary Delirium*. They were not words that she knew.

The doll would be small enough to shuffle between the slats. Eager to feel the doll that she imagined Mrs Mayhew had made, and the enchantment Mrs Mayhew might have laid, Persephone touched the pipecleaner arm. Immediately she felt lightheaded. The pipecleaner seemed to move of its own accord, circling Persephone's finger, and the doll rolled its way into her hand. Was this Visionary Delirium? The doll winked and smiled, then curled up with a pipecleaner thumb in its mouth.

Persephone shifted onto her side in mimicry of the doll's foetal pose, because she was sleepy. Her attention was caught by four hooved feet dragging at the carpet by the bed. She heard the unmistakeable rumble of a horse whickering. Slowly, so as not to startle him, she edged back out from under the mattress.

The man from the painting was on the horse. His hair was long, smooth, dark and parted at the side. His skin was weathered. He was shirted and waistcoated, the tops of his sleeves were puffed, and he wore black trousers that tapered to his ankles. Like the horse, his feet were hooved.

He looked at Persephone with disdain.

"Do you know who I am?" he asked.

He was the Thief. She was certain of that; and yet she sensed this was a title the eyot residents used among themselves, and that he might not like being accused of stealing, whatever the truth of things. Dimly remembering some adult talk, she said: "You're Hedwig's Daddy."

Her conviction that this was the right response grew. Didn't it make sense for him to be here, in Hedwig's home, if he was her father?

He narrowed blue eyes at her. She felt an itch on the back of her hand, and when it didn't subside from scratching, she glanced at it. Ordinarily she bore a birthmark on that spot – an oval the colour of milky coffee – but the mark was shifting over her skin. It reached the end of her fingers and vanished, before reappearing on the Thief's hand that held the bridle. In the same way, she felt the creeping loss of a scar on her knee, sustained from a tumble down the stairs when she was three. Her eyes tingled as she saw the

Thief's eyes turn hazel. He'd stolen her birthmark; her scar; the colour of her eyes. All the things by which she recognised her appearance were being taken. The Thief smirked, reminding her of the day in the playground that Arthur Cantwell crushed her prize-winning Easter Bonnet, grinding the petals into paste beneath his heel. Arthur wore the same smirk, and Mother had said later, *he only did it because he likes you*, but Persephone thought: *he hated that he likes me, and punished me for it.*

"Give me back my things," she said now. The injustice of the thefts emboldened her.

"They're mine." The Thief continued to smirk. "Aren't your eyes at home upon me?"

She was half his size and knelt on the carpet while he rode a winged horse. To insist he was in the wrong was foolish, possibly dangerous. But he had acted unfairly, so she said: "They are *not* at home upon you. They don't belong on you at all."

He raised a single eyebrow. "I might let you have them, if you offer me something better instead."

A pain in her brain and heart and stomach prevented her response. The Thief's gaze narrowed again. "Not much of interest inside you, is there? Some Credulity. Some Ignorance. But they're nice and fresh. Will you spare them?"

The pain stopped. Persephone said: "No. I won't."

"Ah – that's more appealing – *Defiance*. Give me that and you can have everything else."

Persephone knew that if the Thief wanted her Defiance more than everything else, it must be valuable. Why had he not seized it without her say-so, as he'd taken the other things? It must be harder to steal a feeling than a birthmark, otherwise she would have lost Defiance already. Maybe feelings must be given up before they could be taken.

"I don't want to give you any of my feelings," Persephone said.

"As you wish," the Thief said, turning transparent as a stained glass window. He was disappearing, and with him Persephone's birthmark and scar and the colour of her eyes.

"Wait," she said in panic.

The Thief flooded back into solid colour. "What?"

"You can have my Ignorance." Persephone thought she knew what it meant to be Ignorant – it was the word the teacher used if a child forgot their manners – and of all the losses on offer, that seemed the most tolerable.

"Good," the Thief said.

The ginger cat yowled, startling Persephone. She dropped the little peg doll and the Thief vanished, along with his horse. Persephone checked her hand, and her knee, immediately. Her birthmark and scar were back where they should be. According to her reflection in the wardrobe mirror she had eyes of their natural colour, too.

Persephone supposed she should put the doll back under the mattress, but that would necessitate touching it, and she had no desire to feel the Visionary Delirium again. Why would Mrs Mayhew want to feel that way? Surely she couldn't have chosen that enchantment for herself, or made the doll, because nobody would want to be lightheaded and confused with the Thief trying to trick you into bargains. Unless this was one of the adult things Persephone couldn't understand – like drinking, as her father did, until he fell down flights of stairs or was sick, or wanted to start a fight with Persephone's grandfather, her uncle, her mother. Until he wanted to start a fight with her.

The cat picked the doll up in its mouth, and slunk beneath the bed, where it chewed the doll half-heartedly, then sank back into sleep. That, at least, would mean Persephone's snooping went unnoticed.

She crept back downstairs. When she got as far as the lounge, she peeped through the crack in the door. The music had stopped. Mrs Mayhew was sitting on Daddy's lap. They were still; she held the end of his tie. One of her red patent shoes had half slipped from her foot, leaving the soft pink curve of her heel exposed. Persephone turned her head to the wall, alarmed at the prospect of her father or Mrs Mayhew moving, or detecting Persephone's observation. The scene repulsed her, because she had assumed there was a particular order to the world which was now skewed. Women should not sit on her father's lap. She could not have explained why she had this assumption or why the breaking of it disgusted her – nor why the gap in age between Mrs Mayhew and Daddy made it worse. But it did, and she did not want the knowledge such rules could be broken.

Persephone returned to Hedwig's room, and shouted out: "Daddy! Daddy! Daddy!"

He appeared a few moments later. The set of his shoulders told Persephone he'd had a drink. She could always tell when he'd had even a small amount of alcohol, from his posture and the set of his teeth, though a stranger might not notice.

"I need to go home." She spoke mechanically, without

any hint of blame, because accusations would make him angry. "I feel sick."

"All right." He paused. "Shall I come with you?"

"You have to finish the window."

"Yes," he said. "I do."

She walked back to their house alone. He did not follow till several hours later.

9

Conrad Kendrick's kitchen stretched the length of his house. The walls were limed and flagstones paved the floor. A heavy table, scented with carbolic, sat before the range. It was here that Hedwig spent the hours before the masquerade in quiet industry. She roasted pumpkin seeds, and diced the venison in blackberry juice. Ragged sourdough and walnut-studded Roquefort were arranged on boards with careful informality. Just as Hedwig slid poached pears, their flesh flushed with wine, onto a golden plate, the servants' bells vibrated. One specifically: the bell that ran from their front door.

The guests weren't due just yet. When they came, they should be congregating by the riverside behind the house, not arriving at the front. An early interruption was annoying. Hedwig, licking sugar from her fingers, left reluctantly to greet their visitor.

It was Briar Kendrick, dressed in a frock coat. For once

he seemed sober. His hands were clasped, which Hedwig guessed was to hide their tremor.

"What an unexpected pleasure," Hedwig said, because she thought hostesses should be gracious even – no, *especially* – under provocation. "Did you come to help with preparations, Briar?"

"No; it's Conrad that I'm here to talk with. He'll be too in demand later. Can he spare me twenty minutes now?"

She beckoned him inside, and left him waiting in the hallway while she checked. Conrad was stationed at the bedroom mirror, combing the hair that reached his shoulders. Sighing heavily, he said he might permit his twin an audience – for a short while.

"I want you here too," he said. "To remind him when his time runs out."

So she summoned Briar up the stairs, and after his ascent he followed her into Conrad's room. Against the toile that lined the walls, and swags of teal brocade at every window, Briar made a sombre column.

Conrad kept his back to Briar, focused on his own reflection. Holding up his wrist to Hedwig, he requested: "My opalescent cufflinks, if you please."

"I hope that you are well?" Briar ventured.

"Perfectly."

"The business must be doing well – be profitable, that is – if there's cash to take on new employees?"

"You object to me appointing Larkin, do you?"

"Object? I've no objection. I only thought profits must be good," Briar said. Hedwig slid the golden catch through

Conrad's cuff, and Briar spoke again. "I've really come about Persephone."

"Pin my hair up, Hedwig, if you please."

She took the brush that lay on Conrad's dresser. Silently she wrapped a lock of hair around it.

"Seph's not happy," Briar said.

"Happy is as happy does, my brother. If she dwelled on her misfortunes less, then less misfortune would befall her. What do you imagine ails your daughter?"

"She's frustrated with the work available here. Maybe, if she saw the world beyond our little Oxford, then she'd blossom."

"Surely *that* is easily arranged. Dispatch her to her mother's."

"Send her to Berwick-upon-Tweed?" asked Briar, doubtfully.

"Why not? Did you have somewhere more exotic planned?"

"Not planned exactly. I thought she could do some work abroad for you."

"For me?" Conrad twisted under Hedwig's hands, to look at Briar.

"For the workshop. Naturally I'd accompany her."

"You're retired," Conrad pointed out. "What interest have *you* in workshop business?"

"Don't I live on Paxton's Eyot? The workshop's everyone's concern. And I can see it faces competition. Better miniatures are made in Tokyo, and Moscow. They exceed our craft, you know they do, and we've become complacent just because we have enchantments. But Persephone and I could go there, source some new supplies, report on whether they're making things the architects should try here."

"No. I fail to see the need for that," said Conrad. He returned his gaze to the mirror. Hedwig pushed the final grip into position.

"Any fool can see the need." Briar ceased to be hesitant at Conrad's curt refusal.

"If you must know," Conrad said, "Persephone has been ill-motivated, not to mention surly, from the day she started serving in the shop. Be truthful, Briar – how can I reward her with expensive trips away? It wouldn't be fair to the others, now, would it?"

"She isn't the others. She's your niece. And you have money you can spare."

"If she wants to go to Russia, if she wants to go to Japan, she can save her wages. I've provided her with paid work. Additional largesse amounts to favouritism."

"Poppycock. You're nothing but a miser."

Hedwig sensed they'd reached an impasse. "Gentlemen. I suggest the matter's put aside before our guests arrive. I'll show you back downstairs now, Briar."

"Show me?" Briar stared at Hedwig in contempt. "What right have you to show me, when I was born in this house?"

"Of course. I simply meant—"

"The only reason I inherited nothing – not the house, the shop, that blasted mourning doll or any other damn thing – is that our father wished to spite me."

"Hardly, Briar," came the cold reply from Conrad. "Father left it all to me because you'd spend the whole estate on drink."

Briar's lips tightened. He walked away without another word.

"Go back to the kitchen," Conrad said to Hedwig. "We've wasted time enough."

When the hour approached for greeting guests, the master of the eyot and his accomplice donned disguises. A Colombina covered Hedwig's upper face; it shone with crystals and was held in place by white satin ribbon. Conrad wore Autunno, which was painted gold and framed with leaves and berries. Arm in arm they walked through Conrad's garden. By the time they reached the waterside the sun had dropped. They watched a rowing boat turn the river bend, beneath a jaundiced lantern speckled with gnats. Behind were several boats more.

The passengers had also come in masks. The Websters were the first, encased in cats' heads of papier mâché. Hedwig helped them tether their boat, while Conrad stood by regally. The second skiff contained Persephone and Briar. Seph had picked a Moretta, the face without a mouth; while Briar wore the Plague Doctor, that long-faced mask with the elephantine nose. He didn't mention that evening's argument, but nor did he embrace his brother; and when he passed by, Hedwig caught the smell of scotch. She hoped he wouldn't cause trouble – but there wasn't time to dwell on that, because many guests were still to come, and all required a welcome. Third were the Packwoods, followed by the Goldsworthys, and the Reid-Collicotts.

The next arrival rowed alone. He wore the customary

frock coat, and a Scaramuccia: the joker's face, moustachioed and pallid.

"Who is this?" Conrad queried.

"Larkin," Hedwig answered. "Isn't it?"

The loner raised his mask.

"You saw through my disguise."

Not true, exactly. One slight man in a frock coat looks much like another, but she knew no other man was coming unaccompanied. As soon as he'd secured his boat, Larkin joined the Websters and the Goldsworthys and the Packwoods and the Reid-Collicotts, who all were milling near the belvedere. He stayed in Hedwig's thoughts. She had secured a private investigator, for a negligible sum, to check the civil records in Florence, as her lack of language skills had limited her own searches and she didn't trust Daisy's discretion. While waiting for the investigator's findings, Hedwig could sift the newcomer's circumstances further.

So when all the guests had moored, she sought his help. The pyramid of firewood must be checked for living creatures prior to ignition. Conrad owned a thermal camera for the purpose, which she might operate alone, but moving heavy timber would require assistance.

Hedwig held the camera level with her eyes, observing neon colours play over the small screen.

"You could have come from the Tavern with Mama," she commented to Larkin. "Don't you get on with her?"

He shrugged. "Your cousins had first dibs in that boat, and there wasn't enough room for everyone. I didn't mind."

"You can be honest, even if my mama is your landlady.

I know *all* her faults. Are your relations as exasperating as mine?"

"My parents were far worse than Mrs Mayhew. But now they're dead, so no longer."

Such dismissive phrasing! He'd insinuated before that their parenting was poor. Maybe Larkin didn't grieve them. Or he'd benefitted from their premature departure. Deaths meant estates; if Larkin had inherited, it would explain Madoc's allusion to family money.

"Any brothers, sisters?" Hedwig asked.

"No; just me."

"Oh, an only child! That's why you're used to added scrutiny. If Mama does get *too* annoying, there's a cottage standing empty down the lane. I'm sure that you could rent there, Conrad willing."

"I barely see your mother, truly."

"Cottage rental would be more expensive."

"I don't even know what the rent would be," he said, unbothered. "But it's never much mattered to me where I live. At the Tavern I get a clean bed and food. That's fine for now – until my position is permanent."

His reticence frustrated Hedwig. Sighing, she returned the camera to her pocket. "Nothing showed onscreen. I say we're safe to light."

"Wait." He raised a hand – he wore leather gloves – and peered into the heart of the wood stack. "I heard a creature moving, I think."

He took a step or two up the sloping pile, and reached between the branches.

"Got you." He withdrew a baby hedgehog, curled into

a sphere of spikes. His gloves must offer some protection from the spines.

"Let's set him free along the river," Hedwig said. "He should be kept away from harm there."

Larkin nodded. "I'll do it. You better get back to the others. Looks like there's some kind of barracking, up by the belvedere."

She turned to see. A band of people were watching as Briar Kendrick tore away his mask. He lurched to grab his brother's collar. Conrad twisted from his grip, and Briar lost his balance, landing awkwardly upon the ground. Among the spectators was Persephone, her posture rigid. Conrad took advantage of Briar's prone position, by leaning close, as if to kiss him, and Hedwig guessed that he was whispering. Briar shoved his brother back.

It wasn't too late for Hedwig to intervene. She ran towards them.

"The firewood's ready to light," she called out, to encourage a dispersal.

Several guests took a few, half-hearted steps, with glances over shoulders back at Briar, waiting for his next move. He'd been subdued. His ribcage rapidly rose and fell, for he was old, and drunk, and lacked the stamina he once had. He alone was maskless, missing the defence of every other man attending. Sephy scurried to him. She tugged his sleeve, as if she were a child.

Hedwig reached the crowd. She spotted Dennis Botham near the front; he wore a Bauta, or the mask with a prow where the mouth should be.

She told him: "You go light the fire."

He nodded. Hedwig clapped for attention. "Follow Dennis, everyone; the fire'll be a better show than this."

The horde abandoned Briar and Persephone. She led him slowly in the opposite direction, towards the house. From there, imagined Hedwig, they'd go home on foot. No wonder; drunken men and river boats don't mix.

"Should I follow them? To check they actually leave?" she said to Conrad.

"No need. He was stewing all the evening over my refusal. Now he's reached a crescendo, with this scuffle, he'll retreat to lick his wounds. The cycles of his moods are tediously predictable."

A cheer ascended from the guests; the fire was lit. Conrad and Hedwig proceeded through the crowd and stopped before the blaze. Tomorrow winter would begin. The burning timber crackled. Embers caught the air. The circle of masks glowed red and gold. Hedwig saw a flaming sphere, tumbling through the bonfire, and – recollecting the baby hedgehog, the reality that all babies must have a mother – she leapt forward with a cry, her fingers plunged into the pyre.

Her hand was burnt.

"My sweetness!" Conrad exclaimed. "Whatever is the matter with you?"

Wincing, Hedwig answered: "Too much fire and moonlight. It's made me suggestible. I thought an animal was caught in there."

"Hey, Hedwig!" Daisy shouted from the darkness; Hedwig recognised her voice but couldn't see her. "Don't sacrifice yourself!"

"It's not a bad burn," Hedwig said, although she wasn't sure of that at all. "There's salve and bandages up at the house."

"I'll come with you," said Rieko, from behind the face of a Pierrot. "It's hard to dress your own hand."

"Thank you, but please don't. It's barely burnt at all," said Hedwig, who thought that accepting help demeaned her. She wished only to excuse herself, unseen.

It took her ten minutes to reach the house. It would be blessedly quiet and she could inspect the burn in privacy. The side door was open when she arrived, which annoyed her – perhaps all the more because pain had shortened her tolerance. Had Briar been using secret keys again? She had intended to call the locksmith and it slipped her mind... she wouldn't forget again. Tomorrow morning, first thing, every lock would be replaced.

She pushed the door shut behind her. Through the gloom of the hall she could make out the familiar, dark shapes of pictures on the walls, and the sole item of furniture in this narrow corridor, which was a half-moon table. She also saw that a light bulb, and flex, had been discarded on the rug.

That's odd. She looked upwards. Someone had yanked the overhead fitting from the ceiling, leaving wires exposed like the roots of a plant. The light had been whole and working when she and Conrad left the house this evening. Who had destroyed it?

Someone who didn't want to be seen, she thought. *Someone who could buy time in the darkness, if they were disturbed.*

And yet she did not believe she was in any danger. Not yet. For the obvious culprit was still Briar; it must be him, mustn't it? Who else had keys? Who else was known to steal from Conrad, and hadn't the fight left Briar with just the motive he needed? Yes – she was certain it was Briar. Her certainty made her indignant, rather than fearful. Briar knew how to throw a punch and he broke things often enough, but she had expelled him from the house before and she would again.

She turned the corner, into the main entrance hall, and stopped by the suit of armour. She sensed she was not alone – from the acoustics of the room, perhaps; conveying some sound beyond her conscious awareness. Only then did she see, by the spandrel – right before the Paid Mourner's cage – a shadow that looked as solid as a man.

Fresh doubt stopped Hedwig calling Briar's name. The shadow must be Briar – could not be otherwise – but did not resemble him. It was too still. It was too erect of posture.

A moonbeam pierced the fanlight, sudden and bright, illuminating the room before her. The man was real. He wore a Volto Larva mask – the face of a ghost, pale and encasing his whole head, which she had seen no one wear at the party. His frock coat was unbuttoned, revealing a dagger at his hip.

Hedwig ceased breathing. He was armed. She stepped backwards, because to turn her back was unthinkable, when this shadow, this ghost, this man might stab her if he knew he had been seen.

He was intent upon the Paid Mourner. Never taking his gaze from the doll, he placed his hands on the latch – the famous, impenetrable latch – and lifted it, as though no barrier would put her beyond his reach.

How had he opened the cage? Hedwig's mind rebelled against the proof of her eyes. The iron guards of the cage would produce paranoia in any intruder who touched them. Yet they had not deterred this man; and that terrified her more than the wrenched light, more even than the dagger. Because it said he did not feel as normal people do.

The trespasser picked up the Paid Mourner. He cradled the doll in his arms. Conrad's heirloom, worth two million pounds, had been plucked from her pedestal like a ripe cherry.

He stroked the Paid Mourner's head with a gloved hand.

Hedwig cried out as though she had been touched.

The man shot round to face her. Under the moonlight, the eyes of his mask were deep and dark.

His free hand unsheathed the dagger. He held it before him, and the doll crushed against his chest, to warn against Hedwig's approach. She lacked the power for any such thing. Her limbs were frozen.

If he stabbed me now, I could make no move to escape.

He sprinted towards her. As he drew close her legs gave way – she sank to her knees, her hands raised above her head in defence. His coat tail brushed against her skin. The wool raked her weeping palm as he ran on past, from the hall, into the night.

She sobbed, shaking and crouched, uncertain whether he was really gone or might yet return. The clock chimed, and did again a quarter of an hour later, and then a third time, before she tried to stand. With one shoulder to the wall she walked back to the garden.

From the violin music that carried on the breeze she knew the guests had begun dancing. She stumbled into a run, her feet tangling with the thick underskirts of her dress, the burn in her hand raw and screaming. The lacing of her bodice hurt her ribs and still she kept increasing speed, half tripping, half flying in an attempt to leave the empty cage behind her. Her mask slipped as the bow unravelled and she let the Colombina fall to earth.

She only stopped, panting, when she was close enough to identify the dancers – to see the papier mâché cats' heads, the Scaramuccia, the Bauta. She saw no ghost among them. Might he have swapped faces? Who among the dancers would dare terrorise her in the house?

Dennis was the first to see her. He broke from the dancers, to join her.

"What's wrong?" he said, urgently. Her disarray must have caused him alarm. He took her by the shoulders. "Hedwig? What's happened?"

"A man in a Volto Larva mask," she gabbled. "A ghost! He broke the light! He breached the cage!"

"Slow down, Hedwig; I don't understand."

"He *stole the Paid Mourner*."

The other dancers didn't hear Hedwig above the music. Soon, very soon, they would know. They whirled and leapt. Only she and Dennis were still, delaying, for just a while longer, the moment everything would change.

10

That night was a long one. Conrad notified the police, who, when they arrived, insisted that no one leave the grounds. Conrad provided a description of the doll, though when it came to revealing her specific enchantment – a secret hitherto held only by Conrad and his brother – he refused. Why pre-empt the thief by ruining her mystique? She might yet be retrieved, and the thief silenced, particularly if – as Conrad stubbornly maintained – the fae folk were the masterminds behind the crime. The police were unsure how to pursue this angle, and turned their attention to more tangible explanations. They searched the immediate area and questioned everyone, obtaining, in the process, permission to also search the guests' own properties. It was a logical request, because every party attendant lived on the eyot; one of them may have slipped home with the doll in the forty-five minutes before an alarm had been raised.

At seven in the morning the guests were finally allowed to depart. Larkin proceeded to the Eyot Tavern, looking forward to a long bath. His frock coat smelt of firesmoke and damp. Specks of earth had gathered in his glove fingers. Wine and black coffee had soured his mouth. On arrival he found that the police had begun ransacking the Tavern, but still needed more time to confirm the doll wasn't there, which put paid to any thoughts of unwinding. The search team was led by a looming action man, with a thick neck, a soft, meaty complexion, yellow hair, and pale blue eyes. Apparently his name was PC Walcott.

"Will you be long?" Larkin asked. "I was hoping to get out of this costume."

"It takes as long as it takes," PC Walcott stated. "We'd all like some sleep. But the ground and first floors have been cleared for use, so you can get yourself some breakfast."

Larkin went to the kitchen, which was one of the rooms that had been searched already, and left in disorder – much to Mrs Mayhew's annoyance. He assisted her with re-laying the lino and moving the fridge into position and returning the tinned goods to the cupboards. When they'd finished they sat down with mugs of tea.

"That Stanley Walcott," Mrs Mayhew said. "I can't help seeing him as an overgrown boy. He went out with Hedwig for two years. They were at the same school. He's a mite older than her."

Poor Hedwig. "So she didn't go to school on the eyot?"

"She did for primary. There's so few pupils she got a lot of attention. Then I enrolled her at secondary in Iffley when she was eleven. Not much point staying on at the eyot school unless you're going into the doll trade. And she did well, in her A-levels. A bright girl like her should really be at university. But she applied to Oxford, and when she didn't get a place, she refused to try anywhere else. None of the others were good enough."

Larkin pondered how to bring Mrs Mayhew round to the topic that really interested him: whether Hedwig could tell who had stolen the Paid Mourner.

"After the commotion last night, I didn't get the opportunity to speak to Hedwig." He stirred his tea to encourage it to cool. "How is she taking things?"

"Outwardly fine. I can tell she's upset no matter how well she hides it. She's taking it personally – as if she could have stopped a strange man with a weapon!"

"Has she given a good description of the thief?"

"She described the mask, and that he had a dagger. I don't think she could pick him out of a line-up. I reckon she'll blame herself for that as well."

"What a pity." He raised the mug to his lips. Mrs Mayhew made strong, bitter tea. "Does Hedwig have any idea why someone would steal the doll?"

"I don't think so; she only said that the police think it's too recognisable to have resale value. It must be someone with a grudge against Conrad, I reckon."

"Really?"

"There's plenty on that list."

"Briar Kendrick?"

"For certain."

"What's the problem between him and Conrad, anyway? I heard Briar was disinherited, yes?"

"That's the latest, but they've never been on good terms. It was their dad's fault. Felix was a cruel man, the kind who pulls wings from flies for amusement. He poisoned things between Conrad and Briar when they were still boys."

"How?"

"Lots of little games to make them compete against each other... Like, Briar and Conrad are twins – Briar is the elder by a few minutes – but Felix would only buy one of them birthday presents each year. He'd say they could earn his favour with good behaviour, lead one of them to think they were winning, then on the day Felix would say he despised toadying and give the other boy the gifts. He trifled with them, all the time."

"I can see how that might sow discord."

"Briar went off the rails in his early teens and never got back on them for very long. He seemed to settle down a bit when he met Persephone's mother, then she couldn't keep him dry. Still, I'd deal with him over Conrad any day of the week. Briar's broken, but he has a generous heart. Whereas Conrad... He has more of his father's nature." Mrs Mayhew looked at Larkin sideways; her eyes were blue as a Barbie's, even if they were starting to line. Rubbing a flake of nail polish from her thumb, she added: "You should be careful of Conrad."

Larkin laughed uneasily. "Conrad's been very good to me."

"He won't give you those enchantments, no matter what he's promising. He doesn't trust newcomers. He doesn't even trust people who spend too long away from the eyot! I lived in Selkirk for two years before Hedwig was born, and he let me come back but has never treated me the same since. I knew if I didn't come back before the birth he'd never permit me to raise her here."

"But she *was* born here, and Conrad has taken to her."

"For now."

Mrs Mayhew's viewpoint troubled Larkin, because he suspected she was right. Conrad might never willingly relinquish the enchantments and Larkin needed to redouble his efforts to discover the Sorcerers' methods under his own initiative. Still he made a last-ditch attempt to protest: "Conrad doesn't see me as an outsider. I'm family."

Mrs Mayhew opened her mouth to reply, but PC Walcott entered the kitchen. He said the police had completed their search of the Tavern, and normal activities might now resume. Mrs Mayhew went to open the bar. Larkin took the stairs back up to his room, which had been left in a terrible state. The mattress had been shoved at an angle onto the bed, trailing sheets. Floorboards had been lifted and not all of them had been replaced. He knelt by the gap, with the intention of sliding the boards back into position. There, between the joists, lay an abacus, which the police must have deemed irrelevant to their search. Larkin picked it up, disturbing years of grime. He blew dust off a hook at the top, which suggested it was a wallhanging. Was it used for counting? Instead of beads, discs were threaded upon the wooden rods, round face outwards. The discs were half an inch thick and the edges were decorated with a geometric pattern of alternating light and dark triangles.

Larkin remembered, when he was a boy, cutting out a circle of paper and drawing a bird on one side, a cage on the other. When he spun the circle on a piece of string, it appeared as though the bird were trapped in the cage. These wooden discs worked in the same fashion. The face of each disc was painted with a different abstract mark; and the reverse was painted with yet another. You could spin each disc on its rod, so that the two marks blurred into a single, cryptic symbol. Larkin revised his initial impression. Rather than an abacus, it seemed to be an early animation device. The difficulty was, he had no way of establishing what the resulting images meant. He had an inkling the symbols were the alphabet of another language. Maybe the wallhanging was intended as an aid for learning. But what language could it be?

The symbols bore a passing similarity to runes. Runes were used for occult purposes. Might these symbols, too, have a mystical significance? And wasn't there only one thing on this tiny river island that the occult was used for?

Mrs Mayhew might know what the wallhanging was, and why it had been concealed. But he couldn't ask her. If the symbols related to laying enchantments on dolls, he wanted a chance to work out how, before alerting anyone else on the eyot to the wallhanging's existence. He wrapped it in his pillowcase, and placed the lot in his leather bag. It would be safe enough there, while he had that bath.

11

Persephone slept heavily after the masquerade, and rose late. She was making her first coffee of the day when she heard a knock on the front door. Briar was still in bed. She assumed the knock was one of the neighbours – a party refusenik – with complaints about the noise her father made returning last night. People always complained to her, not to him, for there was general consensus she should keep him in line.

But when Persephone opened the door, the half dozen people awaiting her were strangers, and included two people in police uniforms. At the front stood a neat, grey-suited woman.

Persephone stared in consternation. "What do *you* want?"

The woman in grey blinked at this terse greeting, before introducing herself as Inspector Naidu.

"A valuable item was stolen from Conrad Kendrick's property last night," she said. "The doll known as the Paid

Mourner. The thief was dressed in appropriate fancy dress so must have been privy to the details of the party. We're searching the houses of everyone on the eyot."

"The Paid Mourner was stolen?" Persephone's fingers closed tightly round the edge of the door. "We weren't at the party for long. Nobody said anything about a theft while we were there."

"I'm afraid we'll need to know the details of where you went, and with who, after you left." She checked her notepad. "I believe the brother of Conrad Kendrick lives at this address, and there was some kind of disagreement last night?"

If they were asking about that, they must think Briar was involved in the crime. There was, in fact, a brief period of Briar's time unaccounted for. On their way from his fight with Conrad, Persephone had turned her back on Briar when he stopped to urinate in the river. He had also taken the opportunity to wander from her supervision while she wasn't looking, and she didn't find him again for another fifteen minutes. She had roamed up and down the riverbank until she spied him slumped between the roots of an oak tree. But surely, in that time, he hadn't the wherewithal to steal the Paid Mourner?

"My dad and uncle fell out. Brothers argue. He wasn't in a fit state to do anything but come home and sleep it off. In fact he's still sleeping. Does the search have to be done now?"

It would be helpful to buy some time, and check for herself if the doll were in the house.

"You may refuse until we get a warrant. However, the sooner we can establish the doll is no longer on the eyot, the better. All other residents so far have obliged."

So Persephone would draw additional attention to herself if she said no. She sighed, resentfully. "You'd best come in, then."

Half a dozen officers entered. Inspector Naidu said they would take a room each, and confirmed no one besides Persephone and Briar lived at the property. The police would need to roll back carpets, lift floorboards, check cupboards and behind pictures and in the linings of soft furnishings. Persephone led three of the men upstairs, and told them which room was which. She left her father's room till last.

She tapped the door lightly. There was no response, so she pushed it open. The room smelt stalely of alcohol. Her father lay fully clothed on the bed, his arm twisted backwards beneath him; nothing else was amiss.

Persephone touched his shoulder, and shook him gently. "Daddy. Daddy. The police are here."

His heavy lids unglued themselves, revealing narrow, bloodshot eyes. Persephone heard him swallow.

"The police?" he croaked.

"Come into the garden with me. They're here because someone stole something from Uncle Conrad. They need to search your room."

Dazed, he allowed himself to be led downstairs and out the front door.

"They've already asked where you were last night," Persephone whispered.

"I don't remember anything about last night," he said.

"You can't tell them that. Just say you left the party with me. Everybody saw that anyway. You were with me at home until you went to bed. Do you understand?"

He nodded. They waited in silence for an hour while the search was completed. To Persephone's relief, the police found nothing.

That afternoon, Briar returned to bed. Persephone took a few rough wooden shapes from her desk drawer: a head, a torso, two arms, and two legs. She placed the pieces in a paper bag with a three-inch carving knife. Whittling always helped quell her anxiety. Her preferred spot was on the riverbank, where the ditch met the Cherwell, because the sound of the water was soothing. Perhaps that was why Hester once chose to carve there, too. Persephone donned a woollen coat and yellow scarf. She felt lighter as soon as she left the house.

She almost turned back when she arrived at the river, because Hedwig was there, sitting on a fallen tree trunk, smoking a cigarette. But Hedwig had seen her, so they would have to speak.

Persephone approached Hedwig, her hands deep in her pockets. From the bank she could see the river was still thick with autumn leaves, but they had turned from russet to black. They gave the air a scent of decay.

"Sephy. You're the very person." Hedwig's flatness undercut the greeting. "I expect you've heard the news by now? The robbery?"

Persephone nodded.

"I saw the thief," Hedwig continued. "But I couldn't stop him. Just before it happened, I noticed the side door to the house was unlocked. I'd like to ask you – does Briar still have a key?"

"No," Persephone said defensively. The question alarmed her – partly because of Hedwig's implicit accusation Briar was to blame for the theft; and partly because Briar struggled with keys. He was always leaving his house key in places where he'd been drinking. Or sometimes he had the key all right, but he tried to use it in the wrong door, mistaking one of the other terraced cottages for theirs in the dark. On many an occasion, Persephone had lain in bed listening to his shouts to be let in, before she would finally venture out in her nightgown to guide him to the right house.

"Dash it all." Hedwig flicked some ash into the weeds. "The police said an experienced thief can pick a mortice lock. Did you know that? I thought mortice locks were *very* secure."

"The police said the thief was experienced?"

Hedwig shrugged. "Or, they were an amateur who prepared awfully well. He might have learnt to pick a lock especially. A guest could have planned to steal the doll months ago, knowing that the party would give them an opportunity."

"Our house was searched this morning. The police didn't find a thing."

"You're in the clear then, aren't you?" Hedwig smiled.

Persephone nodded. She watched the younger woman drag on her cigarette, and thought: *Hedwig doesn't normally smoke.* Some people whittle for anxiety. Some people imbibe substances.

"The theft sounds frightening," Persephone said abruptly.

"Everyone must be thinking that," Hedwig said. "It won't do. A housekeeper must be prepared for any situation to arise; even armed robbers. If she is frightened, how can she avert catastrophe? Last night needed less fear and more level-headedness."

"You're not a guard dog."

"The distinction may be lost on Conrad."

Was she scared of being fired? It was easy to fire women on the eyot. They rarely knew enough sorcery to be a threat.

Hedwig stood up, with a shiver. "Is that the time? Conrad will be waiting."

She walked away without saying goodbye. Persephone took her place on the log, and removed the wooden head from her pocket. She took her knife to the grained surface, carving subtler contours into its features. The precise work occupied her mind until the light dimmed, and a full moon rose through the pale dusk sky.

Taking a final look at the doll's head she saw that she'd worked well. The face was finely detailed: a dainty upturned nose, a rosebud mouth, and closed eyes. And Persephone realised she had unwittingly carved an imitation of the Paid Mourner.

Her hand shook. It was as though she'd played a trick on herself. If anyone were to see what she had made, they might speculate what she'd used as a model – particularly as Hedwig had already insinuated Briar was under suspicion.

She closed her fist over the head. Without further thought she threw it in the river. Persephone watched it bob on the water for a few seconds before the leaves submerged it, and carried it away; then she walked home, to see if Briar had roused himself to prepare dinner.

12

Somebody pelted Conrad's door with eggs on the morning after the police searches. The job of cleaning them away fell to Hedwig. It was miserable work – she began at eight, below grey skies, her hands immersed in cold water because a higher temperature would cook the eggs instead of wipe them off. To be subject to vandalism so soon after being robbed made Hedwig feel targeted, though she'd never admit it aloud.

A resident approached by the path – Jay Binding, who belonged to the Botham clan by marriage. He was a Geordie with receding auburn hair and a careworn smile, although he wasn't smiling now.

"Is Conrad up yet?"

"Same as normal, Jay. He's free to talk from eleven."

"That's no good to me. I have to hit the road before then."

Jay worked in Didcot at a call centre, having several times declined a post at Kendricks. Conrad disapproved of residents working outside Paxton's Eyot, but gave permission for Jay's alternative employment, as the call centre wasn't in the doll trade and accordingly presented no conflict of interest. Hedwig guessed that Jay preferred to keep his work and home life separate. His wife, Rumour Thornett, had worked since her teens on the Interior Design floor of the workshop – at least until recently; she was recovering from a mastectomy.

Hedwig dropped the sponge back in the bucket, and wriggled her shoulders, to rid them of stiffness. "Conrad won't make any exceptions. If you need to talk to someone straight away, perhaps I'll do?"

They sat on the wrought iron bench in the garden.

"I've come to let Conrad know my feelings on the police search," Jay said. "We weren't even at the masquerade, Hedwig. The first we heard of the theft was the police banging on our door. Was it really necessary to drag Rumour from her sick bed to turn our house upside down?"

"Oh Jay – I'm *so sorry* that happened. How miserable for the pair of you! I'm sure you'll understand that it wasn't Conrad's decision. The police prioritised the line of enquiry."

"They must have heard from him that the residents had a motive for stealing the doll."

"Not at all," Hedwig said, in her most soothing tones. "It was simply that the police thought the culprit was known to us. He was dressed in costume, you see."

"Conrad could have spoken to us. He might have called. We're not stupid – we know sometimes the police have to rule people out when they're looking into a crime – but couldn't Conrad at least have said he's sorry for the disruption? To us, and to everyone else who put up with it? It was humiliating, Hedwig. He goes on and on about loyalty and allegiances. That should cut both ways." Jay paused, then pointed at the door. "Don't you think that might have been avoided? If Conrad had shown some fellow feeling, do you think his neighbours would egg his house? Come eleven o'clock, there's going to be a queue of people to have a go at him, you know."

This was eminently believable. Hedwig's thoughts turned to damage limitation.

"Thank you for bringing this to me, Jay. You're right, you are. I will make sure Conrad hears everything you've said."

Jay stood up, and patted her on the shoulder. "You mean well. Just watch yourself, yeah?"

"I don't know what you mean."

"You're good at cleaning up Conrad's messes, but be careful you don't catch the flack. People might get angry with *you* if he won't speak to them directly."

"I'll make sure he does. And I'm sure he'll make some consolatory gesture," Hedwig improvised. "A bonus in people's pay packets, perhaps."

Jay straightened his tie as he walked away. "Money doesn't make everything better, Hedwig."

It was time to make Conrad's breakfast. Hedwig made her way to the kitchen to prepare everything on a tray, thinking how best to impart the message Jay had brought. It would need to be prudently edited, otherwise Conrad would escalate the situation in an unhelpful way.

All of this immediately left her head when she arrived, tray in hands, at Conrad's bedroom door. He was already up, dressed, and packing luggage.

"*Whatever* are you doing?" she asked.

"Seeking refuge," he sighed. "What man could bear these tribulations, these misfortunes, Hedwig?"

"But – where are you going?"

"Fiji!"

Hedwig watched Conrad fold a series of handkerchiefs, to tuck into the corner of a suitcase. The handkerchiefs were familiar to her. It was her job, usually, to launder and iron them. They all came from the same supplier in London, who – as well as meeting Conrad's needs – held a Royal Warrant of Appointment to provide the Queen's linen. Each handkerchief was made from thin Swiss cotton bordered on every side with Guipure lace. Silently Hedwig had always thought them impractical. She imagined one might dab genteely at a moist eye, and ignore the scratch of those looping white flowers... The lace wouldn't survive a moderate cold. She kept a store of hardier tartan squares in the kitchen dresser.

"Why won't you let me pack for you?" Hedwig implored.

"I know what I'll need," Conrad replied. "*You've* never been to Fiji."

Hedwig strongly doubted that the South Pacific required multiple lace handkerchiefs, but Conrad's remark stung her, because it implied she was ignorant – and that, in turn, suggested incompetence. Conrad had not said outright he was letting Hedwig go; but nor had he invited her to accompany him on this sudden trip.

"Do you want me to call Inspector Naidu?" Hedwig asked, seeking some opportunity for organisation. "I could let her know how long you'll be away for?"

"She is already aware. I let her know yesterday

afternoon." Conrad flipped the suitcase shut. He tugged on the zip, struggling to draw it to the centre.

"Oh. When will you be back?"

"I don't know yet. I only know, if I remain, I will brood on the loss of my dearest treasure; and if I continue to brood, despair will finally submerge me. While the search is ongoing I need not be present. The Inspector will contact me weekly to give a full briefing on their progress." Conrad leant on the top of his suitcase, in an effort to ease the zip's passage. "If you're worried about getting paid, I can assure you you'll receive a full salary for housesitting."

To reassert herself, Hedwig approached Conrad's suitcase and gently nudged him to the side. She neatly drew the zips to the centre, and fastened the buckles.

Conrad didn't acknowledge her assistance. Instead he said: "I don't believe maintaining the house in my absence will be a challenge. You may even fulfil your duties while boarding with your mother, if you prefer. It's not as though anything of value is left in the property to require twenty-four-hour guardianship."

This was surely a point made for effect. There were many items of value in Conrad's house, from paintings to eighteenth-century furniture, from Fabergé eggs to rare Chinese clocks, but the underlying message was that Conrad valued them very little. What he valued, and what had gone, was the Paid Mourner.

"I'd prefer to stay in my room here," Hedwig said.

"As you wish." The rest of Conrad's luggage formed a small tower at his bedside. "I have packed everything needful."

Hedwig speculated what other essentials Conrad had

included. Gold thimbles and ivory combs, she didn't wonder. The problem with Hedwig working so capably was that her work must appear invisible to Conrad, who had forgotten how deficient his own household management was. Hedwig lifted two of the cases, one under each arm, knowing Conrad would never get them down the stairs.

"I'll alert a boatman that your bags are ready to collect." Hedwig walked towards the door. "He can deliver them to your driver in central Oxford."

She felt Conrad's hand on her shoulder.

"I'm sure you'd make my arrangements with great efficiency, my sweet. But who's to say – if the boatman absconded with my belongings, would you stand idly by? I'll depart by car from the Iffley Road. If I telephone Alastair he will cycle my bags to the streetside. He's very reliable, and always ready to indulge me." Conrad patted Hedwig and walked past her onto the landing.

Hedwig wished to protest. The thief had surprised her. He was a man, broader and stronger than she was. He had a *knife*. No reasonable person would expect a nineteen-year-old girl to fight off an armed thief. How unfortunate that Conrad *wasn't* a reasonable person. He needed to blame someone for the crime. Until the thief was named, Hedwig knew the blame would fall on her alone.

An hour after Conrad's departure, just as Jay had predicted, the eyot residents were forming an angry queue at the door. Hedwig opened the landing window to address them from on high, fearing a stampede if they were admitted.

"Ladies and gentlemen," she said. "Conrad will be indisposed for the near future. The theft has placed an *immense* strain on him, and he will be taking a restorative trip. Over the next few days I promise I will visit every house *personally* to address your needs in his absence. You've all been so wonderfully patient and understanding at this difficult time."

"Screw your patience!" shouted Bobby Lush, one of the architects. "The police broke my bathtub!"

Several others joined him in jeering and complaining.

"Bobby – all of you, we're all family; let's show each other some kindness. I promise you'll be financially recompensed for any damage and it breaks my heart to see everyone so upset."

Daisy and Imogen were at the back of the crowd. Imogen's hands were moving too fast for Hedwig to follow, but she saw the sign for *pathetic* clearly enough. Daisy caught Hedwig's eye, and glared. The queue dispersed, as people shook their heads or grumbled to each other. As Hedwig closed the window, the landing phone rang. It was Mama, calling to ask for money, because she was in debt again.

"You are a terror, Mama," Hedwig said. "However do you get in these scrapes? I'm confused; you had money from Larkin for his lodgings. Is he moving out?"

"No, he's still here. It's just my last heating bill was higher than I was expecting."

"Yes, I can see how you'd think it should be a low amount – it *was* the summer quarter."

"Will you help me out with the bills or not?"

"Bills plural?"

103

"As you say, this was for the summer, the next one's going to be higher. And I have the electricity and everything else, too. Please, Hedy – if you could just chuck me a hundred pounds a month for a while... I'll pay you back soon, I promise."

"I *might* be able to help. Only because it's you." Hedwig knew that the money would be a gift, not a loan. Experience had taught her not to expect the money back. She wondered how bad Mama's debt was at the moment. Conrad owned the Tavern, and the bar takings were deposited to Mama's business account, from which a salary was drawn for her. She was permitted to sublet rooms to foreign students, or tourists for short lets. If only she were less of a gambler this life should have served her well. For as long as Hedwig could remember, Mama had been vulnerable to the buzz of a bet. Hedwig told herself that it was impossible to leave Oxford when Mama might risk bankruptcy if left too long unsupervised. This was, however, only half the truth. The fact of the matter was, it sometimes satisfied Hedwig to bail Mama out. Hedwig felt, in some way, that she was justifying her existence if she was relied upon.

"The police were round for their search yesterday," Mama was saying, presumably eager to move on from the subject of money now Hedwig's agreement was secured. "Stanley was with them."

"Stanley who?"

"Really, Hedwig, you are fickle."

"You mean *my* Stanley?"

"First you say *Stanley Who*, now you say he's yours?"

"I didn't mean it that way. I just meant – Stanley Walcott."

She hadn't seen him in over a year, maybe even two. "You caught me off guard. I don't understand why he was there during the search."

"He was with the police, Hedy, that's what I'm saying. A constable."

Hedwig wondered if he had been among the police on the night of the theft. She didn't think so. No matter how in shock she had been, she thought she would have noticed him. They had parted on indifferent terms but surely he wouldn't still hold that against her. A contact in the investigation might have its uses; if Inspector Naidu was updating Conrad every week, and Conrad was inclined to cut Hedwig from the loop, she would need some other way to stay informed. And she did want to be informed about the investigation. Without knowing if the doll was likely to be retrieved, she couldn't know the likelihood of Conrad forgiving her.

"Did you get much chance to talk with him?" she asked Mama now.

"Briefly, but he was busy inspecting my larder."

"He didn't pass on any contact details?"

"No. Hang on though – he said he was still living at his parents'."

That figured. Probably for reasons of thrift. Stanley was deeply sensible. It had always made Hedwig feel competitive.

"Hedwig, are you thinking of calling him?"

"No. The grocer's at the door, Mama," Hedwig invented. "I have to go but it's been so lovely talking to you."

As soon as Mama was gone, Hedwig checked her contacts. She still had Stanley's number. Time to give him a call.

13

The workshop was open as normal, but the police still made their presence felt. At noon Alastair told Persephone that Inspector Naidu wished to speak with her again. He put a girl from Interior Design on the counter and led Persephone to his office, where the Inspector was waiting, in the captain's chair by the desk.

Persephone concealed her anxiety at the prospect of further questioning. She had assumed the search was complete and that was the end of it. To be singled out for more probing could only be cause for alarm. But Alastair smiled when he instructed her to sit down, and asked if she wanted a drink. Both he, and the policewoman, had mugs of tea at their side. Persephone declined, and looked from Alastair to the Inspector in an effort to tell what they wanted from her.

"Miss Kendrick," Naidu said. "I understand that you maintain the records of sales here?"

"Yes."

"Including the customers' personal data – their names, their addresses, their previous purchases?"

"Only where their method of payment or delivery requires it. But that's the majority of our customers. People usually view the dolls by appointment; it's fairly rare for us to have passing trade."

"I need you to provide me with the details of your repeat purchasers. We're particularly interested in those customers you would class as serious collectors."

"Going back how far?"

"As far as your records allow."

"Why?"

The Inspector ignored her question. "Are you friends with the most serious collectors, Miss Kendrick? Presumably you get to know them over time?"

"I've never socialised with any of them." Persephone barely socialised at all. "All that's required is for me to know their preferences well. If a doll is made that I know matches a particular buyer's taste, and it's in their usual price range, I'll telephone to let them know. That usually happens when there's a new doll in a series – wooden dolls made from the same tree, for instance. Our most lucrative transactions are with a fairly small group of people."

"Have any of this small group expressed an interest in owning the Paid Mourner?"

"They all have, as a pipe dream – she's very famous. Are you saying a customer stole her?"

"That, or a customer hired the thief," Alastair cut in. "It seems that whoever orchestrated the theft had a personal motive. The motive can't have been money, because the doll is too famous to sell on without questions."

"A run-of-the mill opportunist might be too thick to realise there was no safe market for it," Naidu added. "But this crime doesn't look spur-of-the-moment. It looks methodical and planned, by someone who'd done their research."

"Whoever planned the crime knew they couldn't sell this doll," Alastair summarised. "They wanted to *possess* it."

Or they didn't think Conrad should possess it, Persephone thought.

"Are you aware of any customer who feels that intensely, Miss Kendrick?" Naidu asked.

"*Every* collector we serve is obsessive. But they'd have to be more than obsessive. They'd have to be able to tolerate the paranoia of opening the cage."

"How long will it take you to pull those records, Persephone?" Alastair cut in.

"I can do it now. The files are locked behind the counter."

"I'll come with you," the Inspector said.

All three of them rose from their seats. Persephone's anxiety had not yet subsided, but it was in her best interests to comply with the Inspector's request as quickly as possible. If her father was no longer under suspicion, and the police were truly shifting their focus to outside the family, she would breathe easier – and might even find her own way back to believing her father was innocent. Hopefully the thief would be found in the customer records, removing the risk of Conrad's retaliation for the crime away from Briar and Persephone.

Alastair was humming a tune under his breath as they

descended in the paternoster – Persephone assumed to cover his discomfort with their lack of conversation. They proceeded to the cabinets, where Persephone entered the pin for the repeat customers' drawer. She took out files for a dozen men – who, despite forming a small group, accounted for a quarter of Kendricks' revenue. Professor Emlyn Madoc; Michael Colman; Julian Brown; the list went on.

The Inspector opened the uppermost file. She ran her finger down the contact and payment details, then paused at the list of prior purchases, which included details of the enchantment borne by each doll.

"Tell me something," she said. "Some of the feelings these dolls evoke – they're not very nice, are they? Rage? Terror? Apprehension? What kind of person buys those?"

"People who need catharsis," Persephone said.

"It's harmless," Alastair reassured the Inspector. "It's like watching a horror film to feel frightened, or a weepy to have a good cry. No one finds that strange, do they?"

"Hm," the Inspector said. "I don't watch horror films. There's enough that's horrific in the world without seeing it in my entertainment."

"You're not wrong," Alastair said. "Still. Some people find it a release, emotionally speaking."

The truth was more complicated than either Persephone or Alastair was acknowledging. Persephone believed that feelings were, in themselves, neither positive nor negative – it was a matter of balance, and what use feelings were put to in one's dealings with the world. She thought of the First World War dolls; Courage was a supposedly positive attribute, but those dolls had helped send boys as young as fourteen to their deaths. And from personal experience Persephone knew that a demand to be Happy could be effacing, even brutal, when you had cause for discontent.

The Inspector produced her phone, and began the process of photographing the collectors' details.

"Do you need me for anything else or can I have my lunch now?" Persephone asked.

The Inspector nodded. "We'll be in touch with any follow-up questions."

Persephone retreated to the cloakroom to fetch her sandwiches. Alastair came after her.

"That was very helpful, Persephone," he said. "You're a good worker."

What did Alastair want, softening her with praise? He didn't step away, so she assumed he had something more to say – but he wasn't meeting her gaze, lending him an air of awkwardness.

"I was thinking," he went on. "When things have settled again, and the Paid Mourner's found, we could maybe discuss a raise?"

"OK," Persephone said uncertainly. More money was welcome and he might change his mind if she showed insufficient gratitude, so she added: "Thank you."

She sat on the bench underneath the coats and peeled back the lid of her lunchbox.

"I never wanted the police involved," Alastair said. "Seemed like a family matter to me, best handled within the family. But if it turns out to have been a customer – it's a good job the police were notified, isn't it?"

So that was why Alastair was offering her money. He felt

guilty. He, too, had assumed Briar was the thief; perhaps he had even suspected Persephone's involvement. The police's new line of enquiry must have given him pause, and now he was salving his conscience for doubting her innocence.

"The Inspector just shouted for you," Persephone fibbed, tiring of Alastair's presence. He left and she wondered if he'd remember her promised raise once the investigation was over – whenever that might be.

14

Several times that week, Larkin took the occult wall-hanging from his leather bag, and tried to work out its function – but failed. On Wednesday afternoon, when Dennis claimed to have seen a rat in the stockroom, Larkin volunteered to pick up poison from central Oxford. He usually avoided town, fearing he'd see acquaintances of his mother, however he welcomed this opportunity to leave the eyot with the wallhanging in tow. To his best recollection, a shop on Turl Street sold zoetropes, and other Victorian optical toys; it seemed to him they might know what the wallhanging was for.

That day the Iffley Road was troubled by few cyclists and fewer cars. Larkin was watchful regardless – and was glad at the token drops of rain falling, because they allowed him to lift the lapel of his coat round his face. No one stopped to speak to him, other than a grey-bearded man on Magdalen Bridge who requested money for a cup of tea. After startling, Larkin fished a two pound coin from his pocket. The High

Street was thicker with people – but that was no bad thing; they were tourists in the main, disembarking from coaches, which were unlikely to carry anyone he knew and may even provide the cover of a crowd. He passed Queen's College, watched by a statue of George II's wife; then the University Church. Shortly after, he took a right onto Turl Street, with relief, where he saw the dark-timbered shop front he remembered. A display of ornate toys and folio books crowded the window.

The bell rang above the door as he entered. Due to the narrowness of Turl Street, the interior received little natural light. However, that added to the premises' cosiness. At the counter, another customer was being served by a lady who put Larkin in mind of a Hitty folk doll. She had black eyes, a neat centre parting, and wore two rosy apples of blusher.

He approached once the other customer had left the shop. The woman didn't seem to mind that he had a query to make rather than a purchase; she accepted his wallhanging and gave it a name.

"It's a thaumotrope. And an elaborate one," she added. "More usually they're just a single bit of paper on string."

"Do you have any idea what the symbols represent?"

"Why should they represent anything? The artist's aim might have been to create something beautiful and momentarily diverting. Do you wonder what the patterns represent when you look through a kaleidoscope?"

"I thought these symbols were letters, or a written character that represents a word."

"Not from any language I recognise – although…" She looked again at one of the discs in the bottom right corner, spinning it thoughtfully. "They all have the same border pattern, don't they? It looks familiar. Bear with me."

She walked to the door and turned a carousel of postcards, stopping at the section which depicted local figures of historical interest.

"Aha. As I thought." She passed Larkin a postcard.

He gazed on it with interest. The picture was of a middle-aged Victorian woman. She was portly and light-haired. Her necklace bore a disc with the same geometric border – but the face of the disc was blank.

"She's a woman of some note," the shopkeeper said. "Her name is—"

"Lucy Kendrick. The maker of the Paid Mourner."

"Quite right," the shopkeeper confirmed.

He bought half a dozen copies of the postcard. It seemed only fair, having taken up the lady's time.

On his journey to the hardware shop he was too absorbed in his thoughts to worry about being seen. A plan was forming: he would ask one of the Kendricks the significance of Lucy's necklace. What could be more innocent? He had seen her in a postcard, quite by chance, he would say. For now, he still wouldn't mention the thaumotrope; instinct told him that, if the symbols were occult, the Sorcerers would confiscate it. He would rather they took a postcard than the thaumotrope, which he might continue to study, privately, if it was concealed.

The rain hit the ground with increasing force. Had this shower come at the weekend, the police might have tracked the intruder's escape route more easily. But the earth had been too dry to receive any impression of footfall. Larkin reached New Inn Hall Street, and hastened down the turning, keen to buy the poison before the weather turned much worse. Who, he speculated, should he ask about the postcard? Conrad, Hedwig, and Alastair were too tight-lipped on anything that might constitute a family matter. Margot Mayhew was so inquisitive she would press and press to find out why Larkin was asking.

He stepped into the shelter of Robert Dyas. It didn't take long to find the right aisle. A bewildering array of poison brands confronted him, and he picked the box at eye level. Mentally he continued his inventory of residents who might help him. Dennis was too shrewd. He might answer Larkin's questions, but he'd tell Alastair and Conrad afterwards. Then there was Persephone. Persephone; the first plausible option. She never *meant* to be helpful. He knew that. But she had shown her willingness to bargain. And he remembered their allyship in the bar. If she knew what that necklace meant – and he could work out her price – she would tell him.

His mobile rang while he was in line for the till. Madoc's name scrolled across the screen. Larkin picked up.

"You're elusive," Madoc said. "This is the fourth time I've called since yesterday. I couldn't get through."

"I told you before. There's no signal on the eyot. What did you want?"

"The police were round here last night, full of questions about my collection and whether I had ambitions to own the Paid Mourner – apparently I was on their list of suspects."

"You?" Larkin laughed. "Of all the people. Do they know how lazy you are?"

116

"My boy you wound me. I'm sure I could orchestrate the perfect crime. Although – it pains me to admit it – the whole interview was boringly routine. My impression was that I was a name to be ticked off a list, and they still think it was an inside job."

Larkin passed the poison to the cashier with a ten pound note. "I thought they'd ruled out the residents."

"Don't be too sure of that. They were asking me a lot about how well I knew different people there, and whether I'd heard of any disputes or grievances between Conrad and his subordinates. I gave them a potted history of Kendricks' succession disputes – told them Conrad's as gay as a daffodil in February and had once thrown over the love of his life for fear of angering his father. Conrad bullied plenty of gay family members himself, afterwards, from twisted jealousy I think. So I gave the police those names. But the family feud they were much more interested in was Conrad and his brother. They asked me quite a few questions about Briar Kendrick. Also – now don't lose your head over this – *your* name came up, what with you being so new to the family."

"Oh, I won't lose my head. Christ, Madoc, why would I do that? It's only the bastard police looking into me, after all." Larkin had enough problems establishing himself on the eyot. He didn't need the police making people wonder if he'd stolen the Paid Mourner.

"Spare yourself the vapours. It was the merest mention. What do you have to worry about? You're an eager-to-impress young man, with a first rate degree behind you and a bright future ahead. Briar's a drunk with a vendetta against Conrad. Who do you think the police are going to pay more attention to?"

"You know it's not that simple."

"It'll be fine. Must dash; I have a lecture."

Larkin didn't leave the shop straight away. It was still raining heavily outside, and he watched through the window, waiting for it to subside. Madoc was right. He must be. The police wouldn't be interested in Larkin when Briar was a much easier collar. Briar had guilt written all over him.

15

On the morning of her thirteenth birthday, Persephone had lain on the bedroom rug, watching the pale octagons of light from the window track their path across the wall. She could hear her father singing in the garden, and her mother, Akemi, on the stair.

A few seconds later the hinge creaked. Her mother's head poked round the door.

"Still in your dressing gown, Seph? Hurry up and wash. You don't want to be late."

"I washed before you and Daddy were up. Hours ago."

"So what are you doing?"

"Waiting." Any kind of ceremony day was the same; the morning of a masque ball she had just this excitement and anticipation thrumming in her blood between the flashes of real incident. Most of such days were waiting.

"Put your clothes on, it's nearly time to go." Mother's head retracted back into the hall as though she were a depressed jack in the box.

Persephone's dress hung at the front of the wardrobe. Mother had finished embroidering it the afternoon before; a chain of stitched dancing dolls adorned the hem. As Persephone pulled it over her face she smelt the clean scent of ironed cotton.

By the time she got downstairs her mother was coated and hatted at the front door, keys in hand. They passed into the warmth of the garden. Father was polishing his shoes on the low wall.

"You go ahead," he told them. "I'll catch you up."

Mother didn't answer immediately. This was another kind of waiting; Persephone recognised the tipping point between the state of tension they normally lived in and the flaring of a row.

"It starts in ten minutes," Mother said. "Just put your shoes on and come with us now."

"I've a thing or two to do first," Father replied.

Persephone pushed by her mother and made her own way to the top of the street. She heard the shouting start but kept walking, till the voices passed from earshot, and she arrived at the workshop alone.

This was a day to mark her place within the family. Because the workshop was part of their heritage, the ceremony was held there, on the top floor. About thirty households would be present. The descendants of Botham and Jackson were permitted but unlikely to attend. As Persephone ascended from the ground floor in the paternoster, the building was near silent – unlike the busy workplace she knew it to be during the week. She hoped she wouldn't be expected to make small talk before the ceremony started. Any social interaction drained her.

She hopped off the paternoster into the Sorcerers' room. Candles had been lit, and by the soft light Persephone saw that all the guests were kneeling in a circle, with a blank space awaiting her at the heart of the ring. Everyone had hassocks to protect their knees, but there wasn't one in her allocated place at the centre, so she remained standing on the glass.

Ten endless minutes followed as they awaited Briar's arrival. The ceremony couldn't start without him. At last Persephone heard her parents' footfall behind her, and Briar joined her in the circle's heart. Alastair approached them, bearing a canvas bag. To Persephone, Alastair said: "This bag contains many wooden discs, passed down by Lucy Kendrick. Every disc is different. When a disc is spun upon a string or a stick, its markings combine, in the viewer's eye, to form a single, unique symbol. We call this a symbol a *hex*, and it has deep magical significance. Each hex represents a specific emotion. To lay an enchantment upon a doll, you must trace the hex upon her with your tongue. Do you understand?"

"I do," Persephone said.

"Every boy descended from Lucy Kendrick, or from her sisters, is entitled to a single hex. On his thirteenth birthday, he selects the hex, sight unseen, from the bag. In privacy, he will lick the hex upon a doll, to learn what emotion it evokes. Do you understand?"

"I do."

"Every man descended from Lucy Kendrick, or from her sisters, is entitled to a further hex for each daughter he sires.

If he so chooses, he may share this with the daughter. Do you understand?"

"I do," Persephone said again, with consternation, because when she was six, Alastair had said there was one rule for everyone on the eyot. That must be a lie. Now she realised any man might keep the shape of his hex secret, even from his family; but the shape of a woman's hex could never truly be her own.

Alastair opened the bag, and held it out to Briar. As soon as Briar had withdrawn a disc Alastair pulled the drawstring tight again. Persephone had the fastest glimpse of the marking on the wood, its curves and angles. Before the disc could be seen by anyone else, Briar concealed it in the pocket of his jacket.

"The ceremony is complete," Alastair said.

People rose from their hassocks. Most of them headed for a trestle table that had been laden with wine. Briar patted Persephone's back, and said: "Good lass. You're a grown-up now." He glanced over his shoulder at the paternoster. "I've a thing or two to do. Won't be long."

He ambled to the lift.

Rieko, still an eyot newcomer and Alastair's bride of just a few months, drew close to Persephone with congratulations. Persephone gave awkward thanks.

"I wore a dress," Rieko said, forlornly picking at her white lace shift. "I always forget you need to have trousers on this floor."

Persephone glanced down into the darkness below the glass. "There's nobody on the other levels to see."

"I hope your hex is one of the happy emotions. It's such

122

a waste," Rieko said hesitantly, "that you won't use it... in the shop, I mean."

"I might. One day I'll make dolls in the workshop. The Sorcerers can teach me how they're made. I'll be their apprentice."

"Really?" Rieko tilted her head. "I must have misunderstood."

The conversation might have continued in that line, but they were joined by Mother, who apologised for her tardiness. The irony of her arriving late because she was scolding Daddy for lateness did not escape Persephone.

"Where's Briar gone?" Rieko asked innocently.

"He's getting pissed," Persephone said coolly.

Rieko reddened, and Mother told Persephone off for swearing. She didn't offer an alternative explanation for Briar's whereabouts. No one but Rieko would have asked the question, because the answer was so obvious. Persephone knew that blush was one of embarrassment and she didn't share in it. Her father's lapses were often disgusting, and always frightening; but they were a fact of life to Persephone, like the eyot flooding when the rivers overflowed. She didn't see any point in pretending they didn't exist.

The women crossed to the refreshment table. Persephone trailed after them. She was dimly aware of Mother and Rieko discussing when Persephone's grandfather would arrive. Eventually, Persephone raised a question that she had previously pondered, and was yet to see a satisfactory answer to.

"Did you both get hexes when you got married? I mean, you weren't here for your thirteenth birthdays."

Mother and Rieko exchanged glances.

"In a way," her mother said. "All brides from outside the eyot are given the same hex by the Sorcerers. You lick it onto a type of doll called a Frozen Charlotte – she's made from a single piece of china – and tie her to the sash of your bridal gown."

Rieko added: "The enchantment is Selflessness."

Persephone's mother said something short and hushed to Rieko in Japanese, which Persephone didn't speak. Rieko nodded, chagrinned. Persephone was glad that she wouldn't have to wait till she got married to have an enchantment. As soon as Briar verified the meaning of her hex, he would grant it to her. Perhaps that evening, if he wasn't too drunk. More likely, she'd be told tomorrow morning.

When the food was finally eaten, and the last guests had gone home, Persephone and her mother left with a sense of grim inevitability: they had a few short hours before pub closing. Father wasn't in the house when they let themselves in. They readied for bed, and Mother sidled in next to Persephone as she often did if it were likely Briar would cause a disturbance on arrival.

Mother rapidly fell into slumber, exhausted by the festivities. Persephone couldn't settle as quickly. She thought of nothing but her hex. Would it make a happy enchantment, as Rieko had wished for her? Or an unpleasant one? Persephone hoped it was a complex feeling, with a contrast of adjective and noun. But even if it wasn't, it would be *her* enchantment to experience whenever she chose.

She heard her father in the street below, calling into the darkness and whooping as he habitually did at this hour. His attempt to gain admittance and then ascend the stairs was protracted. Finally her parents' bedroom door clicked – followed by the wheeze of the bed as he fell upon it – and Persephone assumed further drama was averted for the night. He would sink into unconsciousness, and arise tomorrow afternoon, when he could tell her the meaning of the hex.

Soon after she must have fallen asleep herself; because she awoke, unsure of the hour, and saw his silhouette looming at the foot of the bed. Her feet were damp. He was spilling something; the water hitting the bedspread was muffled, but audible.

Mother snapped on the lamp.

"Get out!" she said.

Persephone winced against the light. A dark yellow stain formed a map upon the bedspread. Her father pulled up his trousers – she closed her eyes, but not before she saw his expression of bewilderment, even anger, that this room should not be the one he expected. His bearings had failed him, leading him here instead of the bathroom, and this must in some way be her and her mother's fault.

"You disgust me." Mother's voice was guttural.

"Oh, no one's as saintly as you," rallied Daddy.

"Get out!" Mother screamed.

He returned to the master bedroom. Persephone could hear him muttering to himself, through the wall.

She got out of bed, to allow her mother to strip the covers. Instead of finding another quilt as Persephone expected, Mother turned her attention to the clothes drawers. Perplexingly, she removed garment after garment, placing them in piles on the floor.

"What's going on?" Persephone checked.

"We're leaving. As soon as the sun's up, if I can get everything together. I've had enough."

"But Uncle Conrad doesn't have any other free houses."

"Don't be silly, Persephone. We're not moving into an eyot house. I'm taking you to your grandparents."

"Will we be coming back?"

"Not if I can help it."

Her grandparents, hundreds of miles away. Persephone thought of her hex, in her father's pocket.

"No," she said.

"What do you mean, no?"

"No, I'm not leaving."

"You can't want to live like this?"

She didn't know how to reply. All her life she had wished her father away, but he had her hex, and if she were removed from the eyot she couldn't persuade the Sorcerers to teach her.

"Conrad will stop you taking me, if I ask him," she gambled. "He'll pay someone. A lawyer. He hates people leaving the eyot."

Her mother paled.

"Why would you do that?" she cried.

"I can't go," Persephone repeated, immovable.

She watched her mother place her head in her hands and sob.

On the following morning, Mother bundled the soiled sheets into the washing machine, picked up her suitcase, and left her keys by the phone. Persephone looked on and knew it would fall to her to tell Briar her mother had gone, because he was still in bed.

"What should I tell him?" she asked.

"Up to you, my love," her mother said. "If you're determined to stay here you'll have to work that out on your own."

Then she left. Persephone didn't look out the window. She heard the rattle of the wheels on her mother's suitcase, followed by the clang of the garden gate. After that, silence.

Persephone focused on the immediate task, which was readying herself for school. She got dressed, ate a boiled egg, and walked to class. Mrs Cadle was there alone; she set Persephone to placing the jotters on her classmates' desks, ready for their arrival. Seven pupils attended the eyot school, including Persephone, and they were all taught in a single class despite their different ages. She had just laid out the seventh book when she realised there was one left over, bearing Hedwig's name.

"Mrs Cadle?" Persephone only called her that in the schoolroom. The rest of the time she was *Brigid*.

"Mm?" Mrs Cadle said, accepting the leftover book. "I put that in there accidentally. I should really pass it on to the Mayhews."

Persephone sat at her desk and folded her hands. Mrs Cadle continued to look thoughtfully at the jotter.

"Hedwig's doing very well, at Iffley Academy, I hear," she said.

"Yes, miss." Persephone was eighteen months older than Hedwig, placing them closer in age than the other pupils, though they weren't friends, exactly.

"Have you ever thought that you might like to go there?" Mrs Cadle pressed.

Had she? Other schools, proper schools as Persephone thought of them, were a source of curiosity. But they sounded ghastly, between the throngs of people moving all over great big buildings and having different teachers all the while. And why, in any case, was Mrs Cadle asking?

"Don't you like teaching me?" Persephone asked.

Mrs Cadle laughed. "What a question. You're an excellent learner. Which is the point – you might be wasted here. You could do more GCSEs there."

"I'll do GCSEs here."

"Yes, English and Maths and Art. But you could do other subjects there."

"I don't need to. I want to work for Kendricks, as a Sorcerer."

"Hardly anyone gets to be a Sorcerer. I'm not saying you shouldn't try. But you can do that even if you go to Iffley Academy. And at least there you'd have other options if sorcery doesn't work out. And Persephone – you would meet people who aren't your relatives."

She meant boys, Persephone guessed; Hedwig certainly seemed to see that as an advantage. Did Persephone want a boyfriend? Or a girlfriend? The prospect of either simultaneously drew and terrified her.

"I don't want to meet people who aren't my relatives," she said firmly. "Anyway. What if Daddy turned up at the school drunk? It doesn't matter if he does that here."

Mrs Cadle looked at her sadly, and Persephone wondered what *she* had to be sad about.

A sharp rap on the window pane made them both jump. It was Persephone's father, instantaneously present as if to prove her point. Although he wouldn't be drunk now. He'd have slept most of it off.

She glanced at Mrs Cadle, for permission to leave.

"You can go," Mrs Cadle said. "Lessons haven't even started yet. But I'll tell him otherwise, if you prefer."

"No," Persephone said, because she wanted her hex, even if her mother had burdened her with breaking bad news to Daddy. Dread swam in her stomach, but she walked out of the schoolhouse and round to the window where her father was standing.

He wore yesterday's dress shirt, but one tail had worked loose from his waistband.

"Where's your mother?" he said. "Her things aren't in the wardrobe. The suitcase is gone."

"I don't know where she is," Persephone hedged. She wasn't lying. There was no way to know how far her mother had got.

"Come off it. You didn't see her before she left? You're not lying to me, Seph, are you?"

She shook her head. "I did see her. She was putting washing on. I don't know where she is now."

Another thing that wasn't a lie.

And her father decided to believe her: he didn't fly into a rage, at least. He was squinting, as he did when he was hungover.

"I'll ring your grandma," he said. "See if she knows anything."

"Daddy," she said.

"Yes."

"You haven't told me what my hex is."

At this he appeared stricken. "That's right, that's right."

"Have you laid an enchantment with it yet?"

"No rush, is there? Always thought thirteen was too young for one of those."

Too young. How could it be too young? He'd received his at the same age, hadn't he, so what was he talking about.

"How about I look after it for you – until you're properly grown up. When you're able to manage it, I'll hand it over."

"Daddy, I want it now. I'm old enough now."

"Are you arguing with me?"

She shrank. "No. I need to get back inside."

"Yes. That's more like it. I'll see you tonight."

By the time she reached her desk again her face was composed.

"Is everything all right?" Mrs Cadle asked.

"He confiscated my hex." That was the right word. Confiscated. He'd taken, as a penalty, what was otherwise rightfully hers.

"Why would he do that?"

"It's because my mother left," Persephone replied. "He thinks I won't go with her, if he's got my hex."

"God, Persephone."

The exclamation told Persephone she, too, should feel distressed. Instead she felt anaesthetised. There was no feeling, nothing, behind her words. Nothing she could access.

"He's clever," Persephone concluded.

"That's not what I'd call it."

"He is. Because he's right; I won't ever leave the eyot without my hex." She opened her jotter, where the letters seemed to wriggle into shapes she no longer recognised.

16

On Friday morning, Hedwig lay in bed with Stanley Walcott, in Conrad's otherwise empty house. She rolled over to face him, and ran a finger down his chest. The skin was clammy and dragged.

"Your boss is barking," he said.

"Be nice," Hedwig coaxed.

"It's true, though. He was on at us about leaving something out for the fairies. Said it would bring the doll back."

"Not the fairies. The Thief on the Winged Horse." Just a few weeks before, Conrad would have asked her to leave the offering. The fact he hadn't, showed that his trust in her had eroded. She wondered whether Conrad had made an offer to the Thief himself, and his despair at the doll's continued absence had prompted his escape from England.

"You don't believe in that nonsense, do you?" Stanley teased. "Naidu says she's keeping an open mind. But you can tell me – you're just pretending to believe, aren't you?"

"It's abominable of you to encourage me in disloyalty.

Conrad is very good to me and I am *not* going to join you in mocking him. Anyway – our sorcery must come from somewhere. Why not the Thief?"

Stanley rolled his eyes. "Sorcery! There's no sorcery in those dolls. It's all the power of suggestion."

Hedwig did not, in fact, care whether Stanley believed in sorcery. The only important measure was the income derived, and enough rich people had faith in the dolls' powers to hand over cold cash. Hedwig recollected the worn path of this argument from their adolescence and had no interest in revisiting it now. She changed the subject.

"Where will you search next, now the residents are in the clear?"

"They're not in the clear as far as I'm concerned."

"You still think the motive was personal?"

"It was personal all right. It was very personal for someone."

"Who?" Hedwig got out of bed, and walked to the en suite. Stanley didn't reply – presumably from professional reluctance – so she prompted as she turned on the taps: "Darling? Do tell who's the theft personal for?"

"Think about it." Stanley raised his voice over the sound of water. "Who knows this house? Who was born here? Who was pissed off with your boss? You honestly believe Briar Kendrick wouldn't have inside knowledge on how to get inside that cage?"

"Yes – but – didn't you search his house?"

"Yes, and there was nothing to find, because he'd already destroyed the doll. I guarantee you that. We know he's broken other dolls in fits of temper."

The doll with the cracked face, that Persephone had offloaded onto Larkin.

"He *was* very angry," Hedwig commented. "He even mentioned the Paid Mourner when he was shouting at Conrad. And it crossed my mind that he may have had a house key."

"There you are then. But the bastard's alibied by that daughter of his, and he's destroyed the evidence. Hard to arrest him without it."

Hedwig let the water from the tap play over her fingers. She was in two minds about Briar's guilt. The assailant had neither the smell nor the posture of a drunken man; but her impression may have been mistaken, given how distressed she was. As for the alibi – Persephone wasn't a liar, in the ordinary way of things, and yet she had shown strange loyalty to Briar over the years. She still lived with him, when her mother had offered her an escape. Perhaps that loyalty would lead her to fake an alibi, too.

"Do you want to get in this bath with me?" Hedwig called.

"No, love. I'll go after you."

She lowered herself into the water, washing Stanley's sweat from her skin. Her status on the eyot was waning already, without Conrad. She needed to secure her position again urgently. Her hopes had been pinned on the police finding the thief, and returning the doll to its proper place. Were that to happen, Conrad would likely be mollified, as no long-term harm could be attributed to Hedwig... but if Briar had destroyed the Paid Mourner, Hedwig could see no end in sight to Conrad's resentment.

"This business has been tremendously draining for everyone," Hedwig said. "If you don't have enough evidence to arrest Briar, is the case at a dead end?"

"It'll stay open. For completion we have to pursue a few other lines of enquiry, before we stop actively seeking the culprit." He appeared in the doorway, pallidly naked. Confident in his appeal for her, he smiled. "When the case does wrap up that won't make a difference to us. I can see you whenever."

Hedwig squeezed a sponge over her shoulder, to rinse the soap away. It wouldn't do any harm to stay on Stanley's good side.

"That would be nice," she lied.

The letterbox clattered, five minutes after Stanley had gone, and Hedwig assumed he had forgotten something; but it was only the postman, delivering two letters for Conrad. Hedwig's secretarial duties included opening mail addressed to her employer. She took both items of post into the study so she could file or shred the contents as soon as she'd checked their importance.

The first was an invoice from the private investigator; she transferred the payment to the man's account there and then. The second envelope came from Conrad's financial advisors, and contained a statement of accounts for the quarter.

She paused. With a lick of the finger, she turned the pages. Conrad's investments had gone from strength to strength under Hedwig's discreet supervision. He could afford to buy many dolls of the Paid Mourner's worth, if only he believed she was replaceable. No doubt he would pay a great deal for her return. Had Briar more sense and less temper, he could have made a pretty penny by stealing the doll and holding her to ransom. Whatever resentment Briar nurtured for being left out of his father's will, Hedwig thought a two million pound payment would be better salve than a few moments' wanton destruction. Fools with money needed someone like Hedwig to suggest these things to them. Clearly Persephone acted as Briar's caretaker, but Hedwig didn't think she was canny enough to look after his interests in the way Hedwig relished doing for Conrad. And should Stanley's theory one day be confirmed, everyone would suffer from Briar's lack of guidance. Conrad would be devastated by the loss of his doll. Briar would be ousted as a vandal; Persephone as his abetter. Hedwig would be fired because her failure to stop the thief led to the doll's destruction.

At this bleak set of prospects Hedwig tucked the statement in the correct section of the filing cabinet, and pushed the drawer shut.

17

Nearly two weeks after the Paid Mourner was stolen, on a clear Thursday evening, Persephone walked home from work in the twilight. Larkin was sitting on the doorstep.

"What are you doing there?" She glanced at the illuminated windows. "You didn't need to chaperone my dad from a ditch, I hope?"

"No. I was waiting for you."

To be pursued was novel, and unsure of the appropriate response, Persephone said nothing.

"How were things in the shop today?" he asked.

"The end of capitalism can't come soon enough."

Larkin stifled a laugh. She'd noticed before that he seemed to find the things she said amusing and she wasn't sure why.

He said: "Good to know, Persephone."

"I hate the current stock. Why must so many of the dolls be twee young girls? It's what you get when you have a bunch of old men making them."

"You don't think dolls should be beautiful?"

"Those men don't want to look at beauty. They want to look at something made for them, to confirm their desire is the most important thing in the world; they want their dolls like they want their women, a painted smile, no internal life of her own and you can blame her for your passions. Japanese doll lore is different, you know. In Japan their dolls have souls."

"I expect there's a market for that."

"There's a market for everything," she said sourly. She remembered a point that would interest him. "Someone took a fancy to your iron doll. They're going to think about it."

Better not to add that she'd steered them to another purchase, because she liked surreptitiously holding the iron girl, with her queer, intense enchantment of Determined Perseverance, and wasn't ready to see her go.

"I'm surprised," Larkin said. "Alastair was convinced no one would take her."

"Alastair doesn't know everything."

"That's why I've come to *you*. I was hoping you could help me with some sleuthing."

He took a postcard from his coat pocket, and gave it to her. She recognised the photograph of Lucy Kendrick. The original hung upon Conrad's landing wall.

"I bought it in town," Larkin said. "Do you see the necklace? I was wondering – does it mean anything to you? I thought you might know, if it had some special significance."

She did in fact know. The disc Lucy Kendrick wore round

her neck was the same as the discs used for their hexes. According to family legend, it had once borne a hex for Lightheartedness. When Jemima died, Lucy sanded the hex away, and fashioned a pendant from the disc, in constant testimony to her grief.

"It's mourning jewellery," Persephone said.

"That's all?" Larkin prompted. "Nothing to do with sorcery?"

"You're playing spies again. I told you before, you need to be careful. If anyone overheard you, they'd tell Conrad you were asking questions you shouldn't."

"No one's listening. Tell me everything. I'd be willing to do something for you in return."

The offer intrigued her. "Say that again?"

"You can have whatever you like – if it's in my means, of course."

His expansiveness was hard to resist. From curiosity, she ventured: "Do you have any tools I could use? Say, a mechanical lathe?"

His expression grew quizzical. "You turn wood?"

"I try, with my own hand tools, but a mechanical lathe gives so much more control – if I could borrow—"

"I'm afraid I don't have my own lathe; I use the Sorcerers' equipment."

"So you do." Persephone handed him back the postcard, feeling foolish. Now he would guess she tried to make dolls; if he hadn't before, when she took the jig. He probably imagined her attempts were amateurish. Her attempts *were* amateurish.

"But I could buy you a lathe," he said. "If that's your price."

Persephone scowled. "Don't be silly. They cost three thousand pounds."

"I know."

Was three thousand pounds so little to him? Or did he want her information so much he would pay more than he could afford? His confidence that she'd comply, with the right offer, irritated her. "Discussing sorcery with you is forbidden. You're so impatient. Conrad's promised you sorcery eventually. Why can't you wait?"

"Why should I wait? I'm a descendant of Ramsay; that entitles me to know. In any case, I'm bad at waiting."

"It shows." Men were bad at many things, and yet they evaded blame. She had the unpleasant premonition that if she broke Conrad's rules, as Larkin wished, all the blame would fall to her, and Larkin would evade any negative consequences; just as friends and neighbours implicated her in Briar's drunkenness. The thought of Briar reminded her she must check to see if he was inside, and still breathing, wherever he had happened to collapse. She addressed Larkin abruptly: "Move out of the way. I need to let myself in."

"A lathe isn't your heart's desire. If it were, you'd do as I ask."

"We're at a dead end then, aren't we?" Persephone put her key in the lock.

"Until I work out what you want," he said.

But he couldn't grant her heart's desire: his own easy autonomy, the assurance that any demands he made to develop his talent would eventually be met without penalty. She stepped into the hallway, and turned to close the door on Larkin. He was already walking away.

*

The cottage, when Persephone entered, was full of light and the scent of stew. Her father was in the kitchen, and she could tell at a glance – from his posture, and expression – that he was sober. This didn't mean Persephone could relax, because he was always capable of volatility. But it would mean he made fewer demands on her attention. She sat down to eat, her feet throbbing from a day standing in the shop and her father joined her. They ate in silence but there was as little tension as there could ever be between them. At the other end of the table, she noticed he had been constructing a wooden model of a spiral staircase. It must be the first bit of miniature architecture she'd seen him undertake in years. Ordinarily his hands shook too badly.

He resumed his woodwork when he'd cleared the plates. Persephone noted that his hands were, indeed, shaking, but he was intent – his tongue pinched between his teeth in concentration as he tried to balance a bead on the head of a tiny newel post. The effort he was investing in a work of beauty made Persephone's eyes prickle.

She stood up rapidly, blinking her tears away, because she didn't want to have a conversation with her father about why she was crying. Her haste disturbed his much strived-for focus. The bead slipped from his grasp, and rolled beneath the cooker. He tutted.

"I'll get it," she said quickly. She didn't want his frustration to turn to anger. "It's my fault it's under there."

She edged past him to the cooker. Gripping it on either side, Persephone shuffled it forward on the lino. The bead

141

was dislodged from the grease it had settled in, and rolled to her father's foot, where he picked it up with a smile and a nod. He turned back to his newel post.

Persephone grasped the sides of the cooker again, to manoeuvre it back. Without warning, she felt a shock of Adrenaline-fuelled Fear. She let go with a gasp, and the fear ebbed.

"It's not still hot is it?" her father asked absently, his eyes trained on his work. "Did you burn yourself?"

"No," Persephone said. "No, I was just clumsy."

She surreptitiously ran her hand down the side of the cooker again. She didn't find the right spot immediately. But then the feeling was back, as sudden as it had been before. Fear. She craned to take a look. A rivulet of translucent wax was barely visible among the food stains. It was solid, and about six inches in length.

Why was there a line of enchanted wax on the cooker?

Someone melted wax on the hob, she thought, *and it spilt or spattered in shaking hands*. Enchanted wax. Persephone envisioned her father melting the Paid Mourner's pretty head in a saucepan.

Her options took on clarity. She could turn the evidence in to the police; Briar had made his bed, so perhaps he should lie in it. But he also still had her hex, and she would never get it if she betrayed him.

She scratched at the wax with her nail, allowing the dust to be lost on the air. She restored the cooker to its original position. No one, now, would know.

18

Larkin was drinking in the Eyot Tavern, which was moderately busy, it being Saturday evening. Briar Kendrick was among the customers. Despite Briar's fondness for beer, he was a rare patron. From word of mouth, Larkin had gathered he usually frequented the Wetherspoons on Castle Street, or else drank at home. This was a chance for Larkin to observe him, and he wanted to observe him, because most people still thought Briar was the chief suspect and that made him compelling. How odd that Persephone would choose to live with such a disaster of a man. She clearly found him a strain, but he must have some hold on her.

That night Briar initially seemed in good cheer, laughing along with some of the other architects at crude jokes, which somehow sounded worse in his Oxford accent. "A woman saw a funny little man at the end of her garden," Briar was saying. "And she thinks, well the little folk have magic powers and they have to grant you your wishes when you catch them. So she lassos him with a hose and says she won't free him till he's given her three. 'Fair enough,' he says, 'what's your first wish?' She has a think and says, 'I want a bigger house.' He says, 'Bigger house, rightio. Second wish?' Then she gives it a bit of thought and tells him, 'I want a bigger bank balance.' 'All right, a million pounds should do the trick, eh? You've one wish left.' And she says, 'I want bigger tits.' He tells her, 'Whatever you want. But to make your wishes come true you have to have sex all night with me.' And she weighs it up and says, 'I can live with that.' Next morning he asks her in bed, 'How old are you then?' She says, 'Twenty-four!' 'Fucking hell,' he tells her. 'Twenty-four and you still believe in magic.'"

The architects all had a laugh at this and Briar fell off his bar stool. When he got up, he ordered another beer; but Mrs Mayhew declined to serve him, because he'd had enough. And then he turned.

"You'd know about bigger tits," he told her. "Only yours aren't magic. They're fucking plastic."

One of the other architects tried to steer him out, but he resisted and broke a glass. They finally got him through the door, and left him sitting on the smoking bench. Mrs Mayhew telephoned Persephone to come collect him. Larkin took a step outside to watch from the shadows. Briar was singing by then, one fragment of a lewd folk song after another.

Persephone approached, from the darkness, without seeing Larkin.

"Come on, Dad," she said to Briar, gently. It was the most placatory Larkin had ever heard her. "Home, eh?"

"You don't tell me what to do," Briar said.

"I'm not telling you what to do. It's more comfortable at home." She placed a hand on his shoulder, as though to steer him.

"I'm your father. You should have respect for me. You giving me orders. I don't take orders."

"I wish you would," she said, with more of the sharpness Larkin recognised. "You fight with people at every turn. Fight with them, steal their things, steal from your own brother!"

He reared, and swung his fist at her. Larkin heard the impact – the thud of his knuckles on her cheekbone – and she fell to the floor. Briar was breathing heavily. Now his anger had peaked he appeared as shaken as she did.

"Back off, Briar," Larkin said, stepping into the light from the pub window. "I think it's time I called the police."

"No," Persephone called out. "Don't. I'm all right."

Larkin approached and offered her his hand. Her temple had caught a jagged stone on the ground, creating a thin line of blood along the side of her face.

She placed her hand in his, and stood, unsteady.

"Go away," she said thickly to Briar. "You've done enough for today."

He nodded; meek now. He shot Larkin a look of some wariness, before weaving up the path. Persephone watched him take the road home.

"Let's get you to the John Radcliffe," Larkin said, meaning the nearest hospital.

"I don't want to. They'll ask questions."

"Has he done this before?"

"No. I mean, I've always got out of his way if he tries. You can, you know, when you know somebody's body language well enough." She repeated: "I should have managed him better."

"That's not true," Larkin said. "You shouldn't have to."

They stood alone for a moment more. She made a move to leave, and Larkin took her hand, again, to delay her.

"You can't follow him," Larkin said.

"I have to. I live with him, Larkin. And I can't move out." She closed her eyes.

"Do you worry he can't look after himself? Is that why you stay there?"

"No. I'm not responsible for him." She sniffed. "But if I move out, he might – look, it's very complicated. You don't have to worry about me going back, Larkin. I do know how to handle him. I've lived alone with him since I was thirteen."

"That was when your mother left?"

She nodded. "She wanted to take me with her – and I – and I refused. I want to be a Sorcerer. I couldn't do that if I left."

So she had ambition. That explained a lot. And she had probably surmised correctly; there was no route into sorcery except on the eyot. But it didn't quite account for Persephone's dogged insistence on staying with Briar. Surely he didn't get power of veto on who became a Sorcerer, and who didn't? She could work at Kendricks while living in any other eyot property. This was a point he could press home.

"The Tavern is available, Persephone. Let me do some

first aid if the hospital's out of the question. And then I'll talk to Mrs Mayhew about you taking a room."

"Mrs Mayhew doesn't like me." But she was wavering, Larkin could see it.

"If you take a room at the Tavern, you'll be walking distance from your father's, and from the workshop. But you won't have to share a roof with an alcoholic. It will give you breathing space."

"That does sound…" Persephone trailed off. "Maybe I could stay here, for the time being."

They walked round to the side door, so Persephone would not be gawked at in the bar. He led her upstairs, into the kitchen, and sat her down with a mug of tea.

"Mrs Mayhew must have a first aid kit somewhere. I'll pop down and ask her."

"Don't," Persephone said. "She gossips."

Larkin didn't bother to deny this. Mrs Mayhew was indeed a gossip. Pragmatically, he said: "She'll know something's wrong anyway, if you can't stay with Briar."

"Just don't tell her he hit me." She wiped some of the blood from her cheek. "How long were you watching, Larkin? Did you hear what I said to him?"

"Nobody else needs to know what I did or didn't hear."

She exhaled. "You promise?"

He nodded.

"Thank you. People can't know my suspicions. They can't. They all suspect him enough already."

"I don't."

She gave a half laugh, half sob of disbelief.

He left her drinking tea, then spoke to Mrs Mayhew

downstairs in the bar. He said Persephone had stumbled while trying to lift Briar from his seat, and needed to clean up a graze.

"The first aid kit's in the wall cabinet by the fridge," she said.

Larkin lowered his voice. "She might need a room here for a while."

"I see." Mrs Mayhew raised an eyebrow. "It's like that with Briar, is it? She's tolerated him longer than her mother, at least."

Larkin ignored the invitation to tittle-tattle. "I thought it might be OK for her to stay, what with you being off season, and having the rooms vacant."

"The other rooms are bigger than yours," Mrs Mayhew said. "She'd have to pay four hundred a week. That's cheap, in Oxford, you know."

He took a roll of notes from his pocket. "I doubt she can cover four hundred on shop assistant wages. Charge her one hundred, and I'll cover the rest. Just between you and me?"

"How thoughtful." Mrs Mayhew gave him an indulgent look, but he detected an acid undertone to her words. "Watch you don't get taken for a ride, though, eh?"

A customer caught her attention. Larkin rejoined Persephone in the kitchen. He took the first aid kit from the wall cabinet.

"Everything's sorted." He filled a small bowl with water and disinfectant. "Mrs Mayhew has confirmed she has a room for you. I've given her some money upfront – just pay me back when you have it."

"What's it cost?" Persephone asked.

"Hundred a week. You will stay however long you need, won't you?"

And Persephone nodded. He sat beside her, to wash the cut. It reminded him rather of glazing the porcelain dolls. She had such a pert face, even in repose.

"Thank you, Larkin," she said suddenly. "You're a good friend."

"For doing something ordinarily decent? You need better friends, Persephone."

"You can call me Seph, if you like. Everyone does."

He checked the cut was clear of grit, before making eye contact. "Is that what you prefer?"

"No." She grinned.

"Good. I like Persephone more. And who wants to do what everyone else does, anyway?"

Mrs Mayhew entered the kitchen, and made a fuss about sticking plasters that ruined the moment. But even that was fine, Larkin decided, because Persephone shot him a glance that made it clear they shared their irritation. He had been right. She thought they were allies, too.

19

Hedwig heard about her mother's new lodger the next morning. Mama had come to the house to pick up the money Hedwig promised, but instead of leaving straight away, she followed her daughter into the dining room where she had been polishing silverware with Brasso. Hedwig resumed her work, Mama unwound her scarf, and launched into second-hand detail. She hadn't seen what occurred herself – she had been working behind the bar – but Briar and Persephone must have fallen out. Briar had been terribly drunk, and Persephone had a cut and a bruise to the head, so it didn't take a genius to work out. He'd telephoned the Eyot Tavern that morning and Persephone refused to speak to him.

"Every cloud, Mama," said Hedwig. "If Persephone's staying with you, there's no need for me to keep loaning you money."

Mama sidestepped the hint. "That reminds me – here's a funny thing. When Larkin told me Persephone needed a room, he said to only charge her a hundred a week. He said he'd pay the other three because she'd never afford the lot on her sales salary. And he said I wasn't to let Persephone know the real cost of the room. I mean, it's all the same to me, but I did wonder what was going on there. He must be soft on her."

Probably. He'd had that drink with Persephone, hadn't he? Hedwig's own curiosity about Larkin had taken a backseat since the Paid Mourner went missing. For the foreseeable future, Stanley had to believe there was a chance of getting back together – no matter how deluded that was – which meant there could be no suspicion of her chasing Larkin. She rubbed the blade of a knife with a cloth, removing traces of tarnish.

"You are incorrigible, Mama. No secrets around you, are there! Now make yourself useful, goose." Hedwig passed her mother a cloth and a handful of cutlery. She wiped the last of the Brasso from her own knife. Briar would have woken to an empty house that morning. He'd need a friend, with Persephone gone.

That afternoon, Hedwig walked into central Oxford. She calculated that Briar would still be sober, it not being so very long after pub opening. It was Castle Street she tried first – the whole eyot knew that was his favoured haunt – and she saw him sitting alone, morose, in a corner booth. His eyes meandered over the silent football match on the television screen.

She ordered herself a lemonade and approached the other seat. He startled.

"Hedwig?"

"It's not taken, is it?"

"No – but – Margot didn't send you, did she? Nothing's happened to Persephone?"

"She's fine as far as I know," Hedwig said. "It's so good to get this opportunity to talk, just you and me. We have such a lot to discuss."

Briar scratched his chin. "Do we indeed?"

"About the Paid Mourner."

His lip curled. "I've got nothing to say about that."

"I've got a friend in the police, Briar. You're his number one suspect. He thinks you stole the Paid Mourner and destroyed her."

Briar downed the dregs of his beer. "They searched my house. They didn't find anything. That's all there is to say."

He put an arm into his jacket.

"Don't be hasty." Hedwig's voice was low. "My contact says that Persephone alibied you. But you've fallen out, now, haven't you? Do you think she'll change her story?"

He stood. "Leave her out of it."

"Don't you see? She's stood by you so far, but if she tells the police you did it, that'll be just the reason they want to look at you again."

"She won't do that," he said, but he sounded unsure.

"We can *help* each other," she said. "I don't *want* the police to confirm the doll's damaged. Conrad would be devastated – bereft beyond repair – can you imagine what that will be like for the rest of us to endure?"

Briar sat down again, with obvious reluctance. "I never took that doll. I don't remember anything from that night."

"Oh, Briar. Hardly a cast iron defence," demurred Hedwig.

"Persephone doesn't really think I took it, not deep down. She just has a temper, like me. Makes her say things."

"If she says them in front of the wrong person, we're all in the shit," said Hedwig sorrowfully. "We need to persuade her, and the police, that the doll is still intact."

"How?"

Hedwig took a deep breath. "We arrange a forgery. There's photos enough of the Paid Mourner to commission a likeness. Then we stage an offering to the Thief on the Winged Horse. It has to exceed the value of Conrad's earlier offering. I'm thinking her worth in gold would be appropriate. All we have to do next is leave the forgery in Conrad's house, as if she's been returned."

"You're mad. Conrad will know the difference."

"Not if the forgery's good enough. And he'll want to believe, Briar. You know how serious he is about appeasing the fae folk. Plus here's the thing, the real clincher. The forgery will have the right enchantment. You're going to lay it on the new doll. Nobody knows the enchantment except him, and you. Is that right?"

Briar left her question hanging. His eyes drifted back to the television screen, but he wasn't seeing the game. Finally he said: "Let's say your forgery is convincing. Everyone accepts the doll's been found. But if I'm not the thief, the real culprit and the real doll are still out there. They could show up at any time. What then?"

Hedwig smiled. "You're right. The plan assumes you're guilty. So the important question is – how sure are you of your innocence? Yes, yes, I know you don't remember, but you have the motive, Briar; and you knew how to open the cage. When you say you didn't do it, not even your own daughter believes you."

He had slumped, unresponsive as she hit home. Hedwig relented for a moment.

"Can I get you another beer?"

Briar nodded.

She stood up to go to the bar, and he caught her arm.

"I can lay the right enchantment," he whispered. "But that forgery better be perfect. Do you understand? If I don't think it'll convince Conrad then I'll have nothing to do with it. Get the doll made well and I'll lay the enchantment on it."

"Brilliant, Briar. Do you have the hex written down?"

"There was never any disc. The hex was visible on the doll's head, beneath her hair, if you knew to look there – Lucy's tongue softened the wax so it left a mark. I remember it clear as my own name."

"You're sure your memory's accurate?"

"Let me worry about that. You just go about arranging a forger."

She nodded. "I already have someone in mind."

20

While Hedwig plotted with Briar, Persephone was at the Tavern, on the telephone to her mother. Persephone gave her new contact details, in case her mother tried to contact her at the cottage.

"You've moved into the *pub*?"

"For now."

"What's he done?"

Persephone did not want to say her father had struck her. As soon as she said that, her mother would insist on collecting her from the eyot.

"I just got tired of his drinking," she said.

"*Something* must have changed."

"Nothing's changed," Persephone said wearily. "That's the problem."

"But the Eyot Tavern, Sephy – you're still on his doorstep. I should never have let you stay there. I should have fought it in court."

"I need to be nearby. If I cut contact, he won't give me my—"

Her mother made a sound somewhere between contempt and frustration. "That blasted hex. Even if he ever gives it to you – and he *won't* – women don't become Sorcerers. Accept that, Seph."

"I'm staying, Mother," she said. "And I won't discuss it any further."

That evening, she slipped from the Tavern back to the cottage. It was in darkness – and thus, she assumed, safe to go in.

She went straight to her own room, eager to pack her things – the clothes and other necessities she had left behind – before Briar returned. The suitcase was nearly full when she surveyed the doll limbs strewn across her bedroom table. With a sigh, she gathered them together in a cloth bag, and placed her finished dolls and whittling tools with them. Whenever she had shown her dolls to Alastair he had dismissed them as juvenile work. But she had practised and practised; she was sure her craft must have improved since her last plea for consideration.

She returned to the landing, and peered down the stairs anxiously. No sign of Briar's return yet. Her mind was on the hex Briar owed her. She had searched the house, numerous times, for his hiding place, and never yet found it. This might be her final opportunity to look again, for the foreseeable future.

To her right, Briar's bedroom door was ajar. It would

make sense to check inside, just in case she found something she'd overlooked.

She saw a plain room, which was tidy enough, though it smelt unaired and faintly musky. The bedclothes probably needed changing. Her attention turned to the storage. She opened the wardrobe and ran her hands over the back and the base. She opened each of the drawers in the chest, and found birth certificates and a passport, with caches of childish crayon drawings in the left hand side – he must have kept them from when Persephone was a girl – but nothing else besides clothes. She glanced under the bed, too. Nothing.

From the floor below, she heard the tell-tale scrape of a key on brass: Briar aiming for the front door lock, and narrowly missing. There would be no way to get past him, and she had no wish to justify her departure when he might rapidly turn aggressive again. She slid up the sash window and dropped her bags onto the flat kitchen roof below. She could escape through the back garden. Just as she heard the key turn, she hoisted herself through the window and landed painfully on the coarse bitumen. Without time to check her scratches, she made the second leap onto the muddy path, her bags over her shoulder, and ran with her gaze straight ahead, no longer caring if Briar saw her getting away. For now, she was out of his reach.

21

Mrs Mayhew passed on a telephone message to Larkin; Hedwig wished to see him at Conrad's house. It was the first time he'd visited since the night of the party. He hoped – though didn't have high expectations – that Hedwig wished to lift his exclusion from the Sorcerers' magic. When he arrived, she led him to the drawing room as she had before; only this time, Hedwig took Conrad's seat. She didn't invite Larkin to sit down.

"It gives me no pleasure to do this," she said. "I'm afraid we need to discuss your position here. When you arrived, Conrad suggested you were a spy. You insisted you had no affiliation."

"That's right."

"Larkin, Larkin, Larkin. I hired a private investigator. He says you were resident in San Niccolò in 2018, with the family of Cristofano Minucci. Signore Minucci owns a long-standing doll-making firm in Florence."

Her findings were potentially disastrous for Larkin's

ambitions. His thoughts turned, immediately, to reducing that risk. "If you're insinuating I'm Cristofano's spy, you couldn't be more wrong. Your investigator can confirm I was never in Cristofano's employ; I paid him for board and he forcibly evicted me—" Larkin hesitated. If he gave a reason for his eviction, Hedwig might be persuaded of his antipathy to Cristofano. But the full truth would do Larkin no favours. He opted for a partial version. "Cristofano's daughter was stealing from me and he took her side. We did not part on good terms. I returned to England a year ago. Since then I've had no contact with Cristofano at all."

"Larkin, you know how fond we are of you. But can you see how bad this looks? At the time of Conrad's job offer you never mentioned living with one of our competitors. What will Conrad say, when I tell him you have history with another doll-making dynasty?"

Will say, not *said*. Whatever investigation Hedwig had conducted into Larkin's background, she hadn't shared her findings with Conrad. It bemused Larkin that she should threaten his position at Kendricks before taking Conrad's orders. Unless, of course, Hedwig was open to negotiation.

Larkin said: "Conrad is far away; he must trust you to make decisions in his absence. Could we reach an understanding without disturbing him?"

"Yes. It would make me so sad to break this news to him. Your duplicity doesn't bother me personally, Mr Larkin. Ideals are no match for pragmatism."

Good. Still, she wouldn't trick him into an admission of guilt. "I'm glad we can resolve this between ourselves. The very idea Cristofano would give me a job is absurd. He despises me. My proper place is at Kendricks, as a member of the company family. I beg you not to undermine Conrad's faith in that."

Dropping her voice conspiratorially, Hedwig replied: "I'll keep this conversation confidential if you will."

"OK." Larkin took the opposing seat. "What remains to be said?"

"It's been brought to my attention that the Paid Mourner has, almost definitely, been destroyed."

"Really?" Larkin was stunned. "Whoever told you such a thing?"

"A friend, with intimate knowledge of the case. Conrad isn't fully aware of all the details yet, and for his sake, I would prefer he never learnt them. To avoid Conrad's heartbreak," Hedwig went on, "I'm seeking to commission a replica of the Paid Mourner. I'll persuade Conrad of a ransom demand from the fae folk. The imitation doll will be supplied to him in exchange for her value in gold. She will be like the Paid Mourner in every respect. It's my intention that Conrad will *never* know the difference."

And she'd be pocketing the gold. Larkin recalled their first meeting, when she'd said the Paid Mourner was worth two million pounds. It wasn't the kind of sum you forgot.

"What part do I play in this?" Larkin asked.

"I need someone to make the doll. From the Sorcerers' reports, your work is *exquisite*, and more indicative of an experienced craftsman than an apprentice. You will craft a replica, and I'll make separate arrangements for the correct enchantment to be laid upon it."

An admirable attention to detail. Other than Conrad,

only Briar knew the correct enchantment. Briar must, then, already be conspiring with Hedwig to work his magic. Maybe she'd extorted his help just as she was trying to extort Larkin's now. The need for Larkin's input was obvious; Briar didn't have the dexterity for basic doll-making, much less for a nuanced forgery. Yet Larkin felt sullied by the offer. He was an artist. Art should transform what had come before; it wasn't mere replication. What was worse, nobody would know the work was his. Where was the appeal of that?

"I do hope you'll accept, Larkin. I did think we were such friends." Hedwig paused. "And – forgive me – you're not in a position to bargain, given Cristofano's testimony."

She was unlikely to be appeased by the reason for his refusal. Larkin offered a humble alternative. "The Sorcerers overstated my talent. Wax isn't a natural medium for my skills. To persuade Conrad, you want a doll maker fully versed in that form."

Hedwig stood and placed some coal on the fire as she thought.

"That's a great disappointment to me," she said eventually. "I'll miss you when you're dismissed."

"If I might suggest a compromise," Larkin said hastily. "What if I were to make a personal recommendation – a forger who fashions wax with breathtaking skill, and will guarantee discretion? I know her very well, and would trust her with my life."

"Who?"

"She operates under an alias, in London. You must go to a butcher's shop on Brewer Street. The butcher is the intermediary – you must tell him you have instructions for Scarlotta Dahl, and he will pass on your requirements."

"I won't be able to speak to the forger directly?"

"It's better if you can honestly say you've never met her, for your protection as well as hers. You don't have to give your own name either, if it makes you feel more secure. She demands payment in cash to avoid a paper trail."

"I hadn't counted on paying for the work at all. Why should I pay a stranger, when I could make you do the work for free?"

So she was definitely intending to keep the gold for herself. Larkin filed this thought, and said: "Believe me, Hedwig – Scarlotta Dahl will mimic the Paid Mourner with far more style than I ever could. Isn't it essential that the doll is convincing?"

Hedwig contemplated the flames. Almost to herself, she said: "The doll needs to be perfect."

"Well, then—"

"I'll consider this Scarlotta. But Larkin, my dear; don't think you're off the hook."

He wouldn't dare. But he had deferred his dismissal, for now.

22

The following morning was Monday, and Hedwig went to the workshop to gather sales information for Conrad. He hadn't requested any such data, but she wasn't going to be caught out if he asked to be briefed on his return. Persephone had phoned in sick; Cosima was covering the sales desk, and she fetched the ledgers at Hedwig's request. Everything looked to be in order. Hedwig scanned for any missed sales deadlines or returns.

"Cosima, do you know why this item was delayed?" Hedwig asked, tapping a fingernail on an entry for Interior Design. *Framed lithograph, pursuant to completed diorama.*

Cosima shrugged. "No idea. They must have told Persephone. Do you want me to ring her?"

"No, I can find out here." Hedwig walked through to the Interior Design department. The atmosphere had changed, she thought, since her last visit; there were more people standing about and chatting rather than at work, and more laughter. Rieko, however, was intent on the room she was furnishing.

"I know the lithograph you mean," Rieko said when Hedwig disturbed her. "I caught a problem with it before it went out. The work had to be redone."

"How tiresome for you! What was the problem?" Hedwig pressed.

"The customer had requested a perfect miniaturisation of a nineteenth-century picture called *Gargantua*, by Daumier. The replica was – imperfect."

Hedwig sensed Rieko was being evasive. "Let me take a look."

At the next table, Rumour Thornett, Daisy Gilman, and Raven Fleetwood had paused their chat to listen. Daisy was grinning, insolently.

Hedwig said: "You oversee the picture making, don't you, Daisy? Would you like to offer me a description of the offending lithograph?"

"I can do better than that," Daisy said. "I can show you."

She apparently took satisfaction in retrieving the picture from her work area. It was about the size of a postcard, in black and white. It depicted a sitting giant, with a ramp running to his mouth. Workers toiled along the ground. They carried offerings on their back, up the ramp, into the giant's waiting maw. The giant had Conrad's features.

"Who was this gentleman *meant* to be?" Hedwig asked icily.

"Louis Philippe II," Daisy said gleefully. "It's an old cartoon by someone who was unhappy with his king. Do you see how oblivious the king is to everyone working beneath him? I thought it was very fitting!"

Rieko cut in: "I've impressed upon the women that it was highly unprofessional to even attempt to send this product to a customer. I would have discussed appropriate discipline with Conrad if he were available. Daisy has received a verbal warning, which I would have brought to his attention on his return."

"Be aware that in Conrad's absence I continue to act as his representative," Hedwig said. "This should have been brought to me, *without delay*. Daisy, your pay will be docked this month in addition to the warning you've already received."

The grin on Daisy's face slipped. "You're a fool, Hedwig. You don't get it, do you? You think we're all expendable, and you shouldn't be. But he can get rid of you as easily as any designer. You're one of us even if you throw your towel in with him. He won't protect you."

"Thank you for the advice. Your pay will be docked *next* month as well." Hedwig glanced around the room, smiling, to show she was unruffled. "I'm sorry I interrupted everybody's work. Please, don't let me delay you any longer."

Hedwig caught the next train to London; from Paddington it was a brisk half hour walk to the Brewer Street Butcher. On arrival, she stepped through the doors and the air had the metallic tang of blood. There wasn't much of a queue; just an elderly lady wrapped in a fox stole. Hedwig glanced around. The walls were cream tile with a red majolica border a quarter of the way up. They were chipped enough to be original features. A man in a vest and striped apron, with his hair beneath a kerchief, apportioned some tripe to the waiting woman and took her cash.

"Yes?" he said to Hedwig. His teeth overlaid each other, as though there weren't enough room in his muzzle for all of them.

The old woman was still standing by the till. She returned her leather purse to her handbag, with her tripe secure in the crook of her arm.

Hedwig checked the wares behind the glass. The first thing she saw was a tray of fat tail segments; each one had a perfect circle of white bone at the centre, with the red meat spilling away in petals.

"A pound of ox tail, please," she said. Before home, she would have to dispose of them. They would keep for the journey, the day was cold, but if the carriage was crowded she didn't relish the idea of cradling a bag of offal.

The butcher pincered the meat and dropped three pieces into his scales. The old woman, finally, left the shop.

The bell above the door was still ringing as Hedwig leant across the counter. She needed to give instructions before another customer arrived.

"I have work for Scarlotta Dahl," she hissed.

The butcher laid down his pincers and removed his gloves.

"What do you require?" he asked.

"An imitation of the Paid Mourner. An exact imitation, good enough to fool the owner."

"Scarlotta Dahl can faithfully replicate the doll's appearance. I can assure you of that. When do you need it?"

"As soon as possible." Persephone could withdraw Briar's alibi at any moment. There wasn't time to be lost.

The butcher laughed. "Have you heard the adage that if you want something good, cheap, and fast, only two of your requirements will be met?"

"I do hope this doll will surpass *all* expectations. What can you provide in a week?"

"The doll will be ready, and Scarlotta will happily accept ten thousand pounds."

"I only have three," Hedwig said, feigning regret. She'd grown up around doll makers. Ten thousand pounds was ridiculous for a wood and wax doll with no enchantment laid on.

"Three what? Three coconut macaroons? Any lower than seven thousand would be an insult." The butcher tipped the pan of ox tail segments back into their tray.

"Surely you should pass on the brief first. Scarlotta may feel differently."

"I handle business." He was implacable. "Seven is my lowest offer."

"Six." She had three of her own saved, and she could pressure Briar into matching her contribution. "That's as very far as I could stretch; and it would be so heroic of you to accept."

"Six thousand, for a ten-day turnaround time."

"Done!" Ten days was longer than she felt comfortable with, but she suspected she'd already pushed hard enough.

"The ten days will start on provision of model photographs, cash, and materials."

"Doesn't Scarlotta have her own wax and wood?"

"If you want an exact replica, you should use the very same source of wax and wood as the Paid Mourner."

Hedwig could see the sense of this. Getting hold of the right wood wasn't impossible – the same tree that had been felled for the doll had been cut up for the workshop floor. She was unsure about the wax, but perhaps Briar could advise.

"Let me see what I can do," she said. "I'll be back later in the week with the cash."

The butcher touched his forelock as she left.

She telephoned Briar as she walked to the station.

"We'll need to split the cost, fifty-fifty," she said.

"Three thousand pounds!" he roared.

Hedwig took a deep breath. Briar was terribly self-indulgent. Unlike her, he came from a monied family, and his current poor finances were entirely down to bad management. Had he been less profligate he could have had a very comfortable life; even a luxurious one, surrounded by the kind of beauty Conrad took for granted.

"Now Briar," she said. "Borrow it from one of the other Kendricks! You can't tell me you haven't gone to them cap in hand before."

"Don't you talk to me with that kind of disrespect. I told you, Hedwig. I need to see the doll's good enough before I have anything to do with this. I'm not putting any money towards it before the doll's even made."

"It's only yourself you're hurting. Don't you see I'm acting for both of us? The moment Persephone gives you

172

up, the police will be on your back. I'm saving you from a certain spell in prison." A tremor of pleasure, at being needed, rippled through Hedwig. She was certain that without her help Briar was doomed. "You have a lot more to lose than me if I call this off now."

She let him think while she waited at a pedestrian crossing.

"All right, I take your point. I can pay one thousand," he said querulously, as the green man appeared. "That's what I've got."

"I know you mean that you'll pay three," Hedwig corrected, "but you'll give me one thousand now, and pay me instalments for the rest."

"All right, all right. I take your point."

She hung up. Five thousand up front would send her into debt. Hedwig was sure it would be worth it if the plan worked, but that only made it all the more imperative that a good forgery was in their hands as soon as possible.

23

The Tuesday after Briar hit Persephone, she returned to work. Bearing in mind her renewed ambition to improve her craft, Persephone had brought her three best dolls with her. She let Alastair know immediately that she wished to talk to him. But he told her he was busy in the morning, and it was mid-afternoon by the time he was able to see her.

"I've only got ten minutes," he said when he finally admitted her to his office.

She sat down with the linen bag of dolls in her lap. He wouldn't look at her directly, and it occurred to her that the cut on her forehead – by now the site of a lurid bruise – made him uncomfortable. All day, the cut had made people uneasy in just this fashion; and although she didn't want their pity, she found it interesting they showed no sympathy. An injury to the head was confrontational. She was sure they suspected Briar of inflicting it. Perhaps they felt they should have intervened when she was younger. Looking at her made them feel guilty. So they looked away again.

"So what's the emergency?" Alastair shuffled some papers into a drawer.

"I've always wanted to work on the top floor. Ever since I was a child."

"There aren't any vacancies." Alastair was decisive.

"There were no vacancies when Larkin arrived."

"He showed exceptional skill."

"You don't know my current skill level. What if my work shows promise, too?" She placed the bag on his desk.

"What's this?"

"My work."

He grunted, and pulled at the drawstring to look inside. He squinted as he said: "It's Conrad's call to make."

"Conrad isn't here. You are." Her voice rose in frustration. "You have a daughter, Alastair. Do you never think about what she might want, and what doors are closed to her because she's a girl? If she wanted to make dolls, shouldn't she have that opportunity?"

His lips tightened. "Now look, I know you might envy a happy family, Persephone, but—"

"*Envy?*"

"But don't use my daughter as a prop for your resentments. What is it you're finding so hard to understand? We can't recruit someone just because she's a girl and we happen not to have any girls on the top floor. We have to recruit on merit."

He stood, dropped the linen bag in her lap, and kept walking to the door.

"You didn't even take the dolls out of the bag," she said.

"I'm going to forget this episode happened. It's obvious

you've had things going on." He gestured at her face. "I'll see to that raise we discussed. An extra fifty pound should be all right."

"Stuff your fifty pound."

"Now look," he said. "You keep telling me you want to make dolls. But who would trust *you* with enchantments, Persephone? You don't have any self-control. It's not your fault, it can't be easy when your mother runs off while you're still a child. But you can't do this work when your emotions are all over the place. I'm sorry, but that's the way it is."

The threshold for not having any self-control was so unjust. Four little words not to Alastair's liking were enough for him to treat her like a hysteric.

He was opening the door. She stood up, and loud enough for the Sorcerers outside to hear, said: "You condescending shit."

He shrugged, as if his point had been made.

She walked past him, her head hot and the bag of spurned dolls in her fist. So absorbed was she in her rage that she didn't notice Larkin was following her until he stepped into the paternoster with her.

"What happened there?" he asked.

"I gave him samples of my work, and asked if I could have an apprenticeship."

"And?"

"He barely glanced at the dolls." She was none the wiser as to whether they were any good. Clearly Alastair didn't think so. She couldn't trust his judgement, and fought against internalising his indifference to her work, but it hurt all the same. She covered her face with her hands. "My mother's right. He's never going to move me away from that blasted counter, and nor is Conrad."

The paternoster had completed a rotation with neither of them disembarking.

"They won't help me either." Larkin was sombre. "I can't teach myself sorcery, and I've failed, utterly, to persuade them I'm ready."

Persephone was tired of following Conrad's rules. There were never any rewards; only punishments for transgressions. They disembarked on the ground floor. Persephone glanced down the hall, to see if anyone might overhear. No one was in sight.

"I'll tell you some things about sorcery," she said. "But not here. Come with me into Oxford, after work."

They took their bikes, along the footbridge, as the moon rose. The temperature had dropped enough for their breath to mist. They cycled and neither of them spoke until they had left the eyot behind.

Persephone began: "Before Lucy Kendrick, or any of her sisters, were born, their parents lived in the house Conrad owns now. The mother, Sarah Horace, miscarried four times. Eventually she left a note upon the threshold of the house, requesting the return of one unborn child, in exchange for her own death on the baby's arrival. She deemed that a like for like exchange. The note was taken, and she expected the bargain would be fulfilled. But instead a week later the Thief left a reply on the same step. It was a request to meet in the orchard at dusk on Friday.

"She arrived at the arranged time, and at first believed she was alone. But the Thief was there – dressed like a gentleman, with hooves instead of feet, and a grey winged steed. He was visible only when the sun was at the right angle in the sky. She asked whether her offer had pleased him, and he said: 'No; I find it boring. There's a better bargain to be struck. First, I offer you all four of your children.'

"This was what she wanted more than anything in the world, but she still felt alarmed. If her death wasn't a sufficient exchange for one lost life, she feared the terms he'd want for four.

"'What's your price?' she said.

"'Your sense of safety,' he replied. 'It will be mine from the second your eldest child takes breath.'

"'And the other three children will follow?'

"'They will.'

"Things passed as he said they would. Lucy was born, and immediately Sarah was fearful. Her mind filled with the terrors of everything that might befall her child. The world never felt safe again."

They were circling the Plain, and anticipating her turn onto Magdalen Bridge, Larkin said: "Not that way; not town. Let's make our way up St Clement's."

So she followed him, in the direction of Headington. He asked no questions about the first part of the story, so she resumed with its next act.

"Lucy was a healthy baby, and also unusual. At the age of six months, she spoke her first sentence – and it was crystal clear. She said: 'Bring me a quill.'"

"Christ."

"She said it as her mother dressed her for the day, then had to repeat it, because her mother was so stunned. 'Bring me a quill, and fine paper' – which would have been paper made from linen. Eventually her mother went to fetch the items and returned with Lucy's father. They watched Lucy make a series of strikes on the piece of paper."

"Babies can scribble, can't they?"

"Not at six months, and it wasn't scribble. She was writing, though her family couldn't tell what language. Her gestures and rhythm and the duration with which she wrote were clearly well controlled. The nanny eventually announced her departure, as she believed Lucy to be a changeling. Her parents were less alarmist, but recognising that the nanny's reaction was unlikely to be an isolated case, they paid the woman for her silence and kept Lucy's strange linguistic abilities a secret."

"Did her parents ever understand what she was writing?"

"No, but her younger sisters were born knowing the language, as she was. It's a language for sorcery, and they'd learnt it while in the company of the fae folk. The sisters recorded words on small wooden discs – you saw a blank one in the picture of Lucy – which their descendants call hexes. Every descendant of the four women receives a hex when they turn thirteen."

"Why?"

"It's a precaution. When Lucy was just entering her teens, she explained to her parents that the fae folk have few natural emotions of their own. In fact the only feeling that is natural to them, and which they feel very deeply, is Envy. They covet human emotions very much but feelings are harder to steal than material possessions, so they try to force a trade through extortion or even abducting the person.

"Now Lucy was a very special child; she understood the language of sorcery, like the fae folk, but she felt emotion, like humans do. So she worked out how to simulate feelings with sorcery. She placed enchantments on her dolls because the fae folk are bad at distinguishing dolls from real people; they could be fooled into taking the doll, rather than its owner. Negative enchantments were included, because they were as attractive to the Thief as positive ones – if not more so. Once Lucy had her sons, she gave them hexes so that they might protect themselves similarly. They gave more of her hexes to their own sons, and it developed into a ritual, which has lasted till the present day, for sons anyhow."

"What a clever myth," Larkin observed. "It feels real because envy *is* the most natural emotion. The myth isn't about the fae folk; it's about us."

Persephone wasn't sure she had understood him. "But envy isn't the most natural emotion."

"Of course it is. It's the most intense; the most primary. It's the most *real*."

"You don't think there are any other feelings that are as real?"

"Lust, maybe. Anger – when the others are thwarted."

"Not – belonging? Happiness? Love?"

"Belonging is an interesting one. There are definitely people with whom one senses a shared goal – and people who are outside that circle. The difference is rather stark, in my experience. I might agree that one is real. But happiness, and love – I think those are rarer than people pretend. Love especially – nearly everyone is pretending about that one. I'm not sure it even exists."

As a bald statement this struck Persephone as absurd. But she admired Larkin – she valued his perspective; and she tried to reverse engineer a truth from what he had said. Hadn't she first been drawn to him by a form of envy? She had wanted his skills for herself, and that was the soil from which her other feelings for him grew.

"I'm not sure I agree with you," she said to Larkin. "But I'll give the matter further thought."

"So what do the Sorcerers *do* with the hexes? Do they paint them somewhere on the doll that's hard to see? I know there aren't any visible paint marks – I'd have noticed."

Persephone was ready to say the words: *you lick the hex on the doll.* He could do nothing with the knowledge, any more than she could; neither of them owned any hexes. Yet she resisted telling him. For twenty minutes now, she had held his attention. The revelation must be spun out, to prolong his focus on her, for as long as possible.

She steered to the kerb, and stopped. "If I tell you, you won't need to talk to me any more."

"What?" Larkin stalled beside her.

"You won't talk to me any more. I'm interesting because I know something you don't. That's true, isn't it?"

"You are peculiar." He laughed. "Imagine *that* being the only interesting thing about you. You're easily the most interesting person on the eyot."

"Damning with faint praise. I'm serious. Let me keep a last secret. For the time being."

"Only one! All right. I can't have done a very good job of persuading you we're friends. I must try harder."

"It's probably me. I'm not used to having friends," she confessed.

"Come make dolls with me tomorrow evening. You wanted Alastair to teach you craft, didn't you? I can teach you craft. I know it's not the same as learning from a Sorcerer, but—"

"Do you mean it?" Persephone asked fervently. "You'll teach me?"

"If you'd like that."

"I would," she said.

They turned their bikes and rode, slowly, towards home.

24

The next morning, the interior designers discovered a break-in. One of the small windows in the lavatories had been shattered. The parquet floor in the designers' workroom was damaged; a square yard of wooden blocks had been dislodged and the pieces had been strewn over the muddy earth behind the building. Rieko notified the police. Inspector Naidu and Sergeant Walcott arrived to rule out any connection with the theft of the Paid Mourner. They solemnly examined the shards of glass, and the hole in the parquetry, and took notes.

Rieko and the other designers began an inventory of their stock to see if anything had been taken. It didn't appear so on first glance, but a small, precious item might easily be missing. Larkin offered to help, less from altruism than curiosity about what the police were doing. He ticked items off a printed list as Rieko checked tiny pieces of furniture.

Her work was charming, and demonstrated a higher level of skill than Larkin had anticipated. He reflected to himself that though her work was interpretive, rather than creative, a Sorcerer might apply his mind to her techniques and elevate them to something truly special.

"How long have you worked here?" Larkin asked, when the first diorama had been fully checked.

"Ten years. I started at the bottom; now I oversee the department. We're doing OK. The press coverage of the theft gave sales a boost."

"It's the same upstairs. Are your customers very different from people who buy the dolls alone?"

"The audience for a full set, including dolls, is smaller, and the proportion of customers who live abroad is higher. We typically make two finished versions of every diorama – one that photographs well, and one that pleases the eye in real life."

"They aren't the same thing?"

Rieko shook her head. "In real life, you want your miniatures to be as finely detailed and as accurately scaled as possible, so the owner can delight in the exquisite craft. But in a photograph, it is easy to read highly realistic miniatures as full scale. To derive pleasure from it as a miniature scene the props must occupy a middle ground of being detailed enough to show craft but just slightly out of scale enough to be recognisable as a model, rather than the real thing." Rieko positioned a bright yellow bentwood chair, five inches high, in front of a grey backdrop patterned with large pink and green flowers. "See how this floral pattern is too large for the scene? That will emphasise the smallness of the chair."

Larkin watched Rieko add a table made from an aerosol top. She placed a trio of glass vases, none taller than his forefinger, upon it and arranged purple sprays of miniature alliums inside them. Finally, she put a doll in position: a welder, her face visible beneath a raised mask, her skin marked with grime. Larkin reached out to feel her evocation.

"Ah ah ah – don't touch," Rieko scolded. "The interior is one part of a story which also includes what the doll looks like and, yes, how she makes you feel when you touch her. Ideally you want all those three elements to contrast with each other, because that's where the drama comes from. But there must be sufficient tension, between the scene and the doll, based on visuals alone. The story must be visual first and foremost, because that is how your customer will, most likely, first encounter it."

At the next table along, a model courthouse was arranged. "This is a commission," Rieko said. "The purchaser expects to receive a highly realistic scene, and the first time they encounter it will be in reality. We have painstakingly painted the wooden panels to imitate correctly scaled grain. The trim is hand carved."

In the dock stood a schoolgirl doll, wearing a gymslip, and holding a hockey stick. Dark plaits fell either side of her face. Thinking to ask this time, Larkin said: "May I touch her?"

"Yes – all three elements must work together."

Larkin brushed the wool of the gymslip with his fingertips. The girl's expression was neutral, a face composed for the avoidance of others' judgement. But he was filling with Upstanding Indignation. Despite her youth, she reminded him, in appearance and mood, of Maria; Maria as she had been in Florence, plotting against Cristofano, before both she and Larkin were cast out.

The Indignation burnt him pleasurably, like a first shot of whisky. He closed his eyes to savour its spreading heat, and breathed deeply.

Rieko observed his reaction. "Enchantments have a powerful effect on you."

"Isn't that true for everyone?"

"Certainly not. That policeman... Walcott? Enchantments barely register with him. He thinks we're all quite deluded, I'm sure of it, when we react to dolls. Naidu feels the enchantment but you can see she resents it. She doesn't like that enchantments affect her. People must have different baselines."

"So emotionally open people feel enchantments more strongly?"

"Maybe. Maybe not. Walcott's dull but I bet he's well balanced; what you see is exactly what you get. Perhaps an enchantment is most potent for those of us who keep our feelings hidden. Hidden from ourselves, as much as other people. The enchantment opens a floodgate."

Larkin didn't like this observation. Rieko seemed to imply he lacked self-knowledge, and even if she was confessing a similar tendency, that wasn't very flattering. He changed the subject. "Do you ever wish you could make the dolls yourself?"

"How do you know I can't?" She veiled the courtroom with a sheet.

"Apologies; I spoke clumsily. I was a hobbyist till lately. I shouldn't assume that the only true doll-making is for the market."

"There are more good doll makers than there are vacancies on the top floor."

"Did you express an interest in sorcery?" Larkin asked, surprised. It occurred to him that his own appointment may have caused resentment among longer-standing hopefuls.

"I never enquired," she said. "I could see that design had better opportunities for advancement. I wouldn't be head of sorcery, if I made dolls for sale."

A passing designer, one of the middle-aged women Larkin didn't know, remarked: "People would only say Alastair was doing your work for you."

All the other designers in earshot laughed, except Rieko, and even she smirked.

"Maybe *I* make *Alastair*'s dolls," she said.

Larkin was far more inspired than he expected to be by Rieko's insights. For his own work, there was so much scope for imagination – in the dolls he would design, in the places he would house them, and most important of all, the enchantments laid upon them. He was sufficiently original to be confident in the first two. And the third he was determined to excel in also.

The inventory was finally completed, and Larkin returned to the top floor. The police were there, discussing the break-in with Alastair. Of the other Sorcerers, only Barnaby and Dennis were present at their workbenches, and they had put down their dolls to listen.

"I take it the alarm is normally set at night?" the Inspector asked.

"Yes. I was last out yesterday, and I set it myself," Alastair replied.

"I was with him," Dennis added.

"But it was off when you arrived this morning?"

Dennis nodded. "It didn't make a peep last night. Would a burglar know how to crack it?"

"Depends how dirty it was." Larkin sat down at his own workbench. "You can work out a code from the cleanest keys – or that's what I've heard."

The Inspector and sergeant exchanged a glance.

"But why go to that trouble and not take anything?" Barnaby asked.

"They didn't come to steal," Naidu said. "Just to vandalise."

"Local kids making trouble," Alastair suggested.

"Maybe. Might also be an employee," Walcott said, "as they were able to turn off the alarm before they were detected. And they seemed to know the CCTV blackspots."

"Can you think of any employee who'd be likely to do this?" Naidu asked Alastair.

"Since your lot ransacked their houses, morale has been low," Barnaby cut in drily. "Are you going to interrogate everyone again?"

The Inspector arched an eyebrow. "We'll take statements from anyone who has relevant information. That will be considerably quicker and less painful with your help. So I'll ask again – does any employee have specific cause for resentment?"

Larkin was tempted to respond: *Briar Kendrick was sacked and has a history of destroying property.* But Persephone would hear of it and he needed her to trust him. So he stayed silent.

"Let's not get ahead of ourselves," Alastair said. "If this latest... incident... was an employee letting off steam, we have our own internal disciplinary procedures. You should never have been called, Inspector. I'm sorry my wife wasted your time."

"She didn't," Naidu said. "A pattern's emerging, Mr Kendrick; it's unlikely to be coincidence that the eyot's experienced this break-in so soon after the last. We have to at least consider they're related acts of sabotage. Now, it may be that someone outside Kendricks is responsible – and if they've left any dabs on the window, we'll have a new line to pursue. But Sergeant Walcott will be speaking to all residents to take down their whereabouts last night and check if they saw anything suspicious in the vicinity. I trust we can proceed with your co-operation?"

Alastair rolled his eyes, but nodded. The sergeant could use his office for the remainder of the day. Larkin was called first, to give Walcott his alibi.

"I was out cycling with Persephone Kendrick," he said. "Then we returned to the Eyot Tavern around eight. It would be impossible for me to leave again without someone seeing because Margot Mayhew was hostessing one of the Kendricks Collectors' evenings in the main bar. They go on till dawn. Another one is scheduled for tonight."

"Who attends those?"

"I'm afraid I don't know any names, but I do know there's a guest list – you have to sign in and sign out at the door – and Margot would have that. Possibly it has times on it, too."

"So there aren't any residents at these things?"

"Cosima Botham helps Margot with hostessing."

"But no one else? No local drinkers? Briar Kendrick wasn't there for instance?"

"No, he'd be a disaster around the collectors. Too volatile." Larkin wondered where Briar *had* been – in one of the town pubs, probably, where he was known by the bar staff and would have his presence verified for at least part of the night by them. But he must have returned home at some point. Then he would have been alone, without anyone to confirm his version of events. Larkin found himself hoping Briar was unalibied. It was right the police should look at him more closely; the man hit his daughter, for heaven's sake. That made him a fair scapegoat, in Larkin's eyes, for vandalising the parquet floor or even stealing the Paid Mourner – irrespective of Briar's actual guilt.

Walcott jotted Larkin's answer down in his notes, and flipped the page. The white paper beneath was heavily grooved from the force of Walcott's handwriting.

"That'll be all for now," he said. "Send in Dennis Botham."

Larkin did so. He returned to his workbench, and absently began sketching the courtroom Rieko had shown him. But he did not place the serious-faced schoolgirl in the dock. The figure he drew was Briar.

25

Hedwig returned to the butcher's on Wednesday afternoon. Seeing that he was busy, and not wishing to repeat the charade of being a normal customer, she slipped along the side alley and let herself in by the back door. She waited between the marble slabs of meat until the butcher had reason to leave the counter. He hawked phlegm into the sink as he passed it. Hedwig wrinkled her nose in distaste.

"Here's the money," she said, offering her carpet bag of notes. She had never been as nervous as she was carrying that money on the train. Nervous, but excited, too. "And here's a bag of elmwood, from the same tree as the Paid Mourner."

She had scattered most of the pieces outside the workshop, retaining just the few she needed, to conceal that a theft had taken place. But there should be more than enough in the bag for Scarlotta to do the job.

"What about the wax?" asked the butcher.

"I couldn't get my hands on any the right age. Can Scarlotta find some that's period appropriate and match it?"

"She can. That will increase the turnaround time to two weeks, and you must pay her the cost of the wax when you collect the doll, otherwise we will withhold it."

More expenditure. Doubtless an outlay was necessary, but she resented being ripped off. "We're working together on this; no need to withhold anything. Now – how much is the wax?"

"Five hundred pounds," he said without hesitation. Hedwig doubted he had based the number on the likely cost. He just knew she was in haste to get the job done. "The ageing of it will be a complex process – the crazing must be meticulous—"

"I look forward to seeing it," Hedwig interrupted. "When I return I'll bring the outstanding cash. You have the wood and the previously agreed payment. Scarlotta can source the wax and get started."

The butcher smiled smugly as he counted the money in the bag.

"I'll be back two weeks from today," Hedwig said.

When she arrived back on the eyot, she went directly to the Tavern. It was a Kendricks Collectors' Society night, which had taken place regularly at the Tavern for the past hundred and fifty years. Attendees paid an annual membership fee to handle a range of dolls, with no need to purchase, on the designated dates. On those evenings the Tavern was closed to the public. Hedwig entered by the main doors, around which Cosima had pulled a velvet curtain. She was there to verify the members' admission and take their coats.

"I need a quick word with Mama," Hedwig explained.

"Go through," Cosima said. "She's popped to the cellar to change a barrel."

Cosima parted the curtains for Hedwig. The divider between the main bar and the saloon had also been folded back, creating a long room where some hundred men were individually seated. Despite the high attendance there was no conversation; only the sound of Imogen Strange playing the piano, and the occasional cough. The atmosphere differed from an ordinary evening. This was where rich men, for they were always men, came for a few hours of oblivion. Candles adorned each table, lending the Tavern a shabby glamour.

As unobtrusively as possible, Hedwig wove through the armchairs in the direction of the stairs. A man in a brown bowler caught her arm as she passed.

"Yes?" she responded quietly, with a slight smile. "Can I get something for you?"

His pores were large and his colour ruddy. At his feet lay a sleeping black Labrador.

"No, my love." The man released her sleeve. His lips glistened. "I just hoped you'd be enchanted."

Hedwig shuddered.

"Is he bothering you, Hedwig?"

She turned in surprise. It was Stanley who had spoken; and he was in uniform.

"No," she said, to avoid an escalation. Gently she ushered him to the bar, away from the customer's earshot.

"Whatever are you doing here? Surely you haven't taken up collecting."

He shook his head. "It's work. I've been taking names. Checking no one was playing silly beggars at Kendricks Workshop in the middle of last night."

"A break-in?" she asked, feigning alarm.

"Yes. I was looking for you earlier."

"I've just got back from London. Shopping."

"And were you there all last night, too?"

"No – at home, as normal."

"Anyone back that up?"

"I sleep alone." She smiled ruefully. "Does this put me on your list of suspects?"

He sighed. "Maybe if you've left fingerprints at the scene of the crime. Or you're carrying several pounds of wood on your person."

Lest her voice shook she didn't reply. She reminded herself that the wood was now far away and off the eyot – and that she had taken care to leave no fingerprints, or so she believed. *But anyone can slip up*, she thought.

Misinterpreting her look of worry, Stanley said consolingly: "Hey. We'll get whoever did it. I know who my money's on. And we'll get him for the Paid Mourner, too."

"I need to go talk to my mother," Hedwig said.

"You do that. Maybe stay the night, if you feel too spooked in that big empty house."

Hedwig nodded, wondering if he expected an invitation back to hers, and choosing to ignore that possibility because she just wanted to get away from his questions about break-ins and his assertions he would catch the culprit.

She pushed through the staff door and took the stairs to the lower floor. Every creak was one she remembered from her childhood. The rail was cold to the touch, and the room still smelt of cold brick.

"Good," Mama said on seeing her. "You can help with the punters while you're here."

"I have to disappoint you, Mama. I'm not stopping long. And I'm terribly afraid you won't like what I have to say." The conversation with Stanley had put her on edge, interfering with her ability to sugar unwelcome messages.

"What's new?" Mama said, brushing dust from her palms.

"I can't keep giving you money."

"Giving? You're loaning me. A nice kind of threat. I'll go under without you chipping in."

"I really think it will be better for your self-esteem to stand on your own two feet."

"You'll see me on the streets." Mama caught Hedwig's eyeroll. "Of all the selfish—"

"Selfish? No, Mama; I know you can't mean that, not really. Ever since I was a child, haven't I kept your finances in order? Would you really have me sacrifice myself till there's nothing left?"

"Don't make me laugh. You love it when I ask for a loan, and the more I beg the better. Is that what you're up to now? Trying to make me beg harder because it gives you a kick? What's that if it's not selfish, eh? Worrying your mother just so you get to feel superior."

"Oh, Mama! There's no talking to you when you're like this, there really isn't."

"Stuck-up mare." Margot shoved her daughter by the shoulders with a strength that Hedwig hadn't anticipated.

"I'm going," Hedwig said. "I'm *sorry*, Mama. You'll thank me eventually."

The piano was silent when Hedwig returned to the bar. Their voices must have carried from below. She kept her head high. Did no harm if people heard her standing up for herself. Stanley, who had been talking with Cosima Botham near the door, said as Hedwig passed: "Do you need walking home?"

"No. Thank you. I don't want to distract you any longer this evening. It's so important, what you're doing here, Stanley. Keeping the eyot safe for us. I can't tell you how grateful I am."

She left the pub, without looking back.

26

When Persephone was fourteen, she saw a person die: her grandfather, Felix Kendrick. Persephone had never been close to him. She saw him often enough – there was no avoiding him; despite advancing years and two strokes, he never relinquished ownership of the workshop. A nurse was employed to administer his medications and wheel him round Kendricks in his bathchair. He presided over every family event. Yet Persephone could never recall him speaking to her. At first it bewildered her to be ignored when she made childish attempts at conversation.

"He thinks children should be seen and not heard," Briar said.

"He doesn't even see me," Persephone pointed out. "He looks in any other direction."

"It's not just you," Briar said. "Does he speak to your cousins?"

No, she had to admit he did not. And once she reached adolescence, she began dreading the day when he deemed her fit to address. But in his final weeks he developed pneumonia, and with his death so clearly on the horizon with never a word passed between them, she suspected he would go to the grave without acknowledging her existence.

On his last day, Persephone was at home with her father, when Dennis knocked at the door to say they should come, quickly, to say goodbye.

"Go along with Dennis," Briar told his daughter. "I'll follow after you. There's a few things I have to do first."

Persephone donned her coat and left, pointing out to Dennis, as they progressed up the lane: "He won't come. The few things he has to do are in the pub. And they're all ordering pints."

"It's not polite to talk about your father that way, Seph."

"Polite?" Persephone struggled with the idea that stating something which was mere fact could be offensive.

"Maybe Briar needs some fortification. You can't know, yet, what it is to watch a parent die."

"But he doesn't even *like* Felix."

"He said that, has he?"

"No. He just looks at him like he hates him. It spreads, too. Daddy always argues more with Uncle Conrad if Felix is in the room."

"All the more reason for him to need preparation before he joins us. Listen, Seph, maybe he doesn't like Felix, but a father's a father, even a bad one, and it'll hurt Briar to see him gone."

They had reached the big Kendrick house. The front door was open, and even from the garden gate Persephone could see the hall was crowded with cousins there to witness Felix's passing.

She expected to wait along with them, taking their huddles for a form of queue. But Dennis told the others to make way, because Persephone was of Felix's direct line. The cousins were not waiting to see Felix – how could they be? There were over a hundred of them, which would be an unreasonable demand on a dying man. They had simply gathered in his house, to be with each other, because Felix's death would mark the end of their community as it had been.

Persephone felt Dennis's hand in the small of her back, pushing her towards the stairs. But he let go as her hand touched the banister.

"Aren't you coming?" she asked.

"I'm a Botham," he said. "I'll show my respects down here with the rest."

"Then I wish my godfather was a Kendrick." Persephone ground her teeth in anger. Her mother was hundreds of miles away; her father was a coward and a drinker. She had at least assumed that Dennis would accompany her all the way to the death bed.

She turned her back on him and walked up the stairs. The exact location of Felix's room was a mystery to her, as she'd never had any reason to venture into this part of the house. Her ear caught voices, and she followed them to an open door at the end of the corridor. The room inside was dimly lit.

Conrad was at the bedside, in a grey suit and a wide-brimmed feathered hat. Beneath the stiff white sheets lay her grandfather, thinned by illness into a greater resemblance with Briar, which made Persephone deeply uncomfortable. An acidic smell pervaded the room. As Persephone moved closer to the bed she suspected the source was Felix's breath. His rasps were short and painful to hear. At first his eyes were closed, but they fluttered open when he heard her. Alarmingly, the white of his left eye had turned red, bright and bloody against the grey of his iris.

"Remind me of your hex," Felix said to Conrad.

Conrad's eyes flickered to Persephone. He clearly didn't want to reveal it in front of her, but nor did he want to disobey his dying father.

"Rivalry," he said.

"Rivalry," Felix breathed. "Yes. That served you well. Is your brother here?"

"No. He's in the pub," Persephone supplied.

"Running the workshop will straighten him out," Felix said, to no one in particular, his eyes closing again. Persephone watched for Conrad's reaction. Her uncle silently tapped the arm of his easy chair. Felix frequently changed his intended heir, even within the space of a single conversation.

She was jolted from her thoughts by Felix grabbing her arm.

"You," he said, speaking directly to her for the first time in her life. "*You're* the one who'll run Kendricks."

Her uncle tutted. Felix laughed wheezily until his chest went into spasm. The coughing gripped him and went on and on till Persephone thought he would vomit.

Then it stopped; for Felix, everything stopped. His eyes, the bloody one and the white, stared through her.

Conrad stood up. He pressed Felix's neck in search of a pulse.

"Persephone. Go downstairs and let the others know."

"Know what?"

"That it's over." Conrad closed his father's eyes with one beautifully manicured hand.

She was glad to leave the room. Conrad's order suggested she should make some kind of announcement, but she told only Dennis, as soon as she located him; and the news made its own rapid journey through the house. Persephone received a series of handshakes and embraces, because Conrad was still upstairs, Briar wasn't there, and she was the next most immediate relative. The encroachment on her space made her want to run home screaming. Why was she there at all? She wasn't going to grieve Felix. The man had spoken one sentence to her in her whole life; and it was a joke at her expense, a laugh at the very idea she might be a worthy successor.

The day after Persephone and Larkin agreed to collaborate, she spent in tension at the thought of sharing her work. She had chosen a maquette that she would take to him, a kind of early draft using wax and pine, so that he might advise her of improvements. Her work sorely needed some guidance, but this didn't lessen her anxiety that he would tell her to give up. Might her work be that bad? Had she, for years, been cursing Kendricks for failing to train her, when really the problem *was* her own lack of talent? Throughout the afternoon she rehearsed telling Larkin: *any expertise you could offer would be wasted on me.* She even took the paternoster to the top floor to tell him there and then, but she saw him through the grille, and changed her mind. He was wholly absorbed in his carving, oblivious to her watching him; and her longing to be in his position eclipsed her fear of failure.

So, after dinner that night, she knocked on the door of his bedroom, and entered at his soft *come in.* He was seated at a small table, with paints and wooden blanks arranged upon it. A very bright lamp cast a white circle in which to work; and the room was otherwise dark.

"Hello Persephone," he said, and smiled.

She liked him saying her name. By means of greeting, she thrust the maquette she had made towards him.

He took it from her. The doll was dressed for the eyot masquerade, in a tiny frock coat, his wax face concealed by a mask.

"Sit down," Larkin instructed, and Persephone accepted the empty chair. Muted music and voices rose from the bar downstairs. She glanced at the room around her. He had made it his own. The shelves were lined with an audience of dolls, varying in size from an inch high to a foot and a half. The faces had a similar snap to each other, sharing some signature that was identifiably Larkin's – an insolent thrust of the chin, perhaps, or the suggestion that the dolls possessed some tantalising secret. Stacks of art books, thicker than Bibles, stood at the foot of his bed. There were a few novels there, too; the children's books of Rumer Godden, and Paul Gallico's *Love of Seven Dolls.*

Larkin was closely attending to the details of the doll

– removing the clothes carefully to examine the joints, and finally slipping the mask off. He half laughed when he saw the waxen face, and Persephone thought, *oh fucking hell, he thinks it's dreadful.*

He saw her flinch.

"Don't worry," he said. "It's good. Tell me your thinking."

"I wanted to make a character from the Commedia dell'arte – the characters roughly fall into four groups: the servants, which includes the clowns; the elderly men; the lovers; and the captains. This is a servant's mask. The servants interest me most. They have the biggest need of masks. Of all the characters they are the ones with the biggest gap between who they are and how they must appear."

"Not the lovers?"

"I don't know about lovers. I know about service."

Larkin looked closely at the mask on the tip of his finger. "Did you consider, instead of the Commedia dell'arte, making characters from our own masquerade?"

"Yes. I almost gave him a Volto Larva, like the man who took the Paid Mourner. But I didn't want to." Because she would have to carve the face beneath; and it would be Briar's face. Anyone who removed the mask would see who she thought was guilty.

"Then you're being too timid. The man in the Volto Larva mask has wrought a great change in your life – the life of everyone on the eyot, really. You're teetering around making masked dolls but ignoring the masked man everyone on the eyot has been affected by."

"I don't understand. You said it was good work."

"The joints are perfect; they allow for some very nuanced

posing. That's important, and difficult to get right with minimal training. You must be a natural."

The compliment warmed her. "But?"

"There's not really a *but*, only things to consider when you start your next maquette. You need a more compelling character. I also think the mask is obscuring a lack of confidence in painting faces."

"I knew the expression was wrong."

"The carving beneath is sound. It's the painting that needs work. You've tried to mimic a real face too closely, and it won't scale. A flaw in the face will always be more noticeable than any other flaw in a doll, because brains are typically wired to pay more attention to faces."

"What can I do to make it better?"

"Simplify. Aim for as neutral an expression as possible, so that people can project emotion onto it. It's best to convey emotion through the doll's posture rather than their face because posture can be made flexible – you can change the emotion then by repositioning. You can't, in the normal way of things, alter a doll's face in a matter of moments. Because your joints are so good it is very easy to make this doll express emotion through posing. Have more faith in that. Let that take the strain more; you don't need the distraction of an overly worked face."

Persephone nodded, relieved that there was something positive to take from his comments.

"Shall we start again then?" Larkin offered her one of the blank wooden doll heads that lay on the table. "We can work side by side companionably, I think, and you can ask me questions as you go."

"All right," she agreed.

As he selected one of the brushes, Larkin said: "Did you consider making Briar?"

Persephone stammered: "Briefly, very briefly. But if anyone found it, I'd be incriminating him."

"Yes," Larkin agreed. "You would. And he deserves it."

"*You're* not going to make a doll of him, are you?"

"No. That's not my story to tell." Larkin picked up a small tube of paint. He mixed a drop of orange into the beige swirl on his palette. "Only *you* can tell that story."

She did not want to talk about her father. Instead she watched Larkin outline a doll's eyes in black: the tear ducts, the apple, the lid. He made a point above each corner of the eye, and joined them with two arcs for eyebrows. Deftly, he shaded in the nostrils.

"This doll will have red hair, I think," he told Persephone. "So let's give her pale, almost translucent skin, and maybe some freckles."

He swapped brushes, checking the softness of the new one with his thumb, and touched the tip to the pool of taupe on his palette. The paint was very slightly darker than the wooden doll head. Persephone tried to memorise the strokes of the brush – the contours around the eyes, and the chin, then the corners of the mouth. Larkin used the orange-beige mixture to create shadows from the temple to the jaw. With the same colour he lightly dabbed the tip of the nose. He paused to tilt the head this way and that, checking it met his satisfaction.

"Lavender for the eyes?" he said.

Persephone nodded. First he filled the small circles with a

pastel blue. He added the lavender in minuscule rings – they reminded Persephone of the rings in tree boughs, except this bough would be no thicker than a pencil. At the centre he painted a black pupil. Black, too, was applied to the edge of the irises, making them rounder in appearance. Larkin switched to brown for outlining the lids and dusting the nose with freckles. He softened the crease of the eye with a toothpick. The doll was completed with the mouth: a sugar pink along the lips, and fawn shadow curving beneath.

With trepidation, Persephone considered the blank doll head in her own hand. She frowned as she picked up a brush, and dipped it into the black, as Larkin had first done. The tip hovered above the wooden eye.

Larkin cupped her hand with his, to adjust the position of the brush.

"Hold it at this angle," he said.

She did, and she marked her own line.

27

Larkin woke, in the early hours of the morning, to the sound of breaking glass in another room. Seconds later he heard a tap-tap on his door.

"It's not locked," he called from his bed.

Persephone opened the door and peered through the gap. Her hair was tousled. She wore a loose checked nightshirt, its cuffs brushing her knuckles. She had the feral look of one stumbling from slumber. It wasn't without appeal.

"Get up," she whispered, one eye scrunched. "Something's the matter with Mrs Mayhew. I can hear her smashing things in her bedroom and I think she's crying."

Larkin raised his head, then let it drop on the pillow. "We could toss a coin, to decide which of us should go."

"It needs to be you, Larkin. She doesn't like me."

He groaned. "Damn your logic."

Persephone retreated to her own room. Yawning, Larkin got out of bed, and followed the call of Mrs Mayhew's sobs. The door to her boudoir was open. Shattered perfume bottles lay upon the floor.

"Margot? What's all this about, hey?"

The poor woman was in a sorry state, slumped atop of her dressing table. She wore her negligee, a satiny gossamer thing, but Larkin wasn't sure she'd been to bed at all; it could barely be an hour since the last of the collectors departed. Her make-up ran from her eyes like tyre tracks in snow.

She sniffed. "Everything's awful."

"I'm sure that can't be true. Let me get you a cup of tea."

He left her briefly, and returned with the promised drink. She took the mug and he pulled up a peach slipper chair that leaked where the cat had scratched it.

"You're a good boy, Larkin," said Mrs Mayhew. "I bet your mother's proud of you."

Not very, he could have said, but he wasn't going to get into that. In any case, it wasn't a genuine enquiry into his background, so much as a segue into talking of Hedwig's callousness as a daughter.

"You wouldn't let your mother struggle, with money, would you? It'd be financial abuse, not to give her a loan if you had the money and more, but she couldn't make ends meet."

Her head fell onto his shoulder, which rather startled him, and the sobs resumed. He could feel her tears seeping through the cotton of his t-shirt.

"I owe so many people money," she said. "The electric and gas people will send round the debt collectors. What am I going to do, Larkin?"

"You're going to get some proper rest before dawn, and then you're going to sit down with me in the morning while we ring your creditors and work out a plan you can manage. How does that sound?"

"It's no use." She bit her lip in a performance of bravery. "Even if they give me more time, where's the money going to come from? I asked Hedwig and she refused to lend me a penny to tide me over."

Larkin knew the pub had a small customer base, but he'd assumed Conrad subsidised it as a common good. It sounded like Mrs Mayhew wasn't really making a living.

"I'll have to put the rent up," she said.

"If you must, you must," Larkin said coolly. The direction of travel didn't surprise him. "But I do think you're doing Hedwig a disservice. She must have misunderstood the severity of your circumstances. I'm sure that – if you approached her in just the right way, and laid it out as to your mutual benefit – she would give you the assistance you want."

"How do I do that?"

"Come now. There's usually a bargain to be made." Particularly because Hedwig would soon be coming into a significant amount of money – if the fraud she had proposed came off. With newly awakened interest, he insisted: "I bet we could persuade Hedwig to see things from a different perspective."

"You really think so?"

"I do. But first you must get some rest. I promise we will sort everything out."

The assurance stemmed Mrs Mayhew's tears. She patted

Larkin's cheek, and he expected this to draw the encounter to a close. Instead she kissed him with surprising gentleness. When he didn't respond she pulled herself away.

"Oh dear." She was matter of fact; the tears still appeared to be at bay.

"Sorry," Larkin said, feeling a vague need to apologise.

"You think I'm old."

She needn't have worried on that score. An age difference was novel to Larkin, and he liked novelty. No. It was her clinginess that repelled him. She was needy, and nothing alarmed him more. Still he could say, with sincerity: "Margot, you're very attractive."

"What then? You belong to someone else?"

Her phrasing touched him with its quaintness.

"Because I don't mind about that," she added.

He laughed. "Margot."

"Is there someone?"

"I'm – halfway in a situation. I don't know yet how things will work out."

"Hm. Yes, I thought as much when you paid for her room."

She stood up, smoothing the creases in her night dress. Larkin watched her lie on the bed, over her quilt. She closed her eyes and ran her hand between the mattress and the bed base, searching for something. But she fell still and silent almost immediately, in what he assumed was a deep sleep.

He needed rest himself. Before leaving he reached for the dressing table lamp, to turn it off; and noticed a tray of seven dolls directly beneath the shade. Dolls that the collectors had toyed with during their society evening, and that would be returned to the workshop tomorrow. The biggest was three inches high. They were all cutesy, white, braid-sporting girls – he remembered Persephone's scorn for the current stock. A label beneath each niche in the tray displayed the enchantment. The first was Homesickness, which compelled a closer look, because Larkin didn't believe he had a home to feel nostalgic for. He placed his palm upon the small tin figure. A lump formed in his throat as he remembered sun-lit bluebells in St Ignatius's churchyard, and kicking a red ball into long grass under the yews. *That's not home*, he insisted to himself, but he realised he was longing for his younger self, not the place, and never having felt homesickness before, wondered if that was true for everyone who spoke of it.

Only a couple of hours remained before he had to get up for work. He departed, taking care to avoid the floorboards that creaked in the corridor. He didn't want to rouse Persephone again. He'd prefer she didn't see the tyre tracks of mascara on his shoulder.

28

While she waited for the forgery, Hedwig concentrated on the remaining elements of the plan. The day after her confrontation with Mama, she sat in Briar's living room, having brought a fountain pen and paper, so that they might compose a ransom demand for Conrad.

"The Thief would write his note by hand," Hedwig said, "but Conrad knows my writing."

"No point me writing it. He knows my scrawl too, remember. Maybe you're getting cold feet? We can still stop this now, you know. Never ignore your instincts because of sunk costs."

"You always offer heaps of excellent life advice, Briar." The very idea she had cold feet was absurd. To demonstrate how absurd, she began to write. Only the words *Dear Conrad*, but the gesture helped strengthen her resolve. She had made her plan, and had to execute it. She had simply to do her best, and rely on the fact Conrad had never received a letter from the fae folk before, so would hardly have a basis for comparison. All would be well.

She continued.

The Paid Mourner is in my possession and diligently cared for. I imagine this is a great relief for you to hear. Your hopes of a safe return must have grown faint by now.

The satisfaction of such hopes depends on your next actions.

I demand her worth in gold.

The following instructions must be followed to the letter. On 10th December at 9 a.m., bury the gold in the burnt-out site of the masquerade bonfire, to a depth of six feet. Provided this action is carried out to the letter the doll will be delivered to you by the next dawn.

Do not, at any point in the future, disturb the burial ground. I will know if you do and will reclaim the doll.

Read and consider.

The Thief on the Winged Horse.

"We need to include what feeling she evokes," Hedwig said. "The Paid Mourner, I mean. That way, Conrad will know the letter-writer really has the doll."

Briar gave her the name of the doll's enchantment, and Hedwig diligently noted the words in a postscript.

"I'll look into old-fashioned writing styles and copy out a fresh draft in a different hand. He'd probably have something eighteenth-century, wouldn't he? Or at least, that would jar Conrad less."

As she walked home, the ransom letter rustled in her pocket. She thought again of Briar's suggestion that she was nervous about proceeding. He was full of rot. A nervous person wouldn't oversee all these details. She wasn't nervous at all. The feeling, she was sure, was excitement. And if her stomach should twist at the sight of Stanley approaching, from the orchard, then that wasn't nerves either – merely annoyance that he should be back to bother her. Not that she should give him cause to suspect her displeasure.

"Back so early?" she called. "You're such a hard worker, Stanley."

He didn't return her smile as he drew level with her. "I was on my way to your place. It's good I caught you."

"Walk with me?"

They continued down the path.

"I wanted to tell you in person," he said. "I won't be working on this particular case any longer."

"Why not?" Hedwig's dismay was genuine. She didn't want to lose the information he could provide.

"The Inspector thinks, given our – prior connection – it may be for the best."

"But you've never hidden that from her, have you? Why is it a problem *now*?"

"Because of this vandalism at the workshop. The

Inspector's not happy about your lack of alibi. Things are getting a mite complicated."

"What do you mean?"

"One of the collectors said that when he left the pub for the night, he saw you, heading in the direction of the workshop."

"That's ridiculous. I told you I was at home all night." She could bluff this out; it had been dark, the collector would be tired, and surely that would introduce sufficient margin for error. "Which collector is it?"

"You know I can't tell you that."

"Was it that man with the wet lips? The one who grabbed me at the Tavern? He's probably feeling vindictive because I rebuffed him. And he probably thought he'd stir up trouble with you. He saw how I looked at you, Stanley – he would have known there was something between us."

"You're quite sure you were at home all night? You don't want to change your answer to that?"

"Stanley!"

"The Inspector wants to keep a closer eye on you. You need to be honest."

"I am being honest." She dropped her voice, and stopped walking to take his hand. "How can I prove I was home alone all night? It would be different – if someone respectable, and credible, like you – had been with me, wouldn't it?"

He extracted himself from her touch, placing his hands behind his back. "I can't do what you're asking me," he said, with disapproval. "I could lose my job. I could face a charge."

"I know." Tears came. She had summoned them, she

assured herself; the better to gain sympathy. This was not a real response to the past weeks of stress and uncertainty. And yet in the normal way of things, didn't she despise crying as a strategy? It was so very like what Mama would do. Hedwig sniffed and swiped at her eyes. "That's enough of that. I insulted you and I'm sorry. Forgive me."

The crying, or the apology, appeared to soften him. "Look, *I* know you're not a thief or a vandal, Hed. You wouldn't have it in you. There's no need to fib to cover yourself. This collector says he saw you; you say he's *mistaken*. It's your word against his."

"It'll end there?"

"Probably." He lacked conviction. "Unless there's any other evidence that comes to light."

"I see. Thank you."

Stanley added, exasperated: "That Briar Kendrick's a sneaky git. If you'd caught him on camera then I could put this whole sorry business to bed."

He put his arms around her. She tolerated his embrace, the blue worsted of his jacket scratching her cheek, the forged letter in her pocket, and she could think only of getting home and shutting the door on the world. Stanley's attentions had outlived their usefulness.

She pulled back from him. "I feel dreadful for affecting your work this way. You're such a rising star, aren't you? And I've made life more difficult for you. Perhaps… while your boss is still investigating here… we should put a break on things?"

The relief on his face was unmistakeable. Stanley was a pragmatist at heart, of a more earnest type than Hedwig,

219

and she was relying on this to end their liaison smoothly. But he didn't have to look *quite* so ready to agree. Some token resistance would have been appropriate.

"You're such an understanding girl, Hedwig," he replied, as though the break were his idea. "And maybe, if Naidu manages to wrap everything up, we can give it another go."

"I'd like that very much." Hedwig had no intention of contacting him ever again.

He kissed her on the forehead before leaving her.

She carried on towards Conrad's house. Now she'd caught the Inspector's attention, she'd have to be even more careful. The sooner the fraud was complete, the better. She couldn't wait for all of this to be over.

29

The next three evenings, Persephone went to Larkin's room to work. She carved, sanded, and joined her new maquette pieces. Larkin was making a doll a day, each one a replica of the Paid Mourner, alike to her in every respect. The heads were wax and he used elmwood for the bodies.

"Isn't it wasteful to make so many maquettes with wood when you could use wax for the body, too?" Persephone asked.

"These aren't maquettes," he said. "I'm making a set piece that needs twenty-one versions of the Paid Mourner."

"Twenty-*one*?" Persephone found his ambition impressive, and also intimidating. It was difficult enough making one doll, let alone a set piece. She added her last peg to the doll's ankle joint, and said: "I've finished."

"Let's take a look at it, then."

She passed it to him. This time she had carved a woman. The face was minimally painted, in keeping with Larkin's advice; six strokes for the eyes, two for the mouth, and the rest was shading. The doll wore a peach velveteen ball gown, and held a cat's eye mask in her left hand. Her little finger was painted gold.

"It's more interesting than the last one," Larkin said. "Explain the gilt to me."

"She's based on a real person. My father tells a story about her – a relative called Esme Palliser, who you won't have seen, because she died a long time ago. But this is about when she was young, in her teens, back in the thirties. The story's about what happened to her at a masquerade. She was very excited about going, and she spent most of the night with her cousin Angela, who was also a teenager. They wore half masks with their prettiest dresses. At the riverside they sipped their lemonades through pale pink paper straws to avoid smudging their lipstick."

"Briar gave you all these details?"

"He was a good storyteller, once. But maybe the flourishes weren't his. Maybe he just repeated by rote what Angela had said. Anyway – Angela and Esme were laughing at their relatives' dancing, and danced themselves to the live band. The river looked transformed under the rose-coloured lights. There were streamers hanging from the trees, drifting slightly in the breeze.

"Around midnight, a masked man asked Esme to dance. She couldn't tell who he was from his voice, but she was very flattered and bashful. He led her to the gazebo. Nervous that her high heels would trip her up, she clung to his arm tightly. But as the music played on they danced with increasing grace, faster and faster, until she was wholly absorbed. She felt as though she were all movement and playing notes and rhythm. She might have been one of the streamers twirling above their heads. Others by the river noticed the change in her and slowed as they watched. Yet there was something disconcerting about the couple, too. A wrongness in the scene that they struggled to identify. It was Angela who noticed what was amiss. She saw, amongst the jostling couples, that the man Esme danced with had cloven hooves instead of feet. She cried out but her warnings were drowned by the clock striking twelve. The handsome stranger pulled Esme to his chest, danced her to the far side of the room and crashed through the window.

"The other dancers ran to the broken pane to see what had happened. Esme lay in the grass, cut by the glass, which was strewn round her like crystals. Her little finger had been sliced clean off. The cloven-hooved man had taken it – and was nowhere to be seen; he was widely thought to be the Thief. At Esme's death, the eyot residents speculated, the Thief would come to collect the rest of her.

"In the months after the masquerade Esme assumed a fearsome air. She wore a false golden finger where her real one should be. Everyone was awed by her. Yet she was riddled with shame and sorrow, that she should be the one who accepted the Thief's invitation. She feared he had approached her because he sensed she was different from the other eyot residents; that she contained some flaw, or weakness, that made her less likely to discern his true intentions."

"What happened to her?"

"She became very reclusive and didn't marry. That may have changed given time; she died young from a Second

223

World War bomb. My father said that they stopped holding the masquerade for years after the Thief stole Esme's finger."

"Do you believe the story?"

"Yes. Stories about the Thief are rarely factual accounts," Persephone said. "But they're still *true* – they're full of the fears and anxieties of everyone who lives here."

"It sounds so obviously an urban legend, doesn't it? A cautionary tale, for young girls, not to dance with strangers. Or sleep with them, more like, given how Freudian fingers are."

"Maybe. When we were teenagers, we *did* used to talk about whether uninvited guests had gatecrashed and blended in among the rest of us. People who weren't the descendants of Kendrick or Botham or Jackson. The rumour was that Alastair sneaked Rieko into the masquerade before they were married, back when I was a child. I suppose that's not the same as Esme. Alastair was a man dancing with an uninvited guest, and maybe people don't think men need cautionary tales. Part of me used to wonder if that was what the masquerade was *for*. A way for men to relax the rules of secrecy while looking like they were keeping them. And to bring in new blood, while everyone was disguised. Otherwise, we'd die out."

"Is that how your mother was introduced to the eyot?"

"I've no idea. I don't ask my parents about their courtship."

"But you're still in touch with her?"

"Yes."

"Do you think of her very much?"

When Persephone looked inside herself, she found only

a numb space. Was that missing someone? Her mother had to leave, and Persephone had to stay; it was simply the way things were.

"I'm sorry," Larkin said. "I'm prying."

"No, it's a fair question. It's just, I could have had my mother, and I was the one who chose to stay. It was my decision. I wouldn't change it. And that means I'm not entitled to cry over it."

Larkin stood the doll on the table, and posed her taking a bow. "You should make a cloven-hooved Thief, too – a matching pair, for a dance."

"I'll think about it."

"You shy away from depicting lovers," Larkin observed.

"I don't know about lovers."

"Yes, you've said that before; but when you don't know how to depict something, you have to study other people's work until you figure it out."

"I'm talking about life experience." She was on the verge of oversharing. But she wanted to overshare with him; and when the admission was enmeshed with her work, to do so felt justifiable.

"Life experience doesn't matter," he said. "You just have to know what the expected tropes and symbols of a story are, and comply with or subvert them."

Persephone shook her head. "You're saying that because you take your own experience for granted. You've slept with a lot of people."

He leant back in his chair. "I *think* you've made a flattering assumption. But I don't know what it's based on; I've lived like a monk since I got here."

"If you hadn't slept with a lot of people, you wouldn't think a couple of months was living like a monk. Anyway, I assumed it because I know how people react to you, and I see you take it as the normal way of things, even if you don't act on the opportunity."

Larkin half smirked, his enjoyment of the digression clear. "How do people react to me?"

"As if they're making an invitation. Like the way Hedwig and Daisy and Imogen whisk you away when they see you in the Tavern – and at the masquerade, Conrad talked about you in a way that was, I don't know, *indulgent* against his better judgement—" Persephone stopped. At Kendricks, if you weren't straight, you pretended to be, and everyone else pretended to believe you. It occurred to her that Larkin's current abstinence might be rooted in a similar pretence. From dismay, she blurted: "It *is* women you like, isn't it?"

"Oh god." Larkin rubbed at his eye. "Yes. Just not exclusively."

She felt a rush of relief and identification. She was not outside of his scope of interest. They were, in fact, alike.

He misinterpreted her silence. "Does it bother you, that I'm queer?"

"No. I'm the same, really... I like both." No one else knew this; but his own disclosure made him seem safe to tell.

He said only: "Maybe that's how you subvert the trope with your dolls – you make a female Thief, with cloven hooves, as Esme's lover."

"Yes – but just switching the gender doesn't help – I don't have experience of any pairings, women or otherwise. For

226

me it's theoretical, being... queer." She tried out the word, tentatively, aware it was a new way to describe herself. "I've only felt attraction in my head. I can't draw on anything *real* if I make a lover for Esme."

"I still don't believe inexperience has anything to do with your doll-making. But if I'm wrong, it's a problem with an easy fix." Larkin held Persephone's gaze a fraction too long without speaking; she was trying to determine if this was flirting, when he tapped the space on the table before the doll. "So. No lover; just Esme. She can't be in the gazebo if she's not dancing. Where does that leave her? What kind of setting does she belong in?"

"For a diorama, you mean?"

"Yes. It's such a shame you're not interested in making the Thief on the Winged Horse – imagine designing his lair. Where does he keep all his purloined goods? Surely it would be very palatial?"

"Yes – it probably would be."

"Then we could go looking for inspiration. Have you seen Titania's Palace?" He was talking about an antique Irish dolls' house currently displayed in Denmark.

"I've never left the country," Persephone replied.

"It probably is a bit far for a flying visit. What about Queen Mary's dolls' house?" Larkin continued. "Less fae, but still luxurious, and much closer to home."

"I've heard of it, obviously. But I've never been to take a look."

"Then let's arrange a morning away from here. In fact we could make a day of things; there's a Ceramics Co-Op in London where I can show you how to make a porcelain doll and they'll fire it for us, too. It's not like you can use the workshop kiln. How are you fixed Monday?"

"I'm working. But Cosima could cover. She said she wanted extra shifts."

"Very well. I will tell Alastair I'm due a day's leave. I've had no holiday since I got here."

"Whatever you think best," Persephone replied. People would surely talk, if Persephone and Larkin were seen leaving the eyot for the day. She found the idea pleasing, although the status of the outing was ambiguous. Perhaps it was no more than another lesson. Sometimes she allowed herself to daydream they might marry. It would solve Larkin's problems, because he could have all the sorcery he wanted if he'd married in; and she envisaged a partnership of creative energy, making and discussing dolls with a true understanding of the depth of each other's obsession. But it was only a daydream. The reality of marriage, she was sure, would horrify her.

30

It had to happen eventually, Larkin knew. He ventured into the centre of Oxford – he wanted to check those animation devices on Turl Street, before using similar mechanisms in his own work – and as he walked past University College, a woman with lank hair and a tired green mac stared at him. He avoided her look until she called his name.

It was his mother.

"You're here," she said. "And you didn't tell me."

"Only briefly." It wasn't a lie. He hadn't been on the eyot very long.

"But why? Your uncle said you were in Italy."

"I had some paperwork to sort out – I lost my birth certificate, and had to pick it up from the original register office." This was complete fabrication. He had no idea why such an excuse occurred to him. But he could hardly tell her he was working for Kendricks. She would be horrified, and might even insist on going there immediately, to tell them all sorts of things he would rather leave in the past. Getting

229

excuses in early, Larkin added: "I'll be catching a flight out at the earliest opportunity."

"I don't know how you could be in Oxford and not tell me." Her voice took the martyred tone Larkin remembered so well.

"I wouldn't know how to contact you."

"I'm where I've always been."

"In that case, I know I wouldn't be welcome."

Unable to contradict him on this point, she stayed silent, and merely looked at him with reproachful eyes.

"If that's all, I'll be getting along." Larkin took a step backwards.

"You might let me buy you a cup of tea."

He rubbed the back of his head. On the other side of the road, he spotted Daisy Gilman weaving through a crowd of tourists. She hadn't seen him yet, and he didn't want her to come over while his mother was there, when it might prompt all sorts of questions.

"All right," Larkin said quickly, and walked past his mother to the nearest café in view, keen to get indoors. He heard her running, in a trotting fashion, to catch up with him.

"What are you rushing for?" his mother said. "Slow down!"

In the café, Larkin made a beeline for the table furthest from the window. The leatherette-covered menus stood to attention at the centre. Mother sat opposite him, smiling to have secured his company for this long.

A waitress approached. Scanning the menu wildly, Larkin said: "Scones and tea and a sundae and some sweet potato fries."

The waitress looked from him, to his mother, and back. "Is that all for you?"

"No. We can share it." While his mother was eating he could excuse himself and slip out the back door, if there was one.

His mother tittered hesitantly. "I don't have much of a sweet tooth. Could I have a cheese sandwich?"

Larkin was shaken. He knew when he moved back to Oxford that he risked exactly this sort of encounter. She was so close – and yet he'd grown complacent in the weeks he'd been there, assuming when he didn't see her that fears of contamination kept her indoors. It had even crossed his mind she wouldn't recognise him. The last time they'd seen each other was eight years ago; he was a boy then and grown now. But of course a mother would know her son.

They were silent until the food arrived. As planned, Larkin said he was going to the gents, but unfortunately no other exit was visible. He returned to the table, and tucked into a scone with resignation. (He wasn't hungry at all.)

She said, shyly: "What have you been doing all these years, son? Your uncle told us you were at college."

"Yes, to study art. Now that's how I make my living." If he mentioned dolls she would go spare. A generic artist was a good enough description. "I don't expect you to approve of such a flamboyant career choice."

"Are you settled? You know, with a girl?" Anxiety crept into her voice. She was always worried he was gay.

"Work takes up all my time," Larkin said, before gulping down some tea.

"I'm glad you found a trade, son," she said. "After You Know. We were worried you'd have a record."

She bit into her own sorry-looking sandwich. Larkin asked: "How long have you been able to leave the house?"

"Hm? A few years now. I went to see someone."

"A therapist?" Larkin clarified.

She chewed, veiling her mouth with her napkin. "A doctor. Father David paid for it."

Of course he had. Larkin abandoned his second scone.

"I was hoping he'd be dead by now," Larkin said.

"That's a wicked thing to say."

"Why? He believes in the eternal life anyway, doesn't he? Or is he as flexible on that as other articles of faith?"

"You should talk about him with more respect," she lectured. "He saved you. If he hadn't—"

"This," Larkin said. "This is why I didn't tell you I was in Oxford. You expect me to humiliate myself at the feet of a man who is wholly and utterly bankrupt."

He opened his wallet, teased out a twenty and laid it on the table. His plan to wait till she had gone was forgotten. The only thought in his head was to get away from her as quickly as possible.

Rather than walk back, he caught the 3 to Iffley Road, thinking that his chances of losing her would be better. Once he was at the entrance to the eyot, he saw she had, nonetheless, trailed him on the next bus and disembarked when she saw him descend ahead of her. Her cunning didn't extend to effective concealment; when she saw Larkin looking at her, she leapt to the side of the path, behind a bin that barely came to her waist. Her shoulders sagged with the futility of what she'd done, and she resumed walking towards him. He was motionless with indecision. He didn't wish to engage in further conversation, but nor did he want her to follow him through the gates to his workplace. It may have been more consistent with his earlier lies to catch the bus to the station – but where would that have ended? With him on the train to Gatwick? She might have insisted on watching him check in for his flight.

By extraordinary bad luck, Dennis was crossing the footbridge over the river – so Larkin faced his imminent arrival on one side, and his mother's on the other.

She reached Larkin first, her face full of dismay.

"I thought you'd be coming here." More reproach. "That wasn't true, about your birth certificate, was it? Were you ever even in Italy? Or have you just been *here*, looking for what you could get?"

Dennis drew near, his face broad with smiles.

"Hello," he nodded at both of them, clearly in expectation of an introduction.

Calmness welled in Larkin.

"Dennis," he said. "This is my mother, Mina. She lied to me about who my father was, for years, after having a sordid little affair."

Her lip trembled and she reddened at the gills.

"I can see you're busy," Dennis replied. "I'll catch up with you later. Lovely to meet you, Mina."

He strode past them, up the Iffley Road.

"Shameful behaviour," his mother muttered.

"I didn't even tell him the worst of it. Serves you right for following me and sticky beaking."

"I just wanted to know you were staying out of trouble."

"I *am*. All the better for keeping my distance from you."

"So you say. How does that man know you? Have you been insinuating yourself?"

"Scuttle off, Mother."

"Does he know about what you did when you were a boy?"

"I've been very open."

She started crying then, because he'd been very open with Dennis about her own horrible conduct. Her tears brought the conversation to a natural stop. Larkin made no effort to comfort her; and she turned and ran in that funny trotting way, towards Iffley.

He didn't think she'd come back. She'd be too worried about being shown up again. But then, Larkin had thought her neuroses would keep her away too, and she surprised him by overcoming them.

He made a point of visiting Dennis later that evening, offering apologies for involving him in a domestic squabble.

"Let's just say the family troubles didn't start and end with Jemima Ramsay's elopement," Larkin said.

"Your mother – she's a descendant of Ramsay too, is that right?"

"No," Larkin said quickly. "That's my father. And we're estranged. It was my paternal uncle who told me our true heritage."

"Huh. But you must have other relatives on that side – surely, now you've made your home here, you should invite some of them to visit? It could be quite the family gathering."

Dennis wasn't stupid. He knew there was something fishy about Larkin's family background, and that it may compromise claims to be a Ramsay.

"For some years now I've felt I'm alone. I've even told people my parents are dead because that's how it feels to me," Larkin said, truthfully. Then, with less probity, he added, "But I will consider whether it is time to bring the other descendants of Ramsay back to the fold."

Dennis gave him a long look. "You do that."

31

Hedwig returned to the butcher's at the agreed date; and obliged him by entering by the front door. He nodded as she joined the queue. When her turn came, he left the counter without being asked, flipped the sign to closed, and walked into the back room. He returned a few minutes later with a branded box.

"Five hundred pounds," he said. "For the extras."

"I'm going to take a look at the goods, if I may." She raised the lid. The doll was an excellent likeness. Hedwig couldn't tell her from real. For now the hex on her scalp would be missing – Briar's imprint was yet to be made; but in every other respect she was perfect. Her dress was peppered with moth holes. The slippers were faded at the toes. The face was crackled as if she had been made two hundred years ago and not this very week.

"Does she meet your satisfaction?" the butcher asked, heavily sarcastic.

"I couldn't be happier." Hedwig replaced the lid, and

took the cash from her purse. The butcher reached out to take it, but she pulled it back. "Just know I'll be back if we find any problem with it."

He grinned. She gave him the money, and the doll was hers.

At home, she laid the fraudulent ransom note on the desk, and telephoned Conrad's mobile number – which went straight to voicemail – then the hotel in Fiji. It would be eight o'clock in the morning there, so Conrad might still be in bed. But the receptionist said there was no response to the call to his room.

"It's a matter of urgency – regarding an ongoing police investigation."

"You're the police?"

"No, I'm Conrad's housekeeper, but I have important information for him."

The receptionist offered to page the communal areas of the hotel, and Hedwig agreed to hold.

Conrad was summoned from the veranda in ill-temper.

"I am in retreat from the world," he said. "Must you disturb me with your petty concerns? Surely the Inspector would impart anything of import."

"I've received a ransom note for the Paid Mourner," Hedwig said, before Conrad could get into full flow. "It was waiting on the doorstep for me this morning. And Conrad… It's signed the Thief on the Winged Horse."

Despite the poor line, Hedwig heard an intake of breath. "But I left an offering! Another doll, a beautiful one! And he didn't take it!"

"Perhaps she wasn't of equivalent worth. He's been specific about what he will accept in exchange."

"Hurry up and read it."

Hedwig read aloud the letter – the letter she had written – with an acute sense that she might, at any second, be seen through. Conrad had no reason to think Hedwig would fake such a thing, and for now, at least, he seemed to take it at face value. She made it to the end, finishing with the revelation of the doll's enchantment.

His reaction was gratifying.

"Preserve us, Hedwig!" he gasped. "That's *her* enchantment. Make no mistake! Whoever wrote the letter must have the doll. How else could they know such a thing?"

"At least we have reason to hope for the best now," Hedwig said. "Will you obtain the gold?"

The Paid Mourner replica was seated next to the phone. She eyed Hedwig with disappointment. Hedwig turned her to face the other way, and gave Conrad a moment to think.

"I believe I will," Conrad deliberated. "Do you think that's for the best?"

Hedwig felt a spreading glow of satisfaction. Conrad was asking her opinion. Already, the possibility of regaining the Paid Mourner was making Conrad better disposed towards her.

"I do," Hedwig reassured him. "And I wouldn't do anything to jeopardise the doll's return to you, Conrad. You can be sure of that."

Hedwig hung up, after a promise to arrange Conrad's flights home. He would speak to his accountant as soon as he arrived.

32

Mrs Mayhew was intrigued by the trip Larkin had planned to Queen Mary's dolls' house. So intrigued that she invited herself – though much to Persephone's relief, on the morning of the trip Cosima the barmaid rang in sick, making it impossible for Mrs Mayhew to leave the Tavern.

"What a crying shame," she complained, while Larkin and Persephone put on their coats.

"Sorry, Margot," Larkin said. "The tickets aren't transferable, sadly."

"You can always go by yourself on another day," Persephone supplied. Mystifyingly, Larkin shook his head at her, but she couldn't believe he wanted Mrs Mayhew's company either. They couldn't talk about craft or sorcery or anything important with Mrs Mayhew around.

"Your broderie anglaise is hanging by a thread, dear," Mrs Mayhew said to Persephone. "I'll sew it on for you before you go."

"Be quick," Larkin said, stepping outside, for a smoke,

probably. "We want to be on the road before the traffic gets too bad."

Mrs Mayhew led Persephone back upstairs to the kitchen and made her wait while she searched for the sewing kit in the cupboard above the kettle. Persephone hoped this wasn't a spiteful gesture – an attempt to delay their journey, now she could no longer attend.

"I'll sew the trim on when I come back," Persephone insisted. "For fuck's sake, Mrs Mayhew, I make all my own clothes, why do you think a few stitches are beyond me?"

"It's all right, I've got it." Mrs Mayhew knelt on the floor, with the sewing kit, to get at Persephone's coat. "Larkin's very kind, isn't he?"

"Yes?"

"Good of him to take you out."

Was this Mrs Mayhew sifting if they were on a date? Surely she wouldn't have tried to come along if she thought so?

"We get on." Persephone winced as Mrs Mayhew's needle jabbed her shin.

"He talks about you so fondly. Getting to be like a sister, he says." Mrs Mayhew bit off the end of thread and patted Persephone's coat. "All done."

"Thanks."

Mrs Mayhew beamed. "You've got such a pretty face, haven't you, Seph? You'd be a little smasher if you lost some weight. I have some diet recipes if you'd like them."

"I am *never* going on a diet," Persephone said emphatically.

"Aren't you ready yet?" Larkin called up the stairs.

Persephone gladly took the cue to exit.

*

They caught the Oxford Tube, with the intention of getting the train from London to Windsor at the other end. Larkin was taciturn initially, and then slept for a while.

When he awoke, he asked: "What was Mrs Mayhew bending your ear about?"

"She thinks I should lose weight."

Annoyance passed over Larkin's face. "She shouldn't be so rude."

"People say I'm rude."

"You're not. Well, you are, but you're not mean. You're just grumpy. That's a different thing altogether."

"I don't want to talk about Mrs Mayhew. Are you looking forward to seeing the house?"

"I am. Since our palace conversation I've been giving house design considerable thought. If I were to design one, I think I'd work with wood, and carve it as intricately as possible, inside and out. The carvings would draw from nature – the flowers of the eyot, the river, the butterflies and bees. And I would paint it polychromatically. The furnishings would be handwoven to my own design."

"You and Ruskin, ignoring the abyss."

"Well what would you do, pour some concrete?"

"I don't care about style. I'd build a house several rooms deep."

"That would be your primary goal? What an odd place to start. People wouldn't be able to see the inner rooms."

"Good. I'd make it hard to see the outer rooms, too. I'd furnish them all, and wire them for lighting. But the shell of the house would have no opening section. I'd fit stained glass windows thick enough to obscure your vision. It would all be perfectly rendered within and completely hidden."

"You might as well only *build* the outer shell! What would be the point of all that inner splendour? It would be wasted. It could have no impact on the person considering the house."

"There would be an impact," Persephone insisted. "The person couldn't observe without growing conscious of their own intrusion. To gain knowledge of the interior they would have to become stalker or thief – their only means of access would be to break the window, or prise open a door. Even then their chief means of sensing the interior would be by feel, rather than sight. A doll's house that is hard to penetrate is, in its own way, confrontational."

"You're the most perverse girl I ever knew."

"Not perverse. Didactic, maybe."

"So you want to school people in the error of their ways? An error you have forced them to make?"

"I wouldn't be forcing them," she corrected. "It would be their choice to gain entry, or to walk away."

"But why create something that they would want to see badly enough to break the windows and doors? You would be provoking them to damage."

"It wouldn't be created for their pleasure."

"Then it's pointless."

"I would know what was there. And that's enough."

"Extraordinary."

"Do you have a person in mind when you imagine who your dolls' house would affect?"

Larkin was quiet. Persephone wondered who he was thinking of, and why he should grow reticent about them.

"A future daughter?" she prompted. "That's who men make dolls' houses for, unless they're making them for money."

"I don't imagine having children. If they were dull-witted I'd be disappointed and if they were clever I'd be jealous. As clever as me, but no cleverer. Can you see me as a father? Don't answer that."

"I don't think I want children either." Persephone enjoyed the children of the eyot; and was drawn to babies, who with their wordless demands appealed to her more than the company of her fellow adults. But babies grew up, and they were damaged en route to adulthood. People replicated the parenting mistakes of their childhood. She might turn out like Briar, one day. And if she already had children it would be too late. You couldn't melt them down and start again if you made an error, the way you could with wax dolls.

Larkin again seemed pensive. It turned out he was still thinking about dolls' house making, not families.

"Queen Mary's dolls' house is a gentleman's residence. But Kendricks mainly makes suburban homes. Or cottages. And shops; we haven't talked about shops. They appeal to the specialist, don't they? They're a good place to showcase a variety of examples in a given category – dresses, or baked goods – when you might only have one on show in a house."

"I don't want to make a shop," Persephone said with certainty. "I spend all day in one."

"But that gives you an advantage," Larkin said. "You would be drawing from a deeper knowledge."

"There's nothing deep about it."

"You discount the knowledge you've acquired working there, because it's familiar to you. But other people who have worked in shops would recognise the truth of your creation, and it would appeal to them. And the people who have never worked in a shop – they would find your knowledge novel."

"Shops are familiar to everyone who's ever bought a packet of teabags. Nobody cares how they look from the assistant's perspective."

"They are intriguing places. I'm amazed you don't see that. Didn't you ever, when you were a child, daydream about being trapped in a shop overnight? Playing with all the toys and sleeping in the beds?"

In fact Persephone had. If people only wanted the products, that would be one thing, but they wanted her time, and her placation. They wanted a particular emotional performance. "I'm not making a shop," she repeated.

Larkin laughed. "A pity. I'd love to see a tiny version of Kendricks, with a grumpy serving woman behind the counter."

After their arrival in London, they took the train to Windsor, and reached the castle at noon. Once inside they followed the arrows towards the dolls' house. It was stored in a dimly lit room, behind a barrier. They took in the miniature rooms: a chequered entranceway with a tiny coat of armour and a sweeping flight of marble stairs; the bedroom with its lilac taffeta; the nursery equipped with thimble-sized toys. The detail was exquisite. And yet Persephone felt subdued by the house. She wondered if Larkin was feeling equally underwhelmed.

"Have you ever seen the baby houses in Amsterdam?" he asked.

"I've never been abroad, remember?"

"They have a naïve charm."

"*This* isn't naïve."

"No. It's very functional," Larkin remarked. "Mod cons. Running taps. Real books in the library. Cars in the garage that run."

"Electricity and lifts," Persephone said.

They took in the details for a few minutes.

"I find it sterile," Larkin said.

"No, it's not that," Persephone said. "It has a sense of humour. Toilets that flush! But when you are used to Rieko's storytelling – that triad of the room and the doll and *you* – it feels like something's missing from displays like this. It's like a documentary, a history documentary. This is a version of how things were, if you were rich, in the nineteen twenties. There isn't any conflict or drama."

"Documentaries have conflict and drama, if they're any good."

Persephone thought how she might document her life in miniature. A Persephone doll that evoked dislike; a Briar doll that evoked pity. The little terraced cottage on the eyot, with a soap dish for the Belfast sink and framed postage stamps on the walls. Waxen figurines, carved from birthday candles, on a desk in the bedroom. And all over the house, concealed behind cushions and under floorboards, real whisky miniatures. That would be where the conflict came in, between the hidden and the visible, though the viewer would have to uncover it – to move objects around – they couldn't simply observe as they would one of Rieko's photographs. Persephone would give it more thought.

"What would you document?" she asked Larkin. "If you made a house as documentary?"

"An incident from my childhood," Larkin said.

"You don't know which?"

"A very specific incident, concerning a boy from school. He was a troubled sort. His mother kept house for the local priest and there were rumours that he was the priest's son."

"A Catholic priest?"

"Yes. Anyway, this boy took to leaving his bedroom in the night. He would spend the dark hours at the cemetery, digging, until he had reached the coffin. Then he'd search the remains."

"The *remains*? What the hell was the matter with him?"

"I don't think he knew. He was looking for *something*, and couldn't tell you what. The first time he was caught he was still a minor, but he could have been charged with desecration of a grave."

"They didn't charge him?"

"The priest never called the police. He had divided loyalties, didn't he? If he was the boy's father. I expect the priest felt he was partly to blame and covered up any further incidents."

"Would you make a doll of the boy? Or the priest?"

"The corpse, I think. I'd use fragments of real bone – there must be an animal bone suitable for carving. With an enchantment of Belonging."

"Would you use the grave as the setting?"

"No, I think I'd put the corpse in the boy's bed. I can remember his room clearly."

"Lots of people have absent or useless parents. They don't all vandalise graves. I didn't."

"Yes. You think it's unforgivable behaviour?"

Persephone didn't believe for a minute the vandal existed. The story reminded her of tales about the Thief; true in some way, but not factual. Larkin was explicating his own past with the symbols of skeletons in closets, and uncovering buried secrets, and he wasn't asking her to forgive a boy she'd never met for ransacking a grave. He was asking whether she accepted him, when his parents had not.

"Sometimes," she replied, "caring about someone means holding them to account, not forgiving them. What happened to the boy?"

"He left the area, cut his ties completely with his mother and the priest. Everybody expected him to be in prison by thirty, I think. Or in the madhouse." His attention was caught by a man in the doorway. She watched Larkin's face illuminate, the seriousness of their conversation drawn to an immediate close; and he walked past her to greet the newcomer.

"Professor," he said. "How lovely to see you."

They clasped hands. The Professor resembled a Victorian magician. He had a black goatee and a sharp, neat face. His eyebrows were a mite too high, which Persephone had initially taken for surprise at seeing Larkin, but she subsequently gathered that was his perpetual expression.

"This is Persephone Kendrick," Larkin said. "Persephone, Professor Madoc."

The Professor's eyes swivelled towards her like he'd spied prey.

"Delighted to meet you." He inclined his head. "I'm a regular patron of your store."

"We've talked on the phone," Persephone said. "I'm the one who dispatches your dolls. How did you two come to know one another?"

"Larkin was my star pupil," the Professor said.

"In which subject?"

"Miniature oils. Portraiture on the smallest scale."

Perhaps that had contributed to Larkin's ability with dolls' faces. He had said he was a self-taught doll maker, but she wondered for the first time how many of his skills might rest on a foundation built by teachers and collaborators, with Larkin retrospectively claiming such knowledge as his own, spontaneous discovery. But facing his old teacher, Larkin was apparently moved to credit him now, and said: "Without the Professor's guidance I think I would have been lost as a young man."

Persephone reflected on how little she knew of him. She supposed that should alarm her, but she suspected it was part of his appeal. He was the stranger on the eyot – with its suggestion of new ways of doing things – and would remain so as long as he deflected personal questions.

"I believe you put the police on my tail," Professor Madoc said to Persephone.

"It wasn't anything personal. They checked all our regular customers."

"I was flattered. A theft of that nature surely takes ingenuity. But how goes the investigation? Are they any closer to finding the thief?"

"I don't know." Persephone flushed, thinking of the wax she had scraped from the cooker. "Nobody updates me. My rank isn't high enough."

"Ah, Kendricks, with its old hierarchies and gate keepers. They've systematically ignored talent in favour of proprietorial cronyism. Which isn't without its own kind of sense – their customers value the sorcery more than the rendering of the doll – but it comes with risks. They've traded this long on their sorcery, but one day *someone* will leak how it works, and then they'll wish they invested more in craft."

"My hope is that Persephone will strike out on her own," Larkin said. "She has craft, and an incipient understanding of sorcery, too."

The compliment filled Persephone's head. She didn't hear the Professor's reply, but it was something that made him and Larkin laugh. She smiled, to disguise her inattention.

"It was very nice to meet you in person, Miss Kendrick," the Professor said. "Larkin, we'll talk soon. *Ave atque vale!*"

He retreated into the assembly of tourists.

"What was he saying in Latin?" Persephone asked.

"Just goodbye, I think. Have we seen enough?" Larkin gestured at the house.

"Yes."

They started their own walk towards the exit.

"I'm not going to start my own business," Persephone said. "I'm a Kendrick. I belong on the eyot. But do you really think I could succeed on my own?"

"Of course. Your dolls are better than Alastair's, you know. Not as good as mine, but—"

She hit him on the arm, with more force than was necessary.

"Ow," he complained.

"Sorry. I will be as good as you, though."

"I know." Larkin added: "There's something I've not told you."

"What kind of thing?"

"Don't worry! Nothing scandalous. Maybe a bit underhand, but in the least offensive of ways. And it might change your mind about starting a business."

"OK. Tell me."

"I'll do better than that – I'll show you, when we get back to the Tavern."

"This is very mysterious."

"I think you'll be pleased. You might even want to tell me how hexes work."

Persephone doubted that, but her curiosity was piqued. They would have all the afternoon for her to speculate what he had in store.

33

Since Persephone had commenced lessons with Larkin, he had been thinking that the balance between them had tipped, ever so slightly towards him. A teacher always holds some power over their student. He felt able to make a tactical gamble: that, by allowing her to see the wallhanging, she would be encouraged to share more again in turn.

And so, when they'd returned to the Tavern, he took the wallhanging from the wardrobe and unwrapped it. She grasped its significance immediately.

"These are hexes," she confirmed.

"Yes. Do you recognise what they stand for?"

"No. But I do know how to work out their meaning, given a bit of time."

"Do you see, with these, you'd be effective competition for Alastair?"

"I don't want to set up a business."

"So you keep saying. But what is all this work for? Stop kidding yourself."

"There's so many of them," she said wonderingly. "Look at the woodworm. I wonder how old they are. Maybe as old as the Paid Mourner."

"Maybe. If they are, imagine how excited the customers would be. Any new dolls with these old emotions would be much sought after."

She was touching the patina on each disc. "You thought, if you gave me these, I'd tell you how they're used?"

"I hoped you might, yes."

"I need to think about that, Larkin."

He longed to shout: *what is there to think about?* It couldn't be that silly anxiety about losing his interest. Maybe she was stuck on the Sorcerers giving her a job, and she feared they never would, if they learnt she'd leaked their secrets.

She stood. "Thank you for showing me this. Can I take it to my room? I'd like to start translating them there."

The thought of losing sight of it troubled him; but he had already photographed every hex with his phone. He nodded.

She didn't say anything further, and retreated to her own room for the rest of the evening.

That night, Larkin couldn't sleep. To curb his wakefulness he dressed, and left the Tavern for a walk. Just as he reached the terrace, he saw Hedwig leaving Briar Kendrick's cottage. It was clearly her, by light of the hallway. The two of them conferred briefly on the step. Their conversation was out of Larkin's hearing but they had the air of plotters.

Briar closed the door, and Hedwig set off down the lane, towards Larkin. She was carrying a wicker basket.

"Being a good neighbour, Hedwig?" he asked her when their paths crossed.

"Briar was the worse for wear," Hedwig explained. "He banged on our door, believing he still lived there, so I walked him back to his house."

Kindly of Hedwig, at half three in the morning. Larkin's eyes fell to her basket, which was empty. It wasn't the first thing you'd grab when escorting a drunkard home.

"He seemed to have sobered up, at any rate," Larkin pointed out. "By the time he said goodbye."

Hedwig tilted her head to one side. Then she laughed, conceding the ruse was up. "All right, Larkin. I'd appreciate it if you don't mention to anyone that you saw me there."

"Don't worry. If I do, I'll just say the pair of you are having a torrid affair."

She shuddered in distaste and laughed again.

Larkin checked up and down the lane that no one was near, then whispered: "I'd been meaning to ask, when I got a moment alone with you. Did my contact's work satisfy you?"

"Very much; thank you, Larkin."

"I hope she wasn't too expensive. The butcher haggles hard, on her behalf."

"Not at all."

"Only, your mother mentioned you were experiencing some financial difficulties."

Hedwig corrected him: "No difficulties – Scarlotta's payment simply took priority over my mother's. I am, in any case, about to be recompensed."

She insisted that she must return home then, for Conrad's flight arrived early in the morning. Larkin continued on his own way. The culmination of her plan must be afoot. He might try to wheedle a detail or two more from her. Or, if not from her, Briar, whose house she crept from in the middle of the night.

34

Hedwig and Conrad stood in the garden, watching the small armoured boat progress along the river. When it came to a stop, they walked to the river's edge in greeting.

Montgomery Delderfield, Conrad's accountant, emerged from the cabin. Hedwig had always thought him blandly nondescript in appearance: you could exchange him for any number of middle managers across the land. His fair hair was thin and his eyes pale. He wore a navy blue polyester suit. But today he was guarding valuable cargo, and that leant him significance.

"Mr Kendrick. Miss Mayhew," he acknowledged with a nod.

"Is everything in order?" Conrad asked.

"It is." A shadowy figure inside the cabin – Hedwig assumed one of Delderfield's employees – passed Delderfield a cash strong box, which he handed to Hedwig; then a second, which he gave to Conrad. The third he carried himself.

"Let's get these inside as quickly as possible, shall we?"

They began the walk up the slope. The shadowy figure remained behind them in the boat, and Hedwig believed she could feel his stare on her neck. It needled her to think someone was party to the transfer of gold and she didn't know who they were.

"Thank you so much for acting swiftly," Hedwig said to Delderfield. The box weighed as much as a young, well-fed child. Her arm strained, but the adrenaline of carrying the gold for her plan sustained her. "I imagine all hands were on deck at the firm to get it? A few people must have helped? I would so like to send my thanks."

Delderfield said: "For administrative purposes, some of my colleagues are aware Mr Kendrick required an immediate release of funds. Obviously they observe confidentiality as they do for any client."

"And that's true of your friend in the boat, is it?"

"He knows only what he needs to," Delderfield said.

They heard the sound of the boat's engine as it finally departed. They walked past the burnt ground of the masquerade bonfire. The gardener, at Hedwig's request, had left a set of spades for her to commence digging. Soon they were at the house, and entered by the side door.

Conrad led the way to his drawing room. On arrival, they placed the strong boxes upon the table. Out of breath from the exertion, Conrad tottered to his seat. Delderfield unlocked the boxes one after the other to reveal layer upon layer of gold bars. The surface, yellow and black, shone softly.

He counted out the bars, placing each one on the table as

he did so. When he had reached sixty-six, silence fell upon the room.

"There's so much of it," Hedwig breathed.

"I believe you have duties to start in the garden," Conrad replied. "I will remain here and discuss the rest of my affairs with Mr Delderfield."

Thus dismissed, Hedwig first went to her room, to change into jeans and a tired shirt and sweater; then in the dusk she proceeded to the bonfire site, where the spades lay. She took the largest and began to dig. The activity warmed her and soon her hands began to chafe on the handle. Her shoulders and lower back began to ache when she was almost halfway down. One by one her fingernails chipped. She wiped her forehead, and kept going, until the hole was six foot deep.

She had envisioned an oblong, as if for a grave. Instead the hole resembled a funnel. It would do. She fetched a wheelbarrow from the head gardener's shed and ran it all the way back to Conrad's drawing room.

Mr Delderfield had seemingly departed, and Conrad was asleep upright in his chair. He was still jet-lagged. The gold lay undisturbed. Hedwig transferred it, piece by piece, to the wheelbarrow. By the time it was full it was unwieldy and her return trip was slow.

She took one of the golden bricks and laid it in the grass, before upending the wheelbarrow into the hole. The clash of one bar falling upon another was tremendous. After allowing herself a few minutes to catch her breath, she retrieved the spade, and shovelled soil over Conrad's wealth. Hedwig regarded it as a type of pension. It would satisfy her to know it lay there, undisturbed and safe from spending, year after year, until she might have need of it – perhaps after Conrad's death. Who else would even know the money lay there? Only Conrad; and Briar, who, if he outlived his brother, might well be silenced with a payment of his own.

The moon had fully risen now. She patted the earth with the spade tip till it was level. She wrapped the remaining bar in her sweater. This would settle her debts nicely and create a comfortable nest egg, too.

This time, when she re-entered the drawing room, Conrad was neither asleep nor alone. Inspector Naidu was with him.

Hedwig cradled the wrapped gold. It resembled nothing more than a tattered jumper, but she still drew it closer to her body with a shiver as the Inspector turned to look at her.

"My sweetness," Conrad said in greeting, apparently unruffled by the presence of the police. "I've just been discussing how you held the fort in my absence. A true Dobermann, an Alsatian in the guarding of all I hold dear."

"It was nothing," Hedwig said. "Forgive me for not shaking your hand Inspector; I've been working in the garden. I must have forgotten you were visiting."

The Inspector maintained eye contact. Hedwig refused to be disquieted. Following her last discussion with Stanley, she had been waiting for questions from Naidu about the vandalism at the workshop. But they never came – and Hedwig had begun to relax again, thinking that perhaps the wet-lipped man had rethought his accusations, or was otherwise found unreliable. It was the most abominable timing that Naidu should come *now*, at a critical point in the execution of Hedwig's plan. What if the Inspector had seen Hedwig burying gold? Or her eyes happened upon the ransom letter, which Hedwig could see from the doorway, face upwards on the bureau? Stanley would deride the very thought of ransoms from the fae folk; he'd snoop till he knew who'd really written it.

"I was terribly naughty," Conrad said. "It slipped my mind to notify the Inspector I was coming home! She rang my Fiji hotel, and they said I wasn't available."

"They said that Mr Kendrick had vacated his room several days earlier than intended, without checking out," corrected the Inspector. "No one knew his whereabouts."

This was what happened when Conrad travelled alone. Without Hedwig necessities escaped him.

"Conrad's back where he belongs," Hedwig remarked. "I'd offer tea, Inspector, only as you can see I'm not dressed for entertaining guests."

"I'm not here for entertainment. Mr Kendrick's house, and more recently his business, have been the target of serious attacks. As a matter of safety we should be informed of his location – or at least that he's in the country. I'm surprised I have to explain this to you, Miss Mayhew. I'd have thought, given your own encounter with the armed assailant, you'd appreciate a degree of risk assessment."

"Very sensible." Hedwig's arms, full of gold, ached. "We so appreciate your protection, and the seriousness with which you've handled everything. It must be frustrating to get here and find everything so very normal. I do apologise for not alerting you myself that Conrad was here."

The Inspector stood up. "If you *could* keep us informed in future. No need to follow, Miss Mayhew; I'll see myself out."

She did so. Hedwig waited for the slam of the front door, and watched, through the window, until the policewoman had left the garden.

"I don't believe for one minute she was worried about my safety," Conrad said. "She thought I'd done a moonlight flit! For the insurance, I shouldn't wonder – stolen the doll myself, then hotfooted it to Fiji before disappearing into the night!"

"Maybe." If Naidu thought Conrad was the bigger catch and Hedwig was merely doing his bidding, it would explain why Hedwig hadn't been called back for questioning. "Whatever she was looking for, she didn't find it. Please, Conrad, please tell me you didn't show her the ransom note?"

"I wouldn't dream of it. I told them once before this was the Thief's work – and they dismissed me, the scoundrels! I won't give them *that* opportunity again."

"You gave them a fair chance at solving things, Conrad. No one could ask for more. But it's time we took matters into our own hands again, isn't it?"

"That it is, Hedwig."

With Naidu's departure a disaster had been narrowly averted. In a few short hours, Briar would bring the magic doll and lay her upon the earth, ready for Conrad to come at dawn. Until then Hedwig would sleep. She would bathe the blisters on her hands, and creep between the covers, with her gold bar stowed beneath the bed.

35

That evening Persephone was working patiently in her room; she started with the first hex on the wallhanging, and licked its duo of symbols on a maquette. Her fingertips stroked the newly magic doll, tenderly. *Justified Aggravation.* She wrote it down, and moved on to the next. *Caring Exasperation.* A third. *Righteous Outrage.* The feelings arrived, pulsed through her, and disappeared. *Vengeful Loathing. Uncovered Grief. Languid Nostalgia. Remorseful Dismay.* The next row. *Dejected Defeat. Wistful Yearning. Docile Acquiescence. Existential Dread.* She paused, dizzy. Then the final row. The purity of the hexes astounded her. *Affection; Exhilaration; Adoration; Longing; Cheer; Contentment; Pride; Rapture; Optimism; Love.* Persephone was giddy with sentiment. She didn't have to wait for Briar to complete her own hex. She had deciphered these treasures without him. And she could not keep that knowledge from Larkin; not any longer. She'd show him how hexes were laid. He wouldn't lose interest in her. They would be bound by their knowledge.

As soon as she'd finished, she went to Larkin's room. He had a finished artwork to show her, and invited her verdict. All the copies he had made of the Paid Mourner were arranged within a type of zoetrope. He had posed them in subtly different stances so that when the zoetrope was spun, and you looked through the sight gaps, it appeared as though the Paid Mourner was running.

"She has escaped." Larkin sipped from an iced glass with misted sides, before pointing at the dolls. "And she won't be caught."

This didn't seem right to Persephone. The doll was running endlessly, but in a circle. You couldn't escape if you were continually returning to the same spot.

She reached out to touch one of the dolls, stopping their motion in the process. It was devoid of feeling.

"Laying an enchantment is simple," Persephone said softly. "You trace the hex on the doll with the tip of your tongue."

Larkin's eyes widened at the suddenness of this revelation. "But that's *ridiculously* simple!"

"Anyone can lick a hex, it's true. *If* you know that's how the symbols work. *If* you are allowed to see the symbols at all. Why do you think the Sorcerers are so secretive? It's because you don't have to be special to do what they do. You just have to have their privileges."

Larkin picked up one of his dolls from the zoetrope. He peeled back the dress and licked the rosewood beneath. Persephone wondered how long he had pored over his wallhanging of hexes, to recall, without checking, the shapes he had seen there.

When he had finished, he stroked the doll's face, and swooned, laughing delightedly. "It works," he said. "Do you know how long I've waited for this?"

"You arrived in the autumn," she said. "When the quince were growing in the orchard."

"No; I've waited since I was a young boy." He put the doll down. "Help me enchant the others. You take half, I'll take half."

The gesture touched her – the offering of his dolls to her in the wake of so recently mastering enchantments himself. She dared to hope their lessons would continue; and wished to secure that likelihood.

Instead of taking one of the dolls, she raised her own wrist to her mouth, and nimbly, silently, traced a hex. She stared at Larkin in challenge as she did so.

"It works upon you too?" he asked.

"It works on any person, as long as there's someone to perceive."

"What's the enchantment?"

"Love."

She extended her hand for him to touch her. As his fingers closed over her she observed his face. He let go as though he had been burnt. He looked back at her, then to her hand again. This time when he grasped it he did so in full knowledge.

"I thought people were lying," he said.

"About what?"

"This." He tapped his heart. "Can I kiss you?"

He was the first man to ask. She said: "Yes."

Larkin pulled her towards him, and their lips collided. The strangeness of tasting another mouth asserted itself. His mouth was cold, and clean, from the chilled water. She felt inept – her tongue clumsy and darting because she knew it was supposed to tangle with his but wasn't fully sure how. *I'm doing it wrong*, her thoughts wailed.

They paused, at just the point Persephone was wondering how she would know when to stop. His face was too close for her to focus.

"You look worried," he whispered.

"I'm bad at kissing."

"Silly." He pecked her mouth. "Who told you that?"

"No one. I just know."

"You're mistaken; but I won't object if you want to practise."

Maybe he was protecting her feelings, because he loved her. And yet – if that were the worst case scenario – she had reason to feel reassured.

"Can we try again?" she asked.

The second time was better. Warmer, their breathing heavier. His hand moved to her breast. Her chest fluttered inside, as if she had been running.

He eased back. "Do you want a drink?"

Persephone shook her head. He picked up his phone from the table and selected some music on low – something old, and shoegazey; she couldn't place it. Then he sat on the bed, and appraised her as he unfastened his wrist watch.

"If you touch your own skin, does the enchantment work on you?" He placed the watch on the window ledge.

She took a seat next to him. "No. Maybe it's there as a constant background hum so I don't really notice it. Because my skin's always touching my skin somewhere, isn't it?"

The cleft beneath her arm; the underside of her breast against her torso; the inside of her thighs.

"So you're not in love with yourself?" he teased.

"The other Kendricks think I am, even without the enchantment. But it's not true – I don't think I'm better than everyone else. I just think I'm better than they give me credit for." Most of the time. Sometimes she feared they'd judged her correctly.

The enchantment only worked on Larkin when he touched her, but he must be sufficiently intrigued by its effects to keep returning, because now he rested his head on her shoulder.

"What are you going to do when people love you just for shaking your hand?" he asked.

"Let go."

"It's that simple?"

"It has to be. I hate shaking hands anyway. I won't do it in future."

"But what if you have to give a customer change, and you brush against their palm? What if you need a haircut? What if you're ill and need a doctor's examination?"

She shrugged. "I'll explain to the doctor. The others, I'll just do my best to avoid. And if they touch me without my say-so they deserve what they get. But the enchantment's laid. I can't remove it."

"Ever?"

"Ever."

"What a ridiculous thing for you to do." He kissed her again, and they lay down, their heads sharing one pillow. Between the breaks in the music they could hear the television where Mrs Mayhew was sitting in the lounge.

"I want to make love to you," Larkin said.

"I know. I can't. It's too fast."

He stroked her head. "All right. Whatever you need."

She woke shortly after midnight. He was sitting at his desk again, arranging the zoetrope.

"What enchantment are you laying now?" she mumbled sleepily.

"It's Faith that All will be Well," he replied.

Persephone thought: *I don't remember that on the wallhanging*. Larkin must have kept a disc back. Larkin, with his secrets. She wondered if he would be less secretive now her touch could inspire Love in him. But lovers weren't always truthful. She drifted back into sleep, dreamlessly, and Faith was forgotten.

36

It was one o'clock in the morning, and Hedwig was woken by the ring of the telephone on the landing. She stumbled from her bed to answer.

It was Inspector Naidu. "We've arrested Briar Kendrick."

"What?" Hedwig was immediately alert.

"Tonight we received a tip that the Paid Mourner was on his property—"

"From *who*?" Hedwig raised her voice.

"The informant withheld his name. However, anyone who'd entered the property would have seen the doll. She was on the kitchen table when we arrived. I'd like to update you and your boss in more detail tomorrow morning, once we've interviewed Mr Kendrick. I'm afraid he isn't currently fit for questioning."

So Briar was drunk. He'd allowed someone to see the forgery, and they'd thought it was real. The police seemed to believe the doll was genuine too – surely they'd say if they suspected Briar, or her, of an attempt to defraud? But Briar might still confess all under pressure, including Hedwig's involvement. Who knows what he would say in an interview.

Naidu went on. "In the meantime, it would help us greatly if your boss would confirm the doll's identity. That's information we'd want to take into the interview room. Miss Mayhew? Are you still there?"

"Yes, yes I'm still here. It's all – quite overwhelming."

"Naturally."

Naidu might know more than she was letting on. The Inspector sounded genuine, but that might be a front, to lure Hedwig into a false sense of security.

"I just don't want to get my hopes up," Hedwig added. "Let's see if the doll's right first."

"It matches the visual description we were given. We're confident of a positive ID."

From his bedroom, Conrad was calling: "Hedwig, Hedwig!"

"I'll bring Conrad to the station immediately," Hedwig told Naidu, and hung up. There wouldn't be any further sleep tonight.

Conrad and Hedwig were at the station within the hour. Inspector Naidu ushered them into a bland side room where the replica of the Paid Mourner lay upon a laminate table.

"Take your time examining it," the Inspector said. "You need to be sure."

As soon as he picked the doll up, Conrad cried: "The enchantment is right! It's her."

"Check her thoroughly. Any case against your brother will depend on it."

"It's her," Conrad said, but he obliged by disrobing the doll and scrutinising the wood beneath, as well as checking through her hair, where Briar had marked the correct hex. Over the years, Hedwig could never recall Conrad taking the Paid Mourner from the cage. If he had done so, it must have been privately, and rarely. He was ready to be convinced by a replica in part because his impressions at close range to the doll were limited – and because he dearly needed to believe she had been found.

"What's Briar said?" Hedwig asked the Inspector. She dared not ask if they thought he'd worked alone. It seemed foolish to plant the idea in their heads before they raised it themselves, but her fear was growing. Once Briar was sober, he would see that he faced prison if he allowed the police to believe the doll was genuine. He might think his chances were better if he told the truth – that he was committing extortion, and fraud, but there was no evidence he was a thief. And if he did that, Hedwig's involvement would surely come to light.

"He claims he was compelled to take her by the fae folk," Naidu said drily. "But that won't affect his legal culpability."

"You're confident of a conviction?" Conrad asked.

"We need to wait until he's fit to interview." Yet the Inspector spoke smugly. Her tone betrayed confidence. "I'll update you as soon as we have anything to report."

They left shortly afterwards, as their presence was no longer required. They departed empty handed, as the crime scene officer was still collecting evidence from the Paid Mourner.

"When she is returned," Conrad said in the car park, "I will expect the clan to come view her glorious reinstatement."

"You must be so relieved she's been found," Hedwig said.

"And she's unharmed," Conrad said. "I'm thankful to Briar for that."

"You're not angry with him?" Hedwig asked, surprised.

"More than I can express; but it sounds as though he was not in full control of himself."

"You think the Thief compelled him?"

"He may have done. I don't think Briar would blame the fae folk lightly. He knows, as I do, that the Kendricks' fate has always been entwined with theirs."

"Do *you* believe Briar?" Hedwig knew that what really mattered was whether the police believed him; but if – by some miracle – she escaped their detection, Conrad's belief was essential to Hedwig's continued position. Hedwig couldn't be blamed for a crime orchestrated by the fae folk.

"I haven't decided if Briar's telling the truth. But I do know that when you buried the gold, the doll was delivered, just as the letter asked. That suggests the Thief was driving events."

"Will you return the gold to Delderfield now?"

"No. You find me superstitious, feign to deny it, but the burial led to the outcome we wanted, and reversing it may reverse the outcome also. At least let us wait until Briar elaborates."

"I wonder what he'll say when they question him tomorrow."

"That, my sweet, may depend on the soreness of his head." He frowned. "There is one thing I can't account for. Before the doll's disappearance, her enchantment was growing faint with age. It's now quite clear and strong – almost as if it had been renewed..."

Hedwig cut in, quick-thinking: "Wouldn't that be natural, if she's kept company with fae folk? The Thief would rejuvenate her power, I'm sure."

Conrad brightened at this suggestion. "Yes. Yes, I'm sure that's true, my sweet."

The chauffeur was waiting. He opened the car door for them, and they settled in for the journey home.

37

Persephone was disorientated in the morning to open her eyes on a room other than her own. The weight of Larkin's arm across her waist reminded her where she was. The cover was over them but she was still in her dress from the day before. Soon she would have to wash and change for work. Till then she could listen to the robin, singing in the darkness beyond the window.

At seven the alarm rang. Persephone reached to turn it off as Larkin blinked, his hair dishevelled.

"You're still here," he said.

"Should I have gone?" She rolled over to face him.

"No." He touched his foot to hers. "It's lovely. You're lovely. Let's stay here all day."

"Just kissing?"

"Whatever you want."

"Not sex."

"I know. You said."

"I'd be bad at it."

"That's why you don't want to? Look, it's not like—" He searched for words, and began again. "You're making a category error. You can't be *bad* at it because I'm not marking your performance. I just want to be close to you."

"If I get things wrong you might laugh at me," she pointed out. "You're always laughing at things I say and I don't always know why."

"I laugh because I enjoy your company, not because you've said something wrong. Well – maybe because you've said something a bit, well, frank – more frankly than most people would. But I like that about you. I thought you knew. Do you want me to stop?"

"No. Not if that's why. Just don't laugh at me if I seem – inexperienced."

"I'm inexperienced. Nobody's ever enchanted me before."

"That's not what I meant."

"I know."

She bit her thumbnail. "We can still do other things."

"Things?"

"Things I know how to do." She kissed him. That, she had the knack of now. Narrowing the space between their bodies, she shifted her leg over his body, her thigh resting on his hip, to move her pelvis closer to his. The long skirts of her black gown rode higher.

"Here," she said, moving his hand over her stomach, over the dark silk, under the cotton of her underwear. "Here. Is that all right?"

He nodded. She guided his hand, moving it the way she liked.

"Keep circling," she whispered, and let his hand go.

She gasped into his shoulder, conscious of Mrs Mayhew's footfall in the corridor. Larkin froze for a second, as Mrs Mayhew seemed to stop at the door. When she walked away, Persephone started to laugh.

"See, laughing's not so bad," Larkin said.

"It's just so embarrassing. Not wanting to be caught out by Mrs Mayhew."

"Ignore Mrs Mayhew," he said gently. He unfroze; she unfroze. Her eyes closed. Those circles, radiating through her body like warm water. She felt herself outpace the speed of his hand, and nearly said, *quicker, go quicker*, but there was something pleasurable in the slowness of his movement – the frustration of it. She imagined that she was a wax doll – that he was shaping her – and the tension peaked; her back arced as she cried out.

She waited for her breathing to steady. Her forehead was hot.

"Your whole face changed when you came," he said.

"Isn't that normal?" she asked, surprised.

"Yes. It's just," he said, "I've never seen you unguarded before."

Persephone learnt of Briar's arrest over breakfast, from Mrs Mayhew.

"I was looking out the window when they came to take him. He made a terrible fuss. Struggled and slapped a policeman, so they'll charge him with that too, won't they? I expect you'll want to ring the station," Mrs Mayhew prompted. "Get some news?"

"If he or the police need me I'm sure they'll call." Persephone wiped her mouth with a napkin. Mrs Mayhew was angling for further gossip.

Larkin was watching Persephone thoughtfully. Once Mrs Mayhew had left to feed the cat, he said: "I can ring the police, on your behalf, if you'll find it too hard."

"What would be the point? We both know they got the right man."

Larkin took her hand, and at her touch, his face softened again.

"I'm annoyed with myself," he said.

"Why?" Persephone asked.

"Because I'm glad your father is in prison. And I don't want to be glad about something that makes you sad."

"I don't feel sad about it. I don't feel anything." And she didn't: just a blank, sedated emptiness.

"He can't hit you, from prison. You're free of him. Let's leave. We have the wallhanging. We can lay on any of the enchantments. We can establish our own business."

"No." Persephone was adamant. "I'm entitled to be here. And so are you."

She sat back in her chair, releasing her hand from his. Larkin mirrored her.

"OK," he said. "You're probably right."

Before Persephone left for work, she called by her room again. She took a dozen of her best dolls, from the ones she had perfected during her lessons with Larkin. She laid them tenderly in her bag.

Larkin was waiting for her at the foot of the stairs. They departed together, walking side by side up the lane.

"How did it get so hard for women anyway?" he asked.

"Haven't you heard? We're crap at the job."

"Four women starting the business should make a difference."

"They only had sons, so there were no women in the next generation to be Sorcerers. Those men decided that their daughters should receive a hex, like the boys, for their own protection from the Thief, but fathers must act as intermediary in translating the symbol. A girl couldn't possibly be allowed to be the only one who knew her hex. Women never regained a proper foothold. Sorcery became *men's work*. That was the company line. The women who did break through were belittled. Usually their dolls had a lower price point, or the maker would get dismissed as just the Sorcerer's sister or wife or lover, or they were treated as freak anomalies."

"Surely, during the wars—"

"Yes, while men were fighting, Kendricks let a few women work as Sorcerers. Mostly they were making dolls for the troops with enchantments of Courage. After the war, both times, everybody said that women had done the job badly, and it was business as usual. The women stayed loyal, the way people always have at Kendricks. But they were broken-hearted. The best of them, a woman named Hester, continued to quietly request the women's re-employment, fearing if she did nothing the lot of women at Kendricks would never improve. She married an architect who supported her efforts. Then she was widowed and had a breakdown. Her uncle committed her. She wasn't released back to the eyot until the nineteen eighties. Everyone said it was the sorcery that sent her mad, but it was just grief, grief for her work, and for her husband."

They were approaching the door to the workroom, where Alastair was letting himself in. He'd regard such talk as seditious. Perhaps sensing as much, Larkin changed the subject. He said to let him know when she was closing up the shop, and he would leave with her. This struck her as official. He fell into step beside Alastair, discussing the work for the day ahead, and they parted ways from Persephone at the counter. She was hanging up her coat when Larkin doubled back to kiss her.

"Go away," she said. "I'm busy."

Which was true, but he laughed on his way to the paternoster, so he must know it was meant affectionately. She had a plan to implement. It was important to act quickly, while she was alone on the shop floor.

First, Persephone removed, at random, twelve of Kendricks' dolls from the shelves. She took them to the stockroom. Their absence wouldn't be missed immediately: in the ordinary way of things, there were always more dolls than were available on the shop floor and they were displayed in rotation. But she did not take a replacement twelve dolls from the stores. Instead she returned to the counter and picked up the bag of her own dolls. She arranged them in the blank spaces that were around the room, and photographed them. Finally, she included the photos in the product list which she distributed, every week, to their collectors.

She sat back. Without Alastair's knowledge or support, she had become a Sorcerer. Her dolls were made; they were enchanted; and they were on sale. It was simpler than she had anticipated. She had done what was in her control, and could now only hope for a buyer before Alastair found out.

38

Conrad slept late the day after Briar was arrested – later, even, than he usually did. Hedwig barely slept at all, but it wouldn't do to let Conrad see it. She brightened her appearance with judicious make-up in readiness for when he finally rang the bell for his morning tea.

His mind, however, was not on her anyway.

"We must discuss Persephone," he said. "She should be summoned here right away, Hedwig – right away, I tell you! Do you believe she could possibly have been ignorant of Briar's crime?"

Hedwig did not; but if Conrad punished Persephone for knowing and saying nothing, Briar would surely be angry. And Hedwig feared an angry Briar was all the more likely to deny he acted alone.

"I find it very possible that he acted without her knowledge," Hedwig said. "They are barely on speaking terms these days."

"Hm."

"You're right, undoubtedly, to raise the question of her innocence. I'm sure the Inspector will consider her involvement too. Perhaps we could leave her questioning to the police?"

"No, I must speak to her myself – it's imperative I do so. We can't allow her to think she's escaped my notice. That wouldn't be proper leadership, Hedwig."

"I'll telephone Kendricks now, and ask her to report as soon as she has finished for the day."

Persephone arrived shortly before six, with Larkin, who hadn't been invited to attend.

"I doubt Conrad will let Larkin in with you," Hedwig said, as the pair took their seats on the pew in the hall.

"Larkin will wait for me," Persephone said shortly. "I won't be here long."

"Very well." Hedwig also thought it best if the meeting were as swift as possible. And if Conrad did decide to be punitive, it would be as well to have two witnesses to Hedwig's greater reasonableness. "Conrad will see you at the stroke of the clock. Would you like refreshments?"

"I wasn't expecting hospitality."

"Tea would be very nice," Larkin added.

Hedwig left them alone while she made tea in the kitchen. On her return she hovered in the doorway, observing them. Persephone was now sitting with her back to the pew's armrest, her feet on the seat, her knees drawn up to her chin. One lace of her black boot trailed.

"Have you ever worked with plastic?" Persephone was asking Larkin.

"No, although I knew people at college who did, with 3D printing mainly."

"I wouldn't know where to begin with that."

"Learning CAD, I expect. It's a popular option for fashion dolls. Did you play with any fashion dolls when you were a child? The ones made by Pedigree or – what was the other one? – Hasbro."

They were just making shop talk in hushed voices, but Persephone slid her booted foot into Larkin's lap, and he tied the lace for her, before running a single finger along her shin. The gesture made Hedwig feel like an intruder.

"I only ever had dolls from Kendricks," Persephone said. "I do remember seeing fashion dolls on TV adverts and being curious about them. They were so shiny and bright. Hedwig had some, I remember, but I'm older than her so I never asked if I could play with them – I would have been mortified – even though I wanted to."

"When I was eight I pinched a fashion doll from a doctor's waiting room," Larkin said.

Persephone laughed. "You wanted one that badly?"

"I guess so. My mother would never have bought me a girl's toy – god, she would have been aghast. So I think I rather liked risking her disapproval. The doll had lost her clothes somewhere along the line. It frustrated me that she couldn't stand up. The design had no stability at all. Every doll I've ever made could stand unsupported. But even though she wasn't very functional I was fascinated with her. She was marked with felt tip scribbles in a few places. At the top of her legs the plastic had deformed slightly – I think it reacts with the air over time – and a previous owner had chewed the feet."

The clock struck six, giving Hedwig an entry point to interrupt.

"It's time to go in," she said. She brought the tray to them, so Larkin could take his cup of tea. He moved his head in her direction without taking his eyes from Persephone. *Sticky eyes*, Hedwig's mother had always called that.

Hedwig backed into the drawing room door. Persephone followed.

Inside, Conrad made an initial show of continuing to read the novel he had on his lap. He waited just long enough for the silence to become uncomfortable, then closed the book with his finger marking the page.

"Be seated, niece," he said.

Persephone took the chair opposite.

"Why did you provide an alibi for your father?" Conrad began.

"I told the police the truth. But I did go to bed as soon as I came home from the party, and Dad must have taken advantage of that. He must have come back here while I was asleep."

"Convince me that you had nothing to do with the theft of the Paid Mourner."

"You've known me all my life," Persephone said. "Have I ever indulged Dad in a vendetta?"

"No, but even disapproving daughters don't want their father to go to prison. Perhaps you didn't aid him in the theft, but you aided him in its concealment."

"Normally, disapproving brothers don't want their twin to go to prison either," said Persephone coolly.

Hedwig winced. Was Persephone confessing that she equalled Conrad in her antipathy towards Briar?

"Touché," Conrad said.

Persephone smoothed the fabric of her skirt. "I don't like him suffering. But the eyot will be better off without him."

Conrad chuckled – callously, in Hedwig's view. "The cock will crow three times, eh?"

"Yes, I'm very disloyal. I have been for weeks. Surely Hedwig explained I haven't spoken to my father in some time?"

"I have," Hedwig said, glad of the opportunity to interject in Persephone's support. "It is my firmly held belief that Briar acted alone."

Persephone rephrased her question to Conrad. "Why would I protect Dad from the police when we're estranged?"

"What caused the rift?" Conrad seized on the reference to discord between man and daughter. "Was it that you knew he was a criminal, and he compelled you to lie for him?"

"No. He drank too much in the Tavern and when I suggested it was time to go home, he punched me in the face."

Finally, Hedwig noted, Conrad looked sheepish.

"So you say," he replied, but his words lacked conviction. Persephone's account was plausible in its simplicity.

"Ask Larkin for confirmation," she said. "He saw it happen."

"That won't be necessary." Conrad reopened his novel.

"I'm sure the police can ask any questions of you that they need. You may continue to live and work on the eyot."

Persephone stood up to leave. "Thanks for your generosity."

He looked at her sharply. "Know I'll be watching you for any signs of insubordination. Do you understand, Persephone Kendrick? If I see any sign that you have acted, or intend to act, against my interests then my generosity will come to an abrupt end."

"I understand perfectly."

Hedwig saw Persephone out, and Larkin with her. It was to be hoped that Persephone had taken in Conrad's warning, and would obey it. For now Briar had nothing to respond to angrily in Conrad's actions. That might change if Persephone failed to stay in line.

At Conrad's behest, Hedwig was to visit the houses of the eyot to inform people that the Paid Mourner would imminently be released by the police. Alastair topped the list. As the Head Sorcerer, he was always the first to be notified of any events.

He lived in the second biggest house after Conrad's, though its style differed in keeping with its later date. While the façade of Conrad's house was relatively plain, Alastair's displayed some Regency flourishes, including wrought iron railings beneath every window. Hedwig was just opening the garden gate when she saw a figure vault over the railings on the ground floor.

Hedwig fell to her knees in horror. The figure wore a

Volto Larva mask, and was running towards her. She shielded her head.

"Sara!" shouted a voice from the doorway. Rieko's voice.

Daring to look up again, Hedwig saw Rieko stride across the garden, and rip the mask away from the figure. This was no thief; a child stood there unmasked. Alastair and Rieko's daughter, Sara, no more than ten years old. The mask had thrown Hedwig into such immediate panic she had failed to distinguish a small girl from a grown man.

"Where did you get this?" Rieko was demanding.

Sara shrugged. "I found it in the mud, near the quince orchard."

"Briar must have dropped it there," Hedwig supplied. "On the night the Paid Mourner was taken."

Unsteadily, she rose and dusted the soil from her knees.

"I'm sorry, Hedwig," Rieko said. "You look terribly shocked. Will you come in for a cup of tea?"

"No." Hedwig shook her head. Sara was looking at the ground, guilty for the effect her dressing up had wreaked. "I was just coming with a message from Conrad to Alastair. The doll will likely be released by the police in the next few days. We will be hosting a party to welcome her, and Alastair's presence will be required."

"That's good news," Rieko said politely. "I will let him know."

The mask was still in her hand. She took it back into the house, Sara following with a glance back over her shoulder.

39

Two of Persephone's dolls sold through the shop within a day of the updated list going out. Although she was initially tempted to substitute another two of her own to the catalogue, she didn't want to push her luck. She put one of Alastair's dolls, and one of Dennis's pieces out instead. In the meantime, she intended to infiltrate some of the other Sorcerers' duties.

In addition to making dolls from scratch, the Sorcerers helped restore private collections, some of which dated back to Lucy Kendrick's days. One of their repeat customers – Julian Brown, a softly spoken man with broken thread veins across his nose – had called into the shop for this reason.

He placed a cherrywood box upon the counter. It was about five inches square. Marquetry spelt out the name *Kendricks* across the side, and the top was decorated with a swirling circular pattern.

"I picked it up for a song because the box no longer opens," he said. "The wood must have swelled. But listen—"

He tilted the box, and Persephone heard the contents softly hit the sides.

"Logic would suggest those are dolls in there," he said. "Given the provenance of the box."

"Probably not a good idea to shake them," Persephone cautioned.

He shot her an exasperated look. "Could I speak to one of the Sorcerers directly?"

She shrugged, then telephoned up to the top floor. Dennis said he would come down. While they waited, Persephone told Mr Brown: "If the contents are enchanted, it's not strong enough to detect the enchantment through the box. That tells us something about the materials. If the dolls were iron, we'd feel the enchantment clearly when we touch the lid. If they were wood, we'd pick up a weak sense of their enchantment. I'm betting they're made from cloth."

"How long will Dennis be?" Mr Brown persisted.

At that moment she heard Dennis hop off the paternoster.

"Julian," he greeted their customer. "What do we have here?"

"That's what I'm hoping you'll help with. You must have the tools to open an old box of yours without damaging it? Whatever's inside may need restoring, too."

"I'll see what we can do. From the lettering on the box, I'd guess it's from 1920 at the very latest. Might be as early as 1900. There's probably a date on the inside of the lid. As for the dolls – bit hard to quote for repairs, when we don't know the extent of their wear and tear, or even what they're made from."

"I have some thoughts on that. You see the enchantment

isn't detectable through the box. So they can't be iron, or even wood. They're probably cotton."

"Mr Brown, wherever did you get that nugget of information?" asked Persephone.

The two men ignored her.

"That's right enough," Dennis said. "I'll tot you up an estimate now, based on a cotton doll, and we can revise it if need be once we've had sight of the blighters. Fair warning – we've got a backlog, so I won't get to look at it until well into the New Year."

Persephone took out her sketchpad from below the counter. She had taken to drawing the dolls she planned to make during quiet periods in the shop, and it was clear that her input wasn't currently required by Julian Brown or Dennis. As the estimate was written up, and accepted, she grew more absorbed in her work. She was startled to hear the shop bell ring when Mr Brown departed.

"File this, would you, Seph," Dennis said, passing her his copy of the quote.

She slid it onto her pad, but not before the underlying pencil sketch caught Dennis's eye.

"Very pretty," he said. "Nice that you've got a hobby."

Persephone put the pad under the counter. "My work's getting better all the time."

"Hm. I heard you'd got a bit upset with Alastair, over the dolls you'd brought in. I wouldn't take him to heart, love. It's his job to be picky about quality control, but there's nothing to stop you doing whatever you like as a pastime."

"It's Alastair's loss," Persephone said, although she'd always thought *it's his loss* was a hollow saying. Clearly she was the person most negatively affected by Alastair's decision. It was nothing to him; he could continue in unchallenged mediocrity. But she thought of her two sales, and she allowed herself a satisfied smile.

"That's the spirit." Dennis hesitated. "And everything's all right, you know, since the Paid Mourner turned up?"

"I haven't spoken to my father yet, if that's what you're wondering."

"No. Understandable. Are you moving back into his cottage? You'd have it to yourself."

"That assumes he's not coming back."

Dennis looked uncomfortable. "I just thought you'd be more at home there. Can't be much fun, living out of one room at the Tavern."

"I've settled in very nicely."

"Yes. I'd noticed you and Larkin get on."

Persephone picked up the estimate, and headed for the wooden filing cabinets at the back of the shop. While her back was turned, Dennis said: "You will be careful, won't you?"

"Dennis – *don't*." The last thing Persephone wanted was a birds and bees talk from her ageing godfather.

"Don't be smutty. I don't mean like that. I mean be careful what you discuss with him."

She pretended to be leafing through the alphabetised tabs. "What do you mean?"

"Our sorcery. He wants it, Seph, and Conrad says he can't have it. Not yet. Don't let him wheedle anything out of you."

Persephone turned back round to face him. "Do you

think I'd reveal everything just because he drops a pretty compliment?"

She'd drive a much harder bargain than that.

"I mean nothing of the sort," Dennis said. "You're a sensible girl. But you're also human."

"Thanks for the advice," she said. "I'll bear it in mind."

"And it'd be a shame if Conrad ended up punishing you, as well as Larkin, for any infringement."

The phone rang, and Persephone gladly picked it up. It was only a recorded sales call, but she faked her side of a conversation in the likelihood Dennis would return to his workbench. He did so, taking the cherrywood box with him.

As soon as she heard his foot on the paternoster, she put the receiver down. The filing cabinet drawer was still open with the estimate resting on the top. Force of habit prompted her to check the figures before putting it away. The total was incorrect; it was a hundred pounds too low.

Sighing with exasperation, she followed Dennis into the paternoster, taking the estimate with her. At the top he was nowhere to be seen.

"Where's Dennis?" she asked Alastair, who was at his own workbench with a paintbrush in his mouth. He didn't answer, but merely nodded in the direction of the storeroom.

She found Dennis in the cramped annexe, looking for a space to put the cherrywood box. He slid it onto a central shelf.

"The estimate's wrong," Persephone told him. "You forgot to carry a one."

He accepted the piece of paper, narrowing his eyes.

"A senior moment." He took a pen from behind his ear and made an annotation on the page. "I can't charge him the full amount now. The hundred pounds can stay off the total as a goodwill gesture. I'll just clear it with Alastair."

Dennis walked past her. She backed into the shelves to avoid his touch, and her hand brushed the lid of the cherrywood box. It was smooth and warm beneath her skin.

She could learn a lot from a conservation project, she thought. Her resolution that morning not to push her luck melted. Her luck was already pushed. She had told Larkin about enchantments. She had sold her own dolls. What was the point of timidity now? Dennis had reminded her that she was already irredeemable, should Conrad think she'd betrayed him.

Her fingers gripped the box more tightly. Rapidly, before Dennis could notice, she slipped it into the pocket of her apron. He'd said there was a backlog. No one would miss the box till the New Year.

She stepped out of the storeroom, and Dennis locked the door behind her.

40

"Congratulations," said Madoc. "You got what you went for."

Larkin had met him for lunch in London, at a restaurant in Coal Drops Yard where every surface was stainless steel or granite. The crowding meant they were yet to receive their starters, but bread was provided, and they were in no hurry.

"How might I lay an enchantment or two?" Madoc asked. "Can I tempt you to tell me?"

"No. Sorry," Larkin said.

Madoc's mouth downturned in mock disappointment. "I would never have given you that glowing reference if I'd known you'd be so mean."

Larkin didn't rise to the bait. Madoc had never faulted his work. He felt safe in his status as star pupil.

"You're saving your enchantments for the highest bidder, I take it?" Madoc pressed.

"I haven't decided yet." Some day Larkin might well need

to sell his new knowledge. But for now, he was enjoying being one of the select few to possess it – for that made the knowledge feel more special. He had other means of making money to exhaust before burning that particular boat. His desire for enchantments had never been about their financial value. He had wanted the control they bestowed over his emotions. He could now feel anything he liked from Lucy's wallhanging of hexes – and stop feeling it, just as easily.

Madoc sipped from his glass of red wine. "When will you leave Oxford?"

"I may not."

"But it's so parochial." Madoc broke off a corner of bread, and swiped it roughly in the butter dish. "Which it hasn't any right to be, given the expense of the place. At least London has the decency to be a truly world class city when you cough up to live here."

"But if I stay – and Conrad officially sanctions my knowledge of the enchantments – I wouldn't be reliant on Maria's money any longer. I'd get proper recognition for my talents if I worked at Kendricks."

"Don't pretend you don't love Maria keeping you. How is she?"

"She's speaking to me again, finally. She's delighted at the opportunity to fool Conrad Kendrick, with that replica. I don't know how she can abide forgeries. It's worse than anonymity – all that talent, attributed to someone else."

"Surely *she'd* never let you stay at Kendricks. She'd tell them all about your nefarious past from spite."

This was too insightful for Larkin's comfort. "Staying wouldn't be without its difficulties," he admitted. "I've been trying to persuade Persephone to set up her own business under the Kendricks' name. Then I could be her partner, but she'd be bringing recognised pedigree. We'd be penniless to begin with – I'd be cutting off the bank of Maria fairly conclusively – so the whole endeavour's dependent on whether I can get another source of funds to come off."

Madoc ran a nail between two teeth, to loosen a morsel of bread. "My boy, you've buried the lede."

It took a moment for Larkin to grasp his meaning. "Persephone isn't the reason I'm rethinking my plans; not in the way you mean. The alliance would be advantageous."

"I find her pretty."

"Yes," Larkin said irritably. "She'd be at home in a Rossetti painting. That hair. But I don't enjoy her company. She makes me anxious."

"How so?"

"I'm always uncertain about what she thinks of me. And it's not exactly a pleasant feeling when I think about her. More like an inability to think about other things. No, that's not quite right; it's like I'm compelled to make her relevant to everything else. She gets into everything."

"Are you having me on? You really haven't felt this way before?"

"No."

"Don't tell Maria that. It sounds like limerence."

"I don't like it."

"It normally wears off quickly."

"There you are! I'm not thinking of marrying her, or any of that palaver; but we could be useful to each other."

"Some people find when limerence wears off, love is left."

Larkin was silent.

"*Do* you love her?"

"Sometimes I'm in love with Persephone," Larkin confessed. "And sometimes I'm not, but I want to be. And sometimes I'm relieved to feel nothing for her at all."

Madoc shook his head. "That poor girl."

When Larkin returned to the eyot, he went directly to Conrad's house, as the residents were gathering there to welcome home the Paid Mourner. She had been released by the CPS and reinstalled in the cage below Conrad's stairs.

The gathering immediately struck him as subdued. Talk barely rose above a hum, though a scan of the hall suggested everyone was in attendance – everyone except for Persephone. She had declined, in emphatic terms, on the grounds of bad taste, for it was hard to untangle a celebration of the doll's return from a celebration of Briar's imprisonment. Her reaction wasn't surprising. Of the other residents, Larkin hadn't expected their presence to be so strained. Surely they couldn't be feeling bad about Briar, too? They had all suspected him – it wasn't as though they believed he was innocent – so wasn't it too late to look regretful about it? Their reaction didn't make sense to Larkin.

Curiosity drove him to the cage. The forgery was astonishing; he wouldn't know her from real. As far as he could tell even the crazing was identical, which couldn't have been easy to achieve.

People were drinking wine, but Larkin couldn't see any for the taking, so he made for the kitchen. There he found

Hedwig, fringe falling in her eyes, as she slid a tray of vol-au-vents from the range.

"Need a hand?" he asked.

"Help me plate these, while they're still warm."

He joined her in arranging the tarts on a willow-patterned server.

"It's going with a swing up there," he commented.

"Oh don't, it's dreadful. What's the matter with everyone?"

"I've no idea. My best guess – they're angry about the police searches."

"Still? It's been weeks."

"Yes, several of which Conrad was absent for, and no apology has been forthcoming."

"He's not going to apologise." She still smiled, but she looked unusually fatigued. Larkin stared past her, to the open door, to check they were alone.

"You did a good thing, Hedwig." He leant in, close enough to whisper. "The doll's perfect."

"Is she?"

"Her appearance is astonishingly accurate. I can't speak for the enchantment – but it must pass muster. Conrad wouldn't be satisfied otherwise."

"He's happy as Larry."

"And he fully accepted the ransom demand was genuine? He didn't hesitate to cough up?" Larkin thought again of that two million pounds.

"Everything went perfectly."

If she'd pocketed most of the ransom she was now a rich woman. He knew for a fact the replica didn't cost that much. Nowhere near. Larkin thought once more of the money he'd need, if he severed ties with Maria. "So you're not at all worried about Conrad finding out?" he checked. "What if Briar changes his story?"

"That possibility has crossed my mind. Even if he were to panic, he's not in a good position to be believed. First he said he didn't remember what happened; then he said the fairies made him take her, which Conrad believes but won't change Briar's legal culpability. Why would anyone believe him if he changes stories again and says she's a fraud? I've never given him the butcher's details, so he can't even say who made the doll." She positioned the last vol-au-vent at the rim of the plate. "I'd better take these up; was there a reason you came down?"

"I was looking for a drink. But on reflection I might head home. The Eyot Tavern calls."

"Larkin," Hedwig stalled him. "You haven't told Persephone, have you? About the replica?"

"No. Why would I do that?"

"Because she's your girlfriend."

It seemed to be the day for this discussion. "I'm not sure I'd call her my girlfriend."

"Would she?"

"No. I don't think she would."

"What is she then?"

"I don't know. Not that. Who told you otherwise?"

"There's only a few hundred of us here, Larkin, did you think people wouldn't notice? You pay half her rent. You take her on trips to nice places. One trip, anyway."

"It was your mother who told you." Margot was acerbic

about Persephone. It wasn't romantic jealousy, Larkin didn't think. It was almost jealousy of Persephone having a father – even one as useless as Briar – when Margot's daughter didn't. But he acknowledged that his own resentments about paternity secrets might make him read motivations into Margot's behaviour that weren't there.

"Mama did tell me, as it happens. I say I would have known even if she'd been discreet. No one's ever looked at me the way you look at Persephone."

"Whatever's between us is expedient. You're clearly no stranger to that, if your stiff of a policeman is anything to go by."

He was rarely openly rude, and regretted it now, because it suggested Hedwig had touched a nerve. Her smile didn't falter; she simply replied: "Spoken like a true Sorcerer."

"What?"

"It's just something I've noticed. All the Sorcerers get affronted when women can make them feel things. Even Dennis isn't immune to it, and he's such a teddy bear in other respects."

This comment struck Larkin as so self-evidently absurd that he felt better disposed towards Hedwig; she hadn't any special insight, and her observations on his relationship with Persephone could be safely dismissed. With more mellowness, he said: "Forgive me; I spoke out of turn. It's been a long day and I really think I should go home."

As he headed towards the back door, Hedwig said: "It's still early, Larkin."

"Yes," he agreed. "Early enough to salvage. Say hello to Conrad for me!"

41

Persephone had lit the fire in her room at the Tavern, and positioned her desk in front of the flames to keep her feet warm. She peered through her magnifier at the cherrywood box. Painstakingly, with a narrow chisel and periodic swabs of alcohol, she scraped the dust and grit that had accumulated along the lid.

On the floor below, the back door opened and closed. Persephone paused to identify the footfall on the stairs. Larkin, not Mrs Mayhew. He knocked for her without first going to his room.

"You're back early," she said when he came in. The tips of his ears were rosy from the cold. Noticing this made her stomach flip, and she thought, *good grief, what kind of infatuation makes you crave to touch someone's ears.*

"The viewing was very odd." He removed his gloves. "No one seemed to be in the mood to celebrate."

Which was fitting, to Persephone's mind. Celebrating the Paid Mourner's return was difficult to distinguish from celebrating Briar's imprisonment, and she couldn't have drunk and danced with the others in good conscience. Her own feelings were less celebratory, and more relieved. Her father's removal from the eyot had led to a drop in her defences. It was as though she had been holding her breath all her life, without even realising it, and could now exhale. She would not hear him shouting in the road. He would not be there to start fights or to break her possessions. The tension had gone from her head and her limbs.

Larkin nodded at the wooden box. "What are you working on?"

"Stolen goods. Like father, like daughter." She laughed nervously. "Sorry. Gallows humour."

"Where did you steal it from?" Larkin asked, apparently unfazed by her bad behaviour. She explained while he picked the box up and examined it attentively.

When she had finished speaking, he said: "There's something funny about this pattern. You don't have a lipstick, by any chance? One with a reflective tube, gold or silver, either would do as long as it reflects well."

"In the top drawer, over there. Why?"

"Wait and see." As directed, he rummaged through the make-up drawer. A couple of lipsticks met with his satisfaction. He returned to her desk, standing behind her this time so they would both have a view of the box from the same angle.

"Now if I'm right—" He placed one of the lipsticks at the centre of the box, right in the middle of the circular pattern. "There! It's an optical trick, called *anamorphosis*."

The swirling patterns were reflected in the golden lipstick

case. But because the case was curved and cylindrical, the reflection formed a different, coherent image. In the shining surface Persephone saw a man and a woman, kissing. He wore a dinner suit, she a feathered veil and white flapper dress.

"How beautiful," Persephone said.

"*You're* beautiful," Larkin told her, and kissed the back of her neck. Her skin effervesced, from the base of her head to her elbows. He kissed her again, where the top of her spine met the zip of her dress.

"Can I undo this?" he asked.

"Yes." She heard the purr of it unfasten. He exposed her shoulder. The bra strap fell with her sleeve and he kissed the pink groove it had left behind.

"Just the same as before; yes?" he asked.

"No," she said, her eyes on the hearth.

"No?"

"Last time I said I didn't want to have sex. I changed my mind. I do. If you still want to." She stood, and added more kindling to the flames.

"You're sure?"

"Yes." The anxiety about her inexperience had relented. At first she was unsure why. But she found sex easier to contemplate now, and it seemed related to the lack of tension in her body; to the fact she was no longer on permanent alert. "I don't have anything, I'm not on the pill, or—"

"It's OK. There's some condoms in my pocket."

She turned to face him. His lips were parted; his eyes trained on her naked shoulder. She shrugged off the other sleeve and let the dress fall to the floor. They stared at each other for a few seconds more. He broke their stillness by swooping in to kiss her mouth, their teeth colliding. His one hand cupped her jaw, the other stroked her waist. The scent of the workroom clung to him – beeswax and varnish – and beneath that was his own odd fragrance, which was as sour and moreish as the tang of a truffle. The wool of his coat scratched her skin. He had so many clothes on. They were removed at speed, the condoms thrown on the bed. She felt, briefly, more shy in the face of his nakedness than her own; more shy about looking, than being looked at. *But I'm here to look*, she thought, warding off self-consciousness. As he moved to kiss her again, she said: "Hang on. I just want to see you."

He was slight, and his skin cream in the firelight. A tattoo of a black and white feather adorned his upper arm. The hair on his chest was fine and symmetrical. His penis was rigid against his stomach. She had thought about what it would look like and yearned to touch. Nerve or initiative failed her.

In a mirror of her thoughts, he said: "Christ I'm scared."

"You are?"

"Yes."

For him, it must be the enchantment raising the stakes.

"I'm not frightening," she said.

"You're terrifying."

She let him kiss her this time. They pressed close, his skin next to hers. They lay on the bed. His mouth traced its way to her nipple, and next to her navel. He moved his hand between her legs. He remembered how she liked to be touched. She peaked quickly, leaving her limbs heavy and her vision pricked with light. Newly languid, she sought to return the favour, watching his face for permission.

"Can you show me how?" she asked. "Like I showed you?"

He placed his hand over hers to guide its motion. She listened to his breath quicken until he said, softly, "Wait."

"Doesn't it feel good?"

"Yes – that's why you need to stop."

The condom wrapper crackled before it tore. She waited until he was ready to hold her. His leg shifted between hers, then he was on top of her. His shoulder tasted of salt. Their skin adhered with moisture. He pushed into her by increments and there was no pain as she'd feared; only the sensation of being stretched past a point she'd known she wanted. She struggled at first with finding a rhythm, and followed his cue. Perspiration made him gleam; his colour was high. At last he cried out and his full weight pressed upon her ribs and pelvis as he relaxed. It was not that they were finished. But they would take their time. They were less apprehensive, and more curious. By sunrise her mouth would be sore and she would throb inside and her legs would be tired, as tired as if she had spent the night walking the Thames Path. With the dawn, Larkin rose from her bed and picked up the cherrywood box. He stood, naked, re-examining it.

"I love you," she told him.

She didn't expect him to reply in kind. He wasn't in touching distance.

But he spoke very cleverly.

"I've never loved anyone as much as you," he said.

The narrow chisel was still on her desk. He inserted it close to the box hinge, and moved the chisel by fractions from side to side, making a shim of it. The lid shifted into better alignment with the box.

"Let's see if that did the trick." He lowered the chisel, and tried the catch. The box opened.

Persephone sat up abruptly. "What's inside?"

"No doll. There's an inscription; and some kind of block wrapped in muslin."

He brought the box to show her. Gold lettering spelt out:

31st October 1920

The Wedding Day of Hester Ashfield to Charles
Wharton

"But I met Hester," Persephone said wonderingly. "I told you – she was a woman Sorcerer. She taught me how to carve dolls once."

"I thought I was your first teacher," Larkin teased. He took out the muslin-wrapped cube. The fabric smelt strongly of alcohol. It unfolded to reveal an ancient slice of wedding cake.

Persephone said: "Julian Brown will be disappointed. But at least he won't be out of pocket."

"I'll take the box with me to work," Larkin said. "I can sneak it back into the stockroom without Dennis noticing. More easily than you can, anyway."

"I wonder why Hester and Charles kept the cake?"

"That's a thing people do after weddings," Larkin said. "Sometimes they keep it for an anniversary, sometimes for a christening. Maybe those dates rolled round and the box had already jammed. Poor old cake never fulfilled its destiny. Shall we eat it?"

She laughed. "No. It must be inedible."

"Fruitcake lasts forever. It's full of sugar and preserved fruit and booze and it's been in a sealed box. I think we can risk it."

"Larkin!"

"I'll go first." He broke off a corner, and removed a shard of royal icing. Experimentally, he tasted it. "It's rather good."

He held out a second piece to her.

"All right," Persephone said, abandoning, for once, her aversion to spirits. She ate from his hand. Rum, and a century-old glace cherry, slipped rich and sweet over her tongue.

42

Six of Persephone's dolls sold within the first week of her putting them on the shelves. This gave her immense satisfaction. But the secret couldn't be kept for long. Alastair was contacted directly, by one of their long-term customers, to congratulate him on a stunning new doll with an evocation of Languid Nostalgia. But Alastair knew they didn't have that hex. On the last day before Kendricks closed for the festive season, he went to the shop floor to investigate.

"Show me the ledger, Persephone," he said. This wasn't unusual. The Sorcerer who made the doll was named whenever a sale was entered. In a show of daring, Persephone had written her own name for her six sales.

She passed him the open book with a smirk.

"What in Jesus' name are you playing at?" he said, when he saw the entry.

"I told you I wanted to make dolls," she said. "You wouldn't let me. I took the initiative. I made some, and I laid enchantments upon them, and I sold them, because I am a good doll maker. I am a good Sorcerer, without your help."

"Where the hell did you get multiple enchantments?" He shook his head. "This doesn't add up, Persephone. These are one of the other Sorcerers' dolls, aren't they? Something they've made privately, and you've taken? Whose are they? Who are you thieving from?"

She laughed. "Get it into your head. I'm a Sorcerer."

"You're not making any sense," he roared.

A few of the interior designers had gathered in the doorway to find out why he was shouting.

"Go back to work," he spat at them, but they only retreated a few steps. To Persephone, he said: "Conrad will have you fired for this. Pretending someone else's work is yours. And he'll fire whoever helped you, too."

"What good would that do?" Persephone said. "I'm not a little girl with no hex any more. I have *dozens*. If he fires me, I'll sell my own magic dolls in competition."

"Women can't lay enchantments," he insisted. "They're not built for it."

Rieko stepped from among the crowd assembled at the door.

"Persephone," she called. "Come with me."

Alastair looked at his wife in confusion. "I'm dealing with this."

"No," she replied. "You have dealt with things too long your own way. Either you believe women are inferior, or you know they are not, but it suits you to pretend otherwise."

"How can you say such a thing?"

"I wouldn't have believed it when we met. But once we had children, I saw. The blithe way you made my work seem nothing."

"This isn't the place for this discussion," he shouted. "This is about Persephone's deception!"

Rieko beckoned to Persephone again. Persephone slid from the stool, and followed Rieko into the paternoster. They stepped out on the top floor.

"Take a seat," Rieko said. Persephone sat at Alastair's bench.

Dennis looked up in puzzlement. "Did Alastair send you?"

Both women ignored him. The paternoster whirred, and the other women began to disembark, in pairs, to gather round the desk.

Rieko looked at Persephone. "You need to teach us the hexes," she said. "All of us on the first floor."

"You want to be a Sorcerer?"

"I want to tell a story; and I can do so better if I conceive of the doll myself."

Persephone nodded. "Conrad will be furious."

"There are many of us. He can't fire us all, still less with what you know."

They would make Kendricks theirs. The women gathered in a circle before her, and Persephone began.

43

Kendricks Workshop shut its doors for the final time that year; but there was no rest for Hedwig, as she was tasked with co-ordinating Conrad's festivities. A waterfall of greetings cards – from residents, collectors, and trade contacts – was cascading through the letterbox each morning. Among them came a different letter, apparently addressed using a typewriter as the words were indented and uneven. As soon as Hedwig saw the envelope she recalled her ransom letter and shivered; as though the Thief on the Winged Horse had discovered her deception, and was writing to let her know.

The contents were brusque.

```
To Hedwig Mayhew


Regarding your recent fraudulent replace-
ment of the Paid Mourner, we demand payment
```

```
to the value of one million pounds as a
price for our silence.

You must obtain the funds by the end of
the week and await further instruction.
```

That was all. The paper creased where Hedwig clenched it. Only a few people could have written such a letter. Briar was one, but as she had told Larkin, she doubted he would be believed if he told the truth now – and that made him less likely to make such a threat. That left Larkin himself; Scarlotta Dahl; and the butcher. Perhaps all three of them, in cahoots.

She went to London, to confront the butcher directly. This time, she disregarded the people waiting in the shop to be served, and made straight for the countertop.

"I need to talk to you," she said. "Now."

He replied, wryly, "There is a queue, madam."

"I've received a bill that's far in excess of what I purchased," she said. "How do you account for it?"

"Wait there, madam."

She endured the slow progression of the queue, and when it had cleared, followed the butcher into the back room, where fridges hummed and the tiles created an echo.

"Well?" she said.

"I'm not aware of any bill. As far as I was aware your balance was settled."

She studied him, for any trace of guile. "Are you the only person here who bills the customers?"

"Yes." The shop bell rang, signalling the entrance of another customer. "Leave by the side exit. I don't want any further theatrics in the shop."

She walked to the side door. At the threshold to the alley, she said over her shoulder: "I won't be paying any more money. Just as long as you understand that."

"You may need to impart the same message to our mutual friend." The butcher checked the point of his knife with his thumb. "Tell him Scarlotta wouldn't be pleased to hear tongues wagging and threats of police action. And if she's unhappy, he'll get his pretty face cut."

Larkin. It was Larkin who sent the letter, the bastard.

44

Persephone had gone to visit Briar in prison – a so far delayed but necessary excursion – and she had declined Larkin's company for the trip. He was thus drinking alone in the Eyot Tavern when Hedwig crashed into the public bar, doors swinging behind her, and demanded to speak to Larkin upstairs. They proceeded to the lounge, where she accused him of blackmailing her by that morning's post.

"It can only be you or Scarlotta," she said. "And the butcher says it's you."

Larkin laughed. "He would, surely, whatever the truth of the matter."

"No, he's probably right. Why would he blackmail me when I could so easily tell the police he acted as intermediary? He would have something to lose."

Spreading his hands, Larkin said: "I can only give you my word. I didn't write you any letter. It might have escaped your notice, but money was never my motivation for being here."

Hesitation flickered over her face. But she wasn't won over. "You and money. It's never made sense. You dress like a scarecrow and you slept in the orchard but you dropped thousands of pounds on dolls. I know what you're earning as an apprentice, it doesn't begin to cover that kind of habit. So where does your money come from, Larkin? Do you survive on extortion – turning the thumb screws on people like me?"

"I have what you might call an allowance," he said. "From – a wealthier family member."

"So you deny any need to blackmail me. As does the butcher. They never learnt my name, Larkin, unless *you* told them."

"I did not."

"Which means you are the only one who could write me a letter. You're either lying about giving them my name, or lying about keeping this confidential, or lying about sending the letter."

"There is an alternative explanation. Didn't you fear Briar would spill the beans?"

"Yes – but – he's taken the full blame – he has never implicated me."

"He's a paragon, I'm sure. Doesn't mean he hasn't said something to a cell mate with few scruples. Maybe while on prison hooch."

She put her face in her hands.

"You could just give them what they ask for," Larkin said quietly. "Conrad has paid his ransom, hasn't he? I assume it's just sitting somewhere, seeing as it didn't actually go to the thief. Surely you could siphon off whatever this blackmailer has asked for? You won't be out of pocket, and Conrad will be none the wiser."

Hedwig looked at him sideways, her eyes glistening with tears. Then she set her mouth, and Larkin knew he had failed to assure her of his innocence, despite widening the scope of possible culprits.

"You've over-reached," she said calmly. "I want you off the eyot *now*. Do you understand me? I'm taking pity on you. Because you should know, Larkin – the butcher threatened to cut you. If I tell him you sent that letter, he's prepared to get your silence. And I *will* tell him, if you're still here when I return this evening."

She left the room.

It was disquieting to hear of the butcher's reaction. If he tried cutting Larkin, then Larkin would cut back. A quick jab in the femoral artery would do the trick. Still Larkin had little to gain from Hedwig telling tales. Better leave, and avoid the aggravation. This was not how Larkin had intended to exit: under threat, and lacking an expected source of income. He soothed himself that he had the enchantments.

There was the small matter of what to do about Persephone. Unaccountably, he found himself reluctant to go without bidding her farewell, and even felt some trepidation about their imminent separation. He attributed these feelings to withdrawal from her enchantment. He was perplexed, and annoyed, that laying the same enchantment on a doll was a weak substitute that utterly failed to sate him. For now, he would check into one of the city's hotels; it would be convenient for Persephone to visit before his departure.

He helped himself to a cigarette from Mrs Mayhew's stash in the kitchen, and then went to his room. What to take with him, when he preferred to travel light? The hexes were in his phone and backed up. He need only take a few clothes, for clothes were easily replaceable. Of his dolls he prioritised the zoetrope, which was too large to take intact, but had been designed for easy dismantling. The parts, and the twelve replica Mourners, fit snugly into his doctor's bag. The clasp strained but remained closed.

There was only one other doll he was certain he must take with him now. On the night of the masquerade, before the police arrived, he'd concealed her in the hollow of a quince tree. It hadn't been safe to bring her back to the Tavern until Briar was in prison. Since then she'd been hidden in the lining of Larkin's coat. He'd pushed her through a hole in the pocket. She still harboured a woodlouse or two.

Larkin put his coat on. He checked the time in the twilight: four o'clock.

Better to avoid the bar, he decided; Mrs Mayhew would have questions. He took the stairs silently, luggage in hand, exited by the back door, and kept going.

45

The prison visitors' room was dispiriting in a bland, grimy way: the chairs were fixed to the green vinyl floors, and a grid of heating pipes crossed the ceiling. The room was too warm for comfort. Persephone could feel the perspiration collecting on her skin as she awaited Briar's arrival.

She saw him enter before he saw her. His gauntness had worsened; his neck looked brittle as a twig, barely able to support his head.

His eyes widened with pleasure when he found her, and he straightened his back – she sensed with the intention to hug her – but he settled again when she, unthinkingly, shrank.

"Are you eating?" she asked.

"Not had much appetite."

They listened to one of the other men improbably discussing entomology with his grandson. Latin names peppered his speech: *Blattodea* and *Demaptera* and *Orthoptera*.

"I received an anonymous greetings card with various news and best wishes. It was from Hedwig, I'll bet. She's the main witness for the prosecution so she wouldn't want to sign it." He paused. "She's a good girl. Will you tell her something for me? Tell her she's got nothing to fear from me."

What reason was there for paternal feeling towards Hedwig? The day he mended the Eyot Tavern window, when Persephone was eight, had taken on additional possibilities over the years. Persephone had speculated whether the nature of Briar's relationship with Hedwig was all it appeared. But Briar had shown no particular affection towards Hedwig – until now. Maybe prison was forcing an adjustment of his priorities.

"All right," Persephone said. "I'll pass the message on."

"Her card said you're selling dolls."

"I am, no thanks to Alastair. He tried to put a stop to it."

"Pompous prick. Sell them somewhere else." His eyes fixed on the bug experts. "Where did you get the hexes?"

"A lucky find." Or Larkin's lucky find. But she didn't want to discuss anything emotional with her father, and Larkin was an emotional subject.

"Ah, that's good," he said absently. "There's something I should tell you, Persephone. About *your* hex."

Persephone's heart shivered, because she intuited this was going to be an emotional conversation after all.

"I did try out your hex," he said. "I was eager. Eager and worried."

"Worried?"

"Let me finish. I made a wax doll, a quick one. I wanted to try out the enchantment. The wax hardened and the sorcery was laid on. It was then I realised your hex was Adrenaline-fuelled Fear."

"Daddy, what have you done?" Persephone said, though she anticipated what he was going to say next.

"I threw the doll back in the melting pan, and I burnt the disc to ash."

"But why?"

"Because I knew how it would feel. I grew up with my disc reading Shame. It weighs on you, knowing that your greatest power is evoking shame in people. Fear is no better. Who wants to make people frightened? I don't regret burning it. But I regret not telling you why. I thought it was for the best. Much better that you never knew what it was at all. That was what I believed. It didn't occur to me that lacking an enchantment would make you sad in a different way. I'm sorry."

"Dad..." She shook her head. "We're a pair of fucking idiots. I found a line of wax, on the cooker, enchanted with Fear. I guessed you'd melted a doll. But I assumed it was the Paid Mourner. That explanation made sense at the time."

At this he began to sob. She couldn't acknowledge his tears, because to do so involved closeness, and she didn't want to be close to him. But she saw the damage that had been done to him by the eyot. For Shame was as valid a hex as any other, put to its proper use; it allowed atonement, when it was shared by a community, rather than shouldered by one, broken man. If everyone on the eyot had been permitted to share their hexes, then no one's life would be dominated by a single, engulfing feeling.

His tears made her prattle. "If I ever cleaned the sides

of the cooker this might have come up years ago. But wax needs scraping. Water and soap runs off it. No one scrapes the side of an oven."

"I need to put something right. Do you have a pen? A scrap of paper?"

Relieved to hear a clear instruction, Persephone checked her bag. There was a biro, and a receipt for a book she'd bought at the station. Briar took them both, and drew a hex upon the blank side.

"Here. From memory," he said. "Your hex."

She examined the looping symbol and then folded the receipt into her purse. The sadness her father raised – the sadness of making people feel fear – made a kind of sense. But fear was helpful in some circumstances. It could propel you from a dangerous situation before further harm.

"Every enchantment has a purpose," she said. "I'll use this for something special."

His expression was sceptical. A final question occurred to her. "If the enchantment on the Paid Mourner wasn't Adrenaline-fuelled Fear – what was it?"

He gave a nervous laugh. "Conrad will worry about the doll losing her mystique if I let on, you know."

"I don't care what Conrad thinks."

"Good." He smiled. "The Paid Mourner's hex is written on her scalp, beneath her hair. It means Faith that All will be Well. But you didn't hear that from me."

The name summoned déjà vu. "Is there any chance you've told me before?"

"No," her father said, but he was melancholy, and she thought how much of his life was lost to blackouts.

"My mistake then."

Persephone left shortly after. She was halfway to the train station when she turned her phone back on. The notifications blinked. Gratefully she relinquished thoughts of the Paid Mourner, and her father's crime, and gave herself over to a message from Larkin. *Booked us a night at the Randolph. As much as I enjoy the frisson of Mrs Mayhew at the door, I want you to myself, for once. Have checked in – you'll come straight here, won't you? I need you.* Persephone sang the last three words in her thoughts for the rest of the journey. He wasn't in touching distance, and he needed her anyway. *I need you. I need you. I need you.*

46

"Dearest," Hedwig said. "You need advice."

She offered Conrad council in his drawing room. He'd been dictating greetings cards in celebration of Sigillaria, or The Festival of Little Figures, which the eyot observed on the twenty-third of December. Conrad would provide his tenants with a gingerbread doll, according to their custom, and a personal note. The beneficiary could add their personal hex, then snap the doll in two to leave one half on the step for the Thief. This ritual reflected their superstition that the Thief was most avaricious during the solstice and the equinox. A token gift was thought to stall him from taking more important things.

Hedwig kept a list of names so Conrad could personalise his message with the gingerbread. They'd reached *Persephone Kendrick*, which had a red line through it.

"You need advice," repeated Hedwig.

"What for?"

"Handling Sephone's defiance."

"I assume you mean her sale of unapproved dolls," said Conrad tartly. "I intend to fire her."

And yet so far he hadn't. He'd been slow to act on Alastair's reports of mutiny, now made two nights ago. The morning's incidents left Hedwig bullish; she'd resolved the blackmail, and her mind was free once more to coax Conrad into the directions she desired.

"Persephone's put you in an intractable position," Hedwig said. "It's no surprise you've given such thought to the issue. The solution isn't obvious."

"It isn't. Briar's family are a source of endless strife. I must admit her actions here have vanquished my resources. She must go – yet I can't make an example of her – if she's shunned, or I evict her, she may set up business in direct opposition to us!"

"She's shared her sorcery already, with the interior designers. And refuses to reveal where she found the hexes."

"I cannot understand it. How did she get them? Has Alastair's stewardship of our secrets been so slipshod? No one but the Sorcerers should be capable of making and enchanting multiple dolls. When that control is lost we have anarchy."

"If harmony can be restored, you, Conrad, are the only man to do it," Hedwig said. "You know you are."

"If I don't have the power, then nobody does," he agreed.

"The main thing we must remember is that Sephy's determined to stay here. She'd only leave Kendricks if her hand were forced. I agree with you that she deserves dismissal... but it may not be in Kendricks' long-term

interest if, as you say, she then sets herself up in competition."
Nor did Hedwig wish to antagonise Briar by making
Persephone's life harder. "Swallow your gall, Conrad. Make
her sorcery position permanent, and you will be setting an
example that loyalty, if not obedience, will be rewarded."

"What is loyalty worth without obedience?" Conrad
scoffed.

"Better a disobedient employee than a disobedient rival."
Hedwig allowed Conrad to think on that. Her point was
made. "There is an attendant, more worrying matter."

Conrad winced, but gestured that she should continue.

"Alastair's stewardship, you say, has failed us. Persephone
may be the least of our problems. What if an outsider has
come by the hexes, too?"

Conrad's eyes widened in alarm. "Do you have reason to
believe so?"

"Only logic – that a breach in security can admit two
people, or two hundred, as easily as one. If we wait until
we're certain of it, there'll be no time to act."

"But we can't silence people who are unknown to us."

"We can do better than silencing. We can profit. Go to
the biggest doll-making firms. Offer them your secrets in
exchange for a stake in each business. Act now, and you
may pre-empt any rogue hex thieves."

"But the Kendrick name—"

"… will adapt, and endure," Hedwig assured him.

"I must take the time to think it over."

"By all means. But the longer you take, the more
opportunity there is for rogues to talk first." She looked

down at the list of the gift recipients, to resume their notes. "Patrick and Unice Low are next. What would you like to say to them?"

47

The Randolph stood on Beaumont Street; it was a tall, yellow-bricked, neo-gothic building with chapel windows and a great entrance flanked by doormen. Persephone had seen it from the outside many times, because it was opposite the Ashmolean Museum, which she visited regularly for the art collections. But she had never been inside the hotel, nor indeed stayed overnight in any hotel off the eyot, and this lent her arrival a sense of occasion.

The interior struck her as baronial: the foyer was dominated by a flight of marble steps with a dark red runner. Larkin had given her the name of the bar in which to meet him, because there were several other bars available to mislead her. She asked for directions at the oak reception desk. The receptionist checked that Persephone was a paying guest, but did not otherwise enquire about her business there, and Persephone was glad of the temporary anonymity that Larkin had bought them. She was happy as she explored the corridors – happier, she supposed, than any daughter who had just visited her father in prison *ought* to be – but wasn't she owed some happiness? She wouldn't chase it away out of duty.

She stopped in the doorway of the wood-panelled bar, scanning the room for Larkin. Hardly anyone was there – one man reading a newspaper; another contemplating a brandy – and she could hear the crackle of the fire in the grate. A grandfather clock struck eight. Then she saw him; he was seated in a club chair, with his back to her, and she knew him by his curls, the shape of his head, the way he rested his temple on his fist. She delayed disturbing him, because it was delicious watching him in the moment before he knew she was there. Perhaps because it felt like watching *over* him, in a protective fashion.

The carpet muffled her footsteps. His first awareness of her presence was when she touched his shoulder. He pulled her into his lap and kissed her with surprising intensity – as though he hadn't seen her for much longer than a few hours – or as though he expected them to soon be parted.

"Hello," she whispered.

"It's an astonishing thing. Once I start holding you I don't want to let you go. You're more addictive than crack."

"Can we go to bed? Now?"

"You haven't even bought me dinner."

"Would you rather go to the restaurant?" she asked primly.

He laughed. "No, Persephone, I wouldn't. Our room's on the top floor."

They made their way to the lift. No one else was waiting, and the lift was empty when it arrived. Persephone admired their reflection, the two of them side by side, as the doors slid closed.

"What are you thinking about?" he asked.

"The same thing I was thinking about the whole train journey," she told his mirror image. "I want you to fuck me. Hard. I've not had any knickers on since Didcot Parkway."

In fact she had removed them in the ladies' loos at Oxford station, planning the line which she thought would amuse him. It did; he laughed again, as he touched her hip to turn her towards him. She closed her eyes – felt his breath on her cheek – and the lift chimed to admit a passenger, forestalling the kiss. Larkin leant against the lift wall. He entwined his fingers with hers. Neither they, nor the third party – a man with a drooping moustache and a long black umbrella – uttered a word. Persephone felt the pulse beat in Larkin's thumb while she watched the remaining floor numbers light up. The lift lurched to a stop when they hit Four. As soon as the hallway revealed itself, Larkin led Persephone out by the hand. She half ran to match his pace. They stopped at the corridor's end.

"We're in here." He produced a card and swiped it through an imposing lock. This, and the door's satisfying heft as it swung shut behind them, pleased her. Inside they were cut off, from men with umbrellas and the rest of the world besides, from the inquisitions of Mrs Mayhew and her patrons, from the tawdriness of doll thieves and prison visiting rooms. Larkin drew her close to him in the darkness. She felt him, hard, against her stomach. He pushed her skirts up to her waist, and the denim of his jeans brushed rough against her skin. She kissed the corner of his mouth – his cheekbone – his throat. His hand was between her legs. Nearly, very nearly inside her, then he said, "I want to taste you."

"No," she said instinctively. "What if I taste bad? What if I smell – wrong?"

"I know how you smell, I can smell you now. You smell of *you*. That's why I want you."

She knew why he wanted her. His perception was filtered through the enchantment. And yet she remembered his statement of need before she caught the train, when they were divided by fifty miles. It swayed her response. "All right," she said. "Yes."

She lay on the white linen of the sleigh bed – like a butterfly, in a shadow box, Persephone thought hazily – and he kissed her from knee to inguen. She tensed when his mouth reached his destination, then she warmed to the movement of his tongue. It was only more kissing, she thought; more of the writing on her body, in shapes from a language they might both be influenced by. She sighed, tilting her pelvis closer to him, and he persisted. Momentum built and built and inexplicably he stopped.

"Keep going," she said. "Please."

"I want you to ache for me." He lay down at her side, and teased loose the buttons of her dress. His hand pushed the cup of her bra from her breast.

"I do ache for you," she said, because her thighs were slick with want and inside she was hollow. She undid his belt.

"The condoms," he said. "They're in my coat."

"Leave them," she said. "You can't feel me with them."

"You're sure?"

"Unless you want them."

"No."

Haste took priority over discarding further clothes. She straddled him. His hand ran up the side of her neck. Their breath was shallow. He slid into her, touching her as deeply as it was possible to be touched, and she came because this was all she had thought of for hours, and now it was real. The glow spread through her. Her climax kindled his almost immediately.

"I do love you," he said, his head dropping back onto the quilt. "I love the shape of your cunt. I love the spaces between your toes. I love the birthmark on your hand. I love the way your brow knits when you paint. I love how you scowl in your sleep. I love everything about you."

She'd think of those words a lot, later.

They made love again; and at ten, showered together, by which point it occurred to Larkin that the restaurant would be closed.

"But room service is probably still available," he said. "What would you like to eat?"

"I'm going to have a big, beautiful steak," Persephone said, drying her ears with a towel warm from the rail. Her hair was tangled, which was a minor annoyance. She didn't think she had a comb in her handbag.

Larkin put on one of the terry dressing gowns and passed her the other. She followed him into the bedroom, where he sat on the bed, his back to her, to look at the menu.

"They do steak," he confirmed. "I think I'll get one, too."

His luggage was tucked beneath the desk. He'd probably packed a comb she could use. She was about to ask, but he'd picked up the receiver and was placing their order.

She pulled the doctor's bag across the carpet. The clasp was tough to release because the bag was bulging – more than you would expect, Persephone thought, for a single night away. The sides sprang apart revealing the tightly packed Mourners; the ones she had seen in his zoetrope. Persephone stared, trying to make sense of why Larkin would have brought his work and little else. She touched one. *Faith that All will be Well.* The Faith faded as she let go. She had forgotten. It was the same enchantment her father said was on the real Paid Mourner.

Larkin was finishing his call. She shoved the bag back under the desk, and joined him on the bed.

"Should be twenty minutes," he said.

"I'm not hungry any more," she said.

He tipped her face up towards him with a finger under her chin, trying to read her expression.

"I'm sorry," he said eventually. "I should have realised you'd be out of sorts, after visiting Briar. And I didn't even ask you how it went. I'm a boor. You are thinking about him, aren't you?"

"After a fashion," she said.

Larkin went to the minibar, selected one of the tiny bottles – vodka, Persephone guessed from the clear contents, though the label was too far away to read. He poured it into a tumbler.

"Did Briar say how he was going to plead?" he asked, casually.

"No. It doesn't matter how he pleads. He had the motive and the means. They found the doll on his property."

"His plea will make a difference to his sentence. For breaking and entering, burglary with a weapon, and taking an item of that value – he's looking at thirteen years minimum, more if he seems unrepentant."

He passed her the drink. She shook her head.

"You should persuade him to plead guilty," Larkin added.

She struggled to imagine what he saw as he looked at her. Could he tell how broken she was? Her face had never matched her feelings.

She took his hand between hers, and his face softened. His stance gave away none of his guilt. He looked relaxed.

She took a deep breath. "Did you steal the Paid Mourner?"

At this he resisted her touch; and she thought – *he loves me, and he wishes to spare me the truth. He wants to be able to lie, and it is harder in my clasp.*

"How would I steal her?" Larkin asked, evading her direct question with one of his own. "Your father knew the mechanism for entering the cage. I did not."

"But you found a way," Persephone said. "I know every doll that passes through the till. That month you made an iron doll, and Dennis laid an enchantment upon it of Determined Perseverance. I remember, Larkin. I was paying attention to everything you made."

"So what?" His cheeks were enflamed.

"You held it, didn't you, when you approached the cage? The determination would be very strong, with iron.

341

Enough to counteract the paranoia of the cage latch. You took the doll; you found the hex etched under her hair, into her scalp; and when I told you how to lay enchantments, you placed that same hex onto the dolls in your zoetrope. How else could you know the hex for Faith? It isn't in the wallhanging."

"You're not making sense. I'd never steal the doll just to plant her in your father's possession. I'd want to keep her."

"Maybe you only wanted the enchantment, not her. You found out how she made you feel. Then you discarded her."

He shook his head. "Only a monster would let someone else go to prison for such a crime."

His hand finally slipped from hers.

"I haven't done what you've accused me of. But if we're talking about the matter, prison is the right place for your father. He *hit* you. He deserves to be locked up."

The self-righteousness in his tone took her breath away. His own capture was less likely if Briar took the fall, but he had used her being hit as justification for covering his tracks.

"Larkin, that's the worst thing you've said yet."

"*If* I let your father go to prison – *if* – it would be for you."

She shook her head, unable to tell if he believed what he was saying.

"You don't love me, Larkin, not really. You love me when you touch me."

"I *wanted* to love you," he cried out. "I kept coming *back*, didn't I?"

She hid her face so he wouldn't see her tears.

"You don't understand," he said, more softly. "Love hardly ever happens. Most people are only presenting a reasonable facsimile of the thing, and they know it's not real, it's just an act we're all agreed on. I did more than that with you. Isn't that consolation?" He pulled her hand from her face, clasping it with deliberation. "We can still do what I suggested. Run away together; make our own dolls, and sell them. I wanted us to have money before we did that, I even made plans, but they fell through. Do you see? I want you near me all the time."

"No. It's no *good*. I can only live with you if Dad stays in jail. I can't be happy knowing that."

Larkin looked away from her, at his luggage beneath the desk.

"Go to the police if you must." His voice was tired. "But allow me a head start; a week, that's all I ask."

"That's all? It's a long time for my father."

"Please, Persephone. If I've meant anything to you at all."

Her eyes brimmed. "I'll give you three days. On one condition. Leave me the replica Mourners."

"Why?"

"I need them as proof. You're in no position to argue."

"You're really going to do it then," he muttered.

She thought how happy she had been an hour ago – no, fifteen, ten minutes ago, though it felt like years – and how he hadn't simply made her unhappy now; he had damaged her, so she would never trust happiness again. She raised his hand to her mouth, in a kiss.

"What are you doing?" he asked.

"Dad gave me my hex, at last," she said. "It's Fear."

"You want people to be frightened of me?" The hurt behind his words pained her; his hand was still in hers, and he loved her.

"I want to give people a fair warning."

"That's not a warning. It's a feature."

"What?"

"You've loved Briar for years. You never stopped because you were frightened of him. The two things will always be tied together for you." He stood up. "You can have the room tonight. I need to get as far away as possible."

She watched him, in silence, as he donned his trousers, his shirt, his shoes. He raked his still wet hair.

"I'm glad you're leaving," she said.

He picked up his coat, which still had no buttons.

"Then it's a happy ending for both of us," he replied.

He walked out of their hotel room, and she was left alone.

48

Hedwig and Conrad were by the fire, playing back-gammon with the cheeseboard in reach. Backgammon is a game of chance, which posed some challenges for Hedwig; she had greater control over games of skill, which she preferred because she could let Conrad win.

Just as she poured his second glass of port, they heard a visitor at their front door.

"Botheration," Conrad grumbled. "Do send them away, Hedwig, do. Who knocks on doors at half eleven? Am I to have no moment's rest, no peace?"

"They'll be gone in two shakes of a lamb's tail."

She left him spreading Camembert across a cracker. Interruptions plagued this week before Sigillaria, as Conrad suffered visits from their large extended family – although this year had seen less interest from the residents in festivities at Conrad's house.

When Hedwig opened the door, she saw Persephone there, ashen-faced, her hair heavy with rain.

"Oh!" Hedwig greeted. "Come inside – I can't let you catch pneumonia!"

Persephone obeyed. The water ran from her fingertips and splashed upon the tiles. "I need to speak to Conrad."

"Hell's bells, he's sozzled, Sephy – I expect he fell asleep as soon as I stepped away. D'you want to join me in the kitchen, and get warm while we talk? No?"

"I don't need to get warm. I'll only get wet again as soon as I go outside. If I have to tell you instead of Conrad, here is fine. The first thing is Larkin has gone. We argued, and he won't be coming back to the eyot."

"Very well; I'll pass that on to Conrad." So Larkin heeded Hedwig's warning. They could draw a line beneath him.

"There's a second thing. I need to leave the Tavern," Persephone continued. "I was only there for Larkin, and your mother hates me."

"Oh, I don't know if that's true!"

"It is. Can I live in the vacant terrace on the lane? I'll pay the rent. Dad's house is empty too and I could go back there, but it makes me sad."

"That sounds so sensible, Sephy. Conrad will agree, you see if he doesn't!" Guilt made Hedwig generous. Briar passed his hours in jail, instead of in his cottage, while she ate and drank her fill by an open fire. His daughter was before Hedwig; wouldn't it be recompense to offer Sephy kindness? Wouldn't that salve Hedwig's restless conscience? "Dearest, we meant to inform you after New Year, but I say you need some good news sooner. Conrad's made his wishes clear. He's offering you promotion. You're allowed to keep using sorcery, and to sell your work through the shop."

Persephone's brow knitted. "He'll allow what I'm doing anyway."

"I wouldn't put it quite like that."

"Ignore me. I know I have you to thank. He wouldn't reach that decision on his own. Don't argue, Hedwig, he *wouldn't*. I'm cynical, because we expect so little of Conrad, and when he gives us less, he expects so much praise. I don't know how you stand it."

They said goodbye. Hedwig made her way to the drawing room, where Conrad was awake, against her expectation. Sephy's words had left her flat and fractious. She'd never felt less inclined to let Conrad win at backgammon.

Conrad smiled at her, genially.

"I've given thorough thought to my estate documents," he said. "The last occasion I amended them was – let me see – November. A great deal has changed since then. It may be time to reinstate you in my will."

Hedwig hadn't known she was ever in his will, much less that she had come out of it. Disinheritance must be the penalty for allowing the thief to escape, and now she was to be restored because the doll had been returned.

"Whatever you think best, Conrad." She took a crumb of Cheddar from her plate, and chewed it absently.

"You'll be my heir apparent," he said. "Future mistress of this house, and of the workshop."

Until the next time she displeased him.

"I thought you were grooming Alastair to take over?" she asked lightly. "He may be surprised."

"Alastair won't go without," Conrad said dismissively. "Anyone would think you were trying to talk me out of remembering you favourably. Don't you want to run the eyot? Don't you long to bear my crown?"

"Your generosity leaves me lost for words, Conrad," Hedwig responded. "And it's bittersweet. Am I to be happy about your eventual death?"

He smiled indulgently at her. "You flatter me," he said, and she knew he approved of her answer.

"Shall I telephone your solicitor tomorrow, to arrange an appointment?" she asked.

"There's no great rush," he said, vaguely. "I can telephone."

He rarely made his own calls. Hedwig sipped her port in the silence. She wondered if he would make the change to his will at all; whether he was telling the truth about her being in his will before; whether he had any kind of will in place. Once she had believed Conrad was too self-absorbed to succeed at manipulation. Now she had to acknowledge that unverified promises of wills and bequeathments were a good way to keep people in line.

"I expect you have years, Conrad," she said. "You'll outlive us all."

She kept her tone level. There was no hint of resentment. This time, his smile wavered.

49

Persephone had promised Larkin three days. She rose early on the first morning, having had no sleep, with a foreboding which she partly attributed to unprotected sex. As soon as the lines were open she made an appointment at a testing clinic for the New Year. She knew she should get emergency contraception immediately, and yet she did not take that step. Rather than examine her reasons, she focused on the practicalities of moving out.

She found Mrs Mayhew in the kitchen, cutting a string of sausages.

"You've burnt the candle at both ends, haven't you, dear?" said Mrs Mayhew. "You can borrow my Touche Éclat for those dark rings. Be a pet and check if Larkin wants breakfast?"

"Larkin's gone," Persephone said. "He's not coming back."

Mrs Mayhew raised an eyebrow. "Met someone else, has he, love?"

"No. I don't want to talk about it."

"I'm afraid we have to. Larkin didn't want me to say anything but I can't see any other option now. You've not been paying full price on your room, love. He thought it would be too expensive for you and was giving me the shortfall."

Persephone's head was splitting. It meant nothing, that he had paid for her and didn't want her to know; it didn't mean he cared for her. It meant he could get the principles of enchantment more easily if she was close by.

"If he's gone, you'll have to start paying full price." Mrs Mayhew ran the tap to wash her hands. "You must have guessed he was covering for you? A bright girl like you can't have believed the rates were *that* low."

"I won't pay you anything extra," Persephone said. "I'm moving into an empty terrace on the lane."

Mrs Mayhew, confronted with her personal dislike of Persephone versus the loss of her rent, said: "If you feel you must. I'll keep the door open if you change your mind. Larkin might come back, you know, love; when the novelty of the other one's worn off."

"There isn't another one. I'm not your love. Sorry, I have to pack."

Packing was a short-lived job. It took less than twenty minutes to stow away her dolls and a couple of dresses. She thought of Larkin's doctor's bag, which had also been packed with dolls, and she supposed they had similar priorities to each other.

She heard Mrs Mayhew on the stairs, heading to the bar in readiness for opening. Reassured that they wouldn't encounter each other for further awkward conversation, Persephone slipped to Larkin's room, lest she had left any belongings there.

His door was ajar. The familiar scents of doll-making greeted her – the wax and varnish she associated with him – even though much of their work had been cleared from the table. His bed was unmade and some shirts still hung in the wardrobe. The postcard of Lucy Kendrick was pinned to the wall, and Persephone tugged it free, to put in her pocket. She imagined framing it when she had redecorated the terrace.

Her dolls with button masks were stacked in a metal crate. Persephone sat on the floor to look at them again. She remembered Larkin's first reaction to them. *You must be a natural*, he'd said, and the words still made her ache. She knew his love was fleeting, and poorly won. She knew he had imprisoned her father. But she still wanted her dolls to please him, because he understood, better than Conrad or Alastair, what made a doll beautiful. When she sketched, when she carved, when she moulded, he was now her imagined audience, every time. It scared her to think she must carry on without the reward of his praise.

She must be self-reliant, and find the inspiration within herself. She pushed the dolls aside in the crate. Underneath lay scraps of fabric; corners of wood. A roll of stiff copper wire, roughly the size and shape of a tennis ball, had acquired a green tinge. As an experiment, Persephone unravelled the wire. With a pair of pliers she twined different sections together, creating variable degrees of thickness and thorn-like protusions. She wound wire round her finger where she wanted curves. Between her palms she shaped the mass of wire into a belly, thighs, a head. The wire might form a woman, twelve inches high, jagged and ridged – a mass of crisscrossing lines that you could see straight through, that could be posed stiffly until her back curved and her arms thrust out from her like horns. You could lick her with the sign for Self-Righteous Outrage. And then Persephone stopped. The woman in her head faded and disappeared. Persephone's hands were messy with wire that she couldn't make sense of. The points jabbed her skin. It was as she'd feared. The doll was going wrong, because Persephone had lost her champion. Larkin wouldn't see this doll. He would never again correct Persephone's mistakes, and she would never make him feel another thing, not anger or love or anything else.

She crushed the wire back into the crate, desperate to be done with the Eyot Tavern. The postcard fell from her pocket as she stood up. Persephone took another look at the portrait; she wished she'd known Lucy Kendrick. Lucy must have worked without validation, because she was the very first, with no one before her to look up to. She had worked things out on her own. If she could answer questions—

Persephone paused mid-thought. Pictures, she recalled, had strange capabilities at the Eyot Tavern; provided you were influenced by the right enchantment. She was uncertain of her ability to control such an experiment. But it was perhaps worth trying.

She checked the corridor and the kitchen, to verify Mrs

Mayhew hadn't come back upstairs without Persephone noticing. The coast appeared to be clear. Persephone removed her boots, and walked soundlessly to Mrs Mayhew's bedroom. It looked identical to Persephone's memory of it: the same nicotine yellow walls, the same painting of the Thief on the Winged Horse. She hastily covered the painting with a satin nightie, which was the first thing that came to hand, because she didn't want the Thief making a personal appearance.

Scooting under the bed, Persephone was relieved to see the cheap peg doll was once again pinned between the slats and the mattress. She took the postcard out of her pocket, stared at it, and reached for the doll that lay above her head.

As soon as she touched Visionary Delirium, the mandalas printed on the mattress fabric started to spin. They glowed turquoise and coral and their motion so entranced her that Persephone forgot her reason for being there until she felt someone's shoulder against her own.

Persephone turned her head. There she was; Lucy Kendrick, matronly and reassuring, with fawn curls pinned above her head. Her dress was gathered at the bust, in cotton which varied from taupe to umber to ecru – the same spectrum of colours permitted by the sepia portrait, Persephone noted.

Lucy sneezed. "Crivens! It *is* dusty under here. Are we hiding?"

"Yes," whispered Persephone.

Lucy dropped her voice accordingly. "From the Thief?"

"No, I took care of him. We have to hide from my landlady. I wanted to ask you something – several somethings."

"I am all ears."

"The wallhanging Larkin found in his room. Was it yours?"

"Jemima made it, during her confinement. She lived in this building after her marriage. The wallhanging was meant for her child – so he might learn the language we were born knowing. But the child died – and she died – and I couldn't bear to see her handiwork, but nor could I bring myself to destroy it. I hid it beneath the floor."

And it had been unseen, for two centuries.

"Jemima didn't run away with a lover?" Persephone watched the bright mandalas fall from the bed, and dissolve on Lucy's skin. Somewhere, beneath the thick haze of the dream they were in, Persephone's heart was cracking. "Jemima didn't take her child to France?"

"The child died, and she died. She never in her life left Oxford."

So Larkin had lied about being a Ramsay. He'd lied while bathing her cut brow; while sharing a slice of wedding cake; while offering her every hex he owned when she had none. With his arrival everything on the eyot had come unstuck, good and bad. Persephone thought again of the difficulty of creating without him.

"Who do you make your dolls for?" she asked Lucy.

"Why, for me!"

"I thought you'd say that. You don't need anyone's help."

"Ah. There's a different matter; help is a different matter. I have help from Rebecca – Jemima – Sally! We help each other."

"The Sorcerers made out it was bad to have help."

"You're not an island. You'll make nothing without help. Nobody does. Have you sisters?"

Persephone thought of Hedwig. She was not sure whether Hedwig had also guessed at the truth of their kinship, or whether she was oblivious to it. Nor was she confident they had anything but Briar in common. Hedwig had never seemed interested in the creative side of their business. Persephone said: "No. I don't have any sisters."

"Brothers?" Lucy prompted.

"No."

"Then you must seek out sisters and brothers, whether or not they're your blood."

"How?"

"Help from above is unreliable. Look for who else is in need, for who else has been denied, and see what you have in common."

Larkin had helped her, after her father and the Sorcerers would not. He had been in need, too. And though his ruthlessness in framing Briar horrified her, hadn't she benefitted? Without Briar's absence she would never have known what it was to feel free of him. He would never have given her the hex that was her due.

But she had sent Larkin away, and now he would never help her again.

"What if you find your champion, and then they let you down?" she asked.

"That's unavoidable; Jemima abandoned me in death. It's why you need many brothers and sisters. An island of two is not much stronger than an island of one."

Persephone was yanked from behind by the collar. Her

first thought was the Thief had caught her; but she dropped the Visionary Delirium doll, and the world swam back into its usual dim palette of colours, and it was the all-too-real hand of Mrs Mayhew at her neck.

"What do you think you're doing?" Mrs Mayhew roared. She towed Persephone out across the carpet.

"I'm sorry," Persephone said, wincing from a friction burn on her elbow. She could acknowledge she'd crossed a line by crawling under Mrs Mayhew's bed. But it was not as though they had a friendship to ruin.

"Get out of this pub now. Talk about liberties!"

"That's rich," Persephone said, rapidly feeling less penitent. "You had a fucking good rummage in my room from time to time."

"Because you're under *my* roof. There's no comparison. You really were dragged up, weren't you? *Leave.*"

"I'm going," Persephone muttered. She picked up her suitcase and boots in the hall on her way.

50

The second day came, and Persephone continued to wait. She had no furniture in the terrace, other than a kitchen table with twin stools, and upstairs, a single bed; for now, that was sufficient. Several times throughout the day she picked up a half-finished doll with the intention of working on it, but each time she put it down again as quickly. She absently tugged on a ragged strip of floral wallpaper in the tiny hallway, and progressed to stripping every room of the ground floor; the simplicity of aiming to finish each wall occupied her hands without requiring any creative thought.

She stopped when the light faded, and she heard music in the lane. The eyot choir sang outside in the evenings before Sigillaria. Persephone opened the front door to hear them. The words were clear now, and were words every Kendrick knew.

> Come sit by the fire!
> Have half my hearth
> And half my table.

Instead of a heart
There's a sigil at my breast
To fill you full of joy.

Cousin Alastair carried a tray of mulled wine to refresh the small audience who had come out to hear. He caught Persephone's eye, and shortly afterwards made his way to her step.

"I hear congratulations are in order," he said.

"They are?"

"You're to be a Sorcerer."

"I'm going to get the title, yes. I've been practising sorcery for some time though."

"I'm aware."

Persephone saw, in his offhandedness, that she would never receive acknowledgement from Alastair of her merit. To get this far had been an act of will for her, and she would have to keep being strong-willed to maintain her place at Kendricks. She was under no delusion that Conrad appreciated her any more than Alastair did; she suspected that her promotion was an attempt to neutralise her role in workshop dissent. Years of combat stretched before her, and the prospect exhausted her.

"You must have a way with Conrad," said Alastair, "if you can smooth talk him into being promoted rather than fired."

"I didn't talk him into anything."

"Have you ever thought of using those powers of persuasion for something less selfish?"

"Alastair, what are you on about?"

"Briar. I'm talking about Briar. The case hangs on Conrad's identification of the doll."

Persephone crossed her arms. "You don't think my father took her?"

"Obviously he did. Don't be dense, Sephy. But he's an old man. Should he spend the last years of his life in jail, for taking something he has a claim to? His claim may be stronger than Conrad's. This should all have been handled without the police. And it still could be – if Conrad said he'd been overconfident with the identification. Why haven't you pointed this out to him?"

"Why haven't *you*?"

"I'm no good at manipulation." Alastair was a bitter man, for one so successful in his field.

Persephone took one of the mugs of wine – to warm her hands; not to drink. "Do you know the story of Pinocchio? There's a cricket on his shoulder, who's supposed to tell him right from wrong when he can't be bothered to work it out himself. You want me to be Conrad's cricket."

"And you're too proud for that, are you?"

"No, not if I thought it would work. You're mistaking me for someone who has any power over Conrad. The cricket gets squashed."

Sara, Alastair's little girl, was calling for him now the choir were between songs. Alastair turned his back on Persephone, with a parting shot: "It might be convenient for you, your dad not living on the eyot any more. That doesn't make it right."

"Fuck off," Persephone muttered. He was already out of earshot. She sat on the doorstep, the stone chilling her thighs through her dress. Alastair was obnoxious, but he'd raised new possibilities. It hadn't occurred to her that the case against Briar would fail if Conrad changed his statement. The case would then likely go cold, because the police would be searching for another doll that didn't exist, and there would be no need to implicate Larkin at all. The relief she felt at this solution told her that whatever anger she harboured against Larkin for stealing, for lying, for laying the blame on Briar, was dwarfed by her need of him. He was despicable, and she loved him.

But she had spoken honestly to Alastair. She didn't believe Conrad would pay her any attention. Who would he listen to then? Hedwig? She might be willing; Persephone remembered the greetings card she sent Briar. And yet, for all Hedwig's influence, the feud between Conrad and Briar was old and ran deep; Persephone didn't believe Hedwig was a match for that.

The singing resumed, a more macabre song this time. Daisy Gilman took the verse in solo.

> Young lad your father asks you,
> "When will you be tamed?"
> Young lad your father asks you,
> "When will you be claimed?
> Don't wander in the snowfall
> Don't skate upon the stream
> Don't daydream in the snowfall
> Don't dawdle on the green
> For the Thief is sure to rob you

And make you do a trade
Yes the Thief is sure to rob you
And say your debt's unpaid."

Persephone smiled. She had thought there was no one more powerful than Conrad on the eyot. But there was – or more importantly, Conrad believed there was. Where she and Hedwig might fail, Conrad would always listen to the Thief.

51

The third day came. It was the twenty-second of December – the eve of Sigillaria; and in the afternoon Hedwig went from door to door with her basket of gingerbread and notes, so that everyone could leave out their share for the Thief that night. It would be the first time Persephone could partake fully in the ritual because she had never before had her hex to do so.

Hedwig rang the bell shortly after two.

"Would you come in for a bit?" Persephone asked.

"I don't have long." Hedwig gestured at the basket, which was three quarters full.

"It's important. I'll help with deliveries afterwards."

"All right – that should be all right. As long as they're given out before dark."

Persephone showed her through the empty living room, to the kitchen, which was the only place where it was possible for them to sit. Hedwig handed over the biscuit doll and the message due to her.

"I'll open it later," Persephone said. "Best just spit this out. Do you think we're sisters?"

Hedwig laughed. "Sorry; it's not funny, really. You sounded so serious and I expected something else."

"It is serious, isn't it?" Persephone asked.

Hedwig fingered the gingham lining of her basket, her eyes lowered.

"Maybe we are sisters," Hedwig said. "And maybe not."

"What does Margot say?"

"She says she doesn't know who my father is, and I believe her. So many men on the eyot are a possibility. Not a Botham man, obviously, but the others. I'm still none the wiser. It's as likely to be a stranger in Selkirk – she lived there a while, you know – or a visiting tourist. Sometimes I'm glad I don't know. There's a certain freedom in being able to imagine your own father. Why do you think it's Briar?"

"A hunch. When I was a child I saw something between him and Margot."

"Hm. Interesting."

"He said you wrote to him in prison. That didn't make any sense to me. Unless you had a hunch he was your dad, too."

"I didn't write to him. Must have been someone else," Hedwig said, but Persephone expected her to deny it, when the action could get her into trouble with the courts.

"He thought it was you. He must think there's a connection between you."

"Connections are borne of all kinds of things – maybe he's holding something over the letter writer. Or maybe the letter writer has reason to be grateful to him. Maybe both."

This contradiction so replicated Persephone's own ambivalence towards Briar that she wondered if Hedwig was being disingenuous by denying his paternity.

"You really don't think he's your dad?"

"What does it matter, anyway?"

"Because if he was, you might help me. I want the police to drop charges against him."

"I don't see how that's possible."

"There is a way, but I need your help. If I explain, and you still don't want to get involved, will you promise not to tell Conrad?" Persephone anticipated this would be a promise too far for Hedwig, but she couldn't risk exposure by proceeding.

"I won't tell a soul," Hedwig said. "You'd be surprised what I've kept from Conrad."

Persephone didn't bother going to bed that night. She opened a book about eighteenth-century miniature portraits, and attempted, but failed, to read it; she maintained this effort until four in the morning, with the bedroom curtains open, bowed before her reflection in the night sky. Then she turned off the lamp. She stretched, and watched the still, moonlit eyot. This was the time she'd agreed with Hedwig.

Larkin's zoetrope stood at the end of her bed. She had assembled it to see its intended form one final time. There they were; twelve Paid Mourners, at a standstill in a circle. Persephone gave them a last spin. She looked through the slats to see the dolls merge into a single illusion of a running girl. First the girl sprinted, then the smoothness of her movement steadily declined, until she split back into her multiple selves, and stopped. Persephone reached inside and detached every doll from its station. She swaddled them in a towel apiece, and packed them, upright, in a rucksack.

Her winter coat, with the plush collar, was dark and would provide some camouflage on the way. There was always a chance she would meet someone before her destination. If so, she would have to claim insomnia, turn back and try again another night. The plan's success depended on her not being seen.

With the rucksack on her back, she left her room and then the house, pulling the front door closed soundlessly. She listened for footfall or voices. But there was only the sway of the trees; a distant ambulance siren; a few notes of robin song, mournful on the breeze.

She walked at speed and as lightly as she could given the load on her back. The straps dug uncomfortably into her flesh. A fox ran from a hedge, causing her to jump. He glanced sideways at her, his chartreuse eyes gleaming palely. But as quickly, he was gone; and she passed through the quince trees. They were leafless, with dried husks of unpicked fruit still on the bough.

She emerged from the orchard to see Conrad's house. An upstairs light was on. This gave her pause; she tried to remember what she knew of the layout. It might be Hedwig, awake as Persephone was, and watching for her arrival. But if it were Conrad – roaming for the bathroom, say – she couldn't risk him seeing her from the window. For now she stayed at a distance, on the shaded side of the path. Though the walk had warmed her limbs her nose was icy and her ears throbbed with cold. She longed for this job to be done, and to be at home, in the warm again.

The light in the house went out. Persephone checked the time on her phone. She waited a further ten minutes, to be on the safe side, squinting for any sign of a face at the window. Finally confident she was unobserved, she walked across the track, through the gate, and up the garden path.

She slid the rucksack from her back and rested it on the doorstep. Her shoulders tingled with the loss of weight. One by one she withdrew the dolls and unwrapped them. She arranged them in a semi-circle before the front door. They were on their backs, in the gravel, pointed feet first. Persephone was glad of their enchantment: twelve small doses of Faith kept her believing the plan would work. She squashed the towels back into the bag and gave the dolls a final look. They were identical to each other, and indistinguishable from the real thing – at least in Persephone's opinion. She hoped Conrad would be of similar mind.

When she reached home again, she ate her half of the gingerbread doll slowly, and opened the envelope containing Conrad's message. *Your grandfather had a gift for prophecy*, it said. *Kendricks may yet be yours*. She yawned, her lack of sleep catching up with her. Cradling her head on the kitchen table she closed her eyes with the intention of a moment's rest before bed. She fell into a doze. During her half-waking, half-slumbering state, her dreams and her surroundings melded confusingly. She roused enough to watch the Thief, on his Winged Horse, pass through the wall from the garden. The kitchen was barely large enough to contain them all. The Thief dismounted, and picked up his share of the gingerbread. He bit the head first.

"Do you like the taste of my Fear?" Persephone asked.

"It's delectable. I watched you tonight. You've been trespassing on my terrain."

"And what are you going to do about it?" she said. "I'm not afraid of you."

"No." She could hear a smile in his voice. "You're not frightened by the same things as other people."

She sank back into sleep again, as he laughed.

52

The sun rose on Sigillaria and Hedwig was awake. She saw the dolls, but didn't touch them. Neither post, nor personal callers, came to cause disruption; and this made it easier to feign, when at ten she roused her master, that she'd woken him as soon as she'd laid eyes upon the new arrivals.

Conrad, coated in his paisley robe, perused the dolls himself, stooping for a close view, though he did not touch them. In bafflement his lips parted.

"What means this display?" he asked. "You say this is exactly as you found them? And you saw no one approach, or leave?"

"I found the dolls, just the dolls, exactly as they are. Why don't you pick one up, Conrad? Any of them."

He eyed her warily. He knelt, with effort, and extended bony fingers to the nearest Mourner. As he touched the wax, he cried: "She bears the right enchantment!"

Hedwig stayed silent, as this knowledge shouldn't already be in her possession.

Shaking, Conrad patted every doll in turn, then fell back on his heels. "I've grasped the truth of it. My brother Briar knew the hex; he told Persephone, and she has used her new sorcery to cast that same enchantment on her copies."

All the care they'd taken to conceal Persephone's arrival! Wasted effort; but the larger game was still to be won. Persephone and Hedwig had discussed an alternative course of action if Conrad guessed correctly how the dolls came to be in his garden.

"You are so astute, Conrad," Hedwig said. "That is the likeliest explanation."

"But whatever can she mean by it?"

"Perhaps she doesn't know."

"Doesn't... know?"

"You've always told me that the Thief on the Winged Horse works through people. Perhaps he did so here; he used Persephone as his channel, to provide you with a gift."

"These dolls are – very beautiful. I couldn't tell them from the work of Lucy Kendrick." Conrad touched the nearest doll again. "I'd like to keep them. What do you believe he wants for them? More gold?"

"He has enough gold." The words felt new and alien – to have *enough gold* was strange for her to contemplate, and to believe was possible. "The Thief may want a more precious thing."

"A feeling."

"Yes."

"My hex; my Rivalry."

"It's deep and long held. Who might be your greatest rival?"

"My brother. Always."

"And you've bested him on every measure. You own the estate; you run a thriving business and that gives you stature. He has nothing but a failed marriage, an excessive taste for drink, and a prison cell. Perhaps the time to drop your rivalry has come?"

"But how?"

"The case depends on your ID of the doll. Lie, Conrad, for your brother. Tell the police you're no longer confident of her provenance. The guarding of enchantments isn't what it was; haven't twelve convincing replicas been left here? You will know the Paid Mourner in the cage is real; so will us all who live here… but the police, the courts, need not. So let the case go cold. Whoever matters will see order is restored by you – because you showed compassion to your brother."

"I must think this over."

"Yes. A man of your sense would never act rashly. I am sure the Thief will wait, for a very little while."

She helped her master stand again. His breathing laboured, heralding a cough; she rubbed his back. They walked to the stairs.

"Please bring those dolls in," Conrad said, with one hand upon the banister. "They must be safe from the elements. I'll take a moment alone to lock them in the cage as soon as I am dressed."

She turned to do as she was told. He hadn't finished.

"What if your advice is wrong?" he asked. "How can I rely on your knowledge of the Thief?"

She smiled her broadest smile. "You know the answer to

that, Conrad. The Thief is my father; who would know his wishes better than I?"

Suspicion faded from Conrad's face.

"Forgive me. I'd let that slip my mind, amidst the morning's strangeness." He placated: "You're a good girl, Hedwig. When you've brought the dolls in, make a start on breakfast."

She watched him scale the marble staircase. Sephy would be waiting for her call; she'd telephone from the kitchen, with the good news.

53

The Archway campus of Central Saint Martins was unprepossessing: flaking, cream, and mansard-roofed, with numerous grid windows. From the opposite pavement Persephone watched students pass in and out through the doors. Not so very long ago Larkin had been one of them. That, at least, he hadn't lied about. Since his departure, Persephone's geography had split into places she recalled being with him, places she knew he had been without her, and the rest of the world. There was also a peculiar, negative group of places she now realised he'd avoided. While working at Kendricks he usually wriggled out of trips through the middle of Oxford with offhand suggestions to take another route or the sudden recollection of somewhere else he had to be. She had noticed his aversion but taken it for a dislike of tourists, which was hardly rare in the town. It didn't occur to her he was avoiding people he knew. Not until he'd gone.

"Are you lost?" A young man, with a buzz cut, had

stopped to ask her. He carried a portfolio case and the heels of his shoes were unevenly worn down.

"No." She scowled. "I'm just early."

He nodded in acknowledgement and continued walking.

Maybe she looked suspicious, staring grimly at a public building for minutes on end. But she needed the time to cool down. She had walked across London, from Paddington Station, and it had taken an hour and a half. These days it was unthinkable to use the Underground. Too many people might be pressed together, their arms and backs disastrously crammed against her own. All she needed was for a ring of strangers to be convinced they loved her from Edgware Road to Tufnell Park. She shuddered.

Bells pealed, four times, from the church around the corner. The same bells he would have heard. It was time for her to go in, and she crossed the road, thinking: he crossed this road, often, for years.

The receptionist let her in and directed her upstairs. Professor Madoc's office was only a single flight up. She had brought with her a Frozen Charlotte, the little bridal doll enchanted with Selflessness. More men would benefit from a Selflessness enchantment, she believed.

"Miss Kendrick!" Madoc greeted her on opening the door. "Do come in. And disregard the mess – it is shameful."

It was barely messy, and she would not have taken it for the office of an artist. He must create elsewhere. This was a room for admin: beech laminate chairs, a blue grey carpet, the cork board upon the wall with various memoranda and flyers.

She took an empty seat.

"I need to know where Larkin is," she said.

"Then you've come to the wrong place. He isn't here."

"But you know him well. You can guess where he's gone, better than me." Persephone took the Frozen Charlotte from her bag, and told him its value. "Take it. Just answer my questions."

Madoc leant against his desk as he turned the doll over for inspection.

"Very well," he said. "I will sing like a canary. But as soon as the conversation is over, I will deny it ever happened."

"What can you tell me about Larkin?"

Madoc laughed. "That isn't his name, for a start. Legally, he's Callum Lorcan. There was a rift from his parents that prompted the change."

"He didn't speak about them," Persephone said. "But I guessed there was some paternity issue – was his father a priest?"

"Assuredly; and the priest is my brother. Miss Lorcan was the housekeeper. A sordid business. While still a minor, Larkin got into some trouble for desecrating a grave. The church is – now I always get it wrong – St Ingrid's?"

"St Ignatius," Persephone said. "The burial place of Jemima Ramsay."

"Yes. You may draw your own conclusion."

"But we were never notified of her grave being desecrated."

"My brother covered it up. Maybe he felt guilty about his bastard offspring. Or maybe he didn't want word to get out, and that was easier if the boy was kept out of trouble."

"And Larkin's not Jemima's descendant?" Persephone asked, remembering her vision of Lucy, and Lucy's insistence Jemima never ran away. "He just lied about that?"

Madoc snorted. "He's a fantasist. Jemima Ramsay's child died, there was no secret lineage – Larkin made the whole thing up, and forged parish records. Eventually, I fear, he came to believe his lie. I've always felt uneasy about my own role in it – you know I love dolls; I may even have pointed out Jemima's grave to him when he was a boy, and perhaps that seeded something. His poor mother has always been utterly bewildered by the story, but then, she shares her portion of blame, too. If you bring up a child telling them to pretend to the world that their family situation is significantly different from the reality, should you be surprised when they weave another familial fiction they prefer? Lies and family secrets were the air he breathed."

"You're in regular contact with his parents?"

"Indeed, though I don't often update them of Larkin's whereabouts. If he thought I was too pally with them, he'd cut me out, too."

"So there's no chance his mother knows where he is?"

"I doubt that very much." Madoc pursed his lips and shook his head. "He tried to maintain as much distance between them as possible. I'm afraid he'll avoid you in the same way. He's very slippery, and you can be sure he's already left the country."

"Does he have *any* other family?"

"His wife, obviously."

Persephone swallowed. "Larkin's married?"

"Technically; the union is more often in the breach than the observance. She's Italian, from a doll-making family in Florence. Her father hated Larkin – he thought Maria had been led astray. She did end up in a lot of trouble, she even spent a spell in prison for fraud, I believe, but the girl was capricious without Larkin's help. These days she continues to do a fine line in art forgeries, under a pseudonym, and she tends to be secretive about her whereabouts. She and Larkin are one of those tiresome couples who explosively split up and reunite at regular intervals."

This was not the account Persephone had hoped for, though it made an intuitive sense. "They must love each other, to try again."

"Love? Good lord, no. Larkin likes having money and she has plenty of it. Normally he goes back when he runs out, and he's canny enough to offer her something in return."

"This time he has the enchantments."

"Yes – but in fact he hasn't offered them to her – as of yesterday morning she doesn't know where he is any more than you do. She rang me to check if I knew anything."

Don't read too much into that, Persephone warned herself. It was dangerous to think he had ended his marriage because he was pining for her.

"I suppose it's only a matter of time until he sells the enchantments to someone. He can tell who he likes."

"Does that thought bother you?"

"No," she said with certainty. Keeping enchantments a secret had done her no favours. Having fought to access the enchantments herself, how could she protest other people doing the same? It would affect business, no doubt. But who said Kendricks deserved to benefit from contrived scarcity? The knowledge wasn't their property, although they had convinced themselves it was.

"My dear," Madoc said. "Why are you looking for him?"

"Why do you think? It's safe for him to come back again now; I fixed things so that I didn't have to tell the police."

"It would be better to forget him. I'm fond of him, as you know. In his own way he's fond of me, or so I hope. But the only way to engage with him is on very narrow terms. He is incapable of ordinary depths of feeling."

"He once told me that envy is the only real emotion," Persephone remembered. "And love and happiness could only be felt with the help of enchantments."

"What is it people say – when someone tells you who they are, believe them? I've always suspected that Larkin feels less than most people do, and that's behind his bad behaviour – a drive for *sensation*, because ordinary things don't get through to him. He wanted the enchantments for the same reason. They give him something he's missing. He lacks a conscience, he shirks responsibility, he is impulsive, and he doesn't understand what truly loving someone is. What a vacuum to fill!"

"But he could fill it, if he wore the right enchantments all the time."

"He won't. Larkin enjoys the transient thrill of un-accustomed emotion; that is not the same thing as wanting to be a better person. He is now a Sorcerer; if he were willing to permanently develop the qualities he lacked, he could do so himself. And if he did, perhaps he would no longer be the same person, in any meaningful sense." He paused. "Ask yourself this, Persephone; I believe, when he stole the Paid Mourner, he was armed. Do you think – if his escape had depended on it – he would hesitate to use that knife?"

The question was pertinent. Her hope that things might

still come right was false, and his words made her confront a harder truth.

"Do you know," she said softly, "I'd love Larkin no matter how he behaved, as long as his talent remained. That means I'm not a very nice person."

"But it's natural you should love him for his talent. It is the one truly good thing about him."

"He said he saw my talent, too. I'm scared he's taken it with him."

"Tosh. I saw your creations in the catalogue, Miss Kendrick, and it is obvious you are your own artist. Believe me – I've taught for more years than I care to admit. You will be fine."

In her lower back, Persephone felt the familiar cramp that augured her period. She had never taken the emergency contraception, and now she knew there was no need. It was a relief – for she doubted that she would be a decent parent, and knew Larkin would be less so – and yet it was also the loss of a fantasy, that she and Larkin might be the kind of people with that kind of mundanely meaningful future, making a family and a business.

She took a blister packet of painkillers from her bag. "I need some water."

Madoc walked to a water fountain in the corner, and filled a paper cup, which he brought back to her. She swallowed the chalky tablets and drained the cup.

"I'm sorry I wasted your time." Persephone closed her bag.

"No, no – not at all. I'm only sorry I couldn't give you better news."

He reached out to shake her hand.

"I don't do that," she said.

"Very sensible." He gestured towards the door. She saw, as she had not when she entered, a small automaton to the right of the frame. It stood upon a plinth. The work was clearly Larkin's. The material was battered tin, and the subject was a young woman, her flesh dimpled and undulating from the impressions of the hammer.

"It's the Maiden of Spring," Madoc said, seeing where her attention had fallen.

"May I activate it?"

"Be my guest."

She turned the handle at the side. The maiden touched the rocks around her, and a series of ceramic flowers spiralled from their crevices. They reminded Persephone of the porcelain wreaths that Victorians had laid upon graves. But the strangest thing of all was the feeling that swept over her. An unaccountable, Uncovered Grief.

"When did he give this to you?" she asked.

"It was in my pigeon hole, two days ago."

She accepted then, for the first time, that he had really left. It would be easy to interpret the doll as a portrait of her – and the Grief as Larkin's regret, for what he had thrown away. That might have sent her deeper into denial that they were over. But she grasped that you only grieve what is dead.

54

On the second of January, Persephone went to work early. Now no one could say that she was trespassing if she strayed from the service counter. The building was empty, apart from Rieko, who was contemplating the Interior Design floor with dissatisfaction. Persephone wondered what Rieko was distracting herself from to be there before anyone else. Possibly Alastair was yet to forgive her betrayal, as he saw it.

"The whole building needs reorganisation," Rieko said. "The current arrangement is impractical; six men take up the top floor, the whole floor, and as doll makers they have least need of the space! Building and decorating houses requires a far larger working area."

"Let's look at areas of overlap," Persephone suggested. "The tools for wooden doll-making and wooden house-building should be in the same place. There's no need for wooden dolls to be made on the same floor as ceramic or metal or cloth ones. House design and interior design should happen in the same space, too, surely?"

The two women commenced a tour of the building, labelling equipment and tables with Post-its signalling where they should be moved to. On the third floor, Persephone saw Larkin's workbench, still bearing the last project he was working on: a porcelain shoulder bust, with a kid leather body. The torso was half stitched, with the needle jabbed into the doll's heart till work resumed.

Rieko put a Post-it on the bench top. "This should be moved one floor down, along with the others."

"Hm. Yes."

"We also need to do something about *this*." Rieko tapped her foot on the glass floor. "To make it walkable for anyone with a skirt."

"Most of the workers wear overalls."

"You don't."

"No. But we can't cover the floor. It lets natural light through the building."

"We could obscure it," Rieko said. "There's frosting spray in the paint store."

"All right. If we do that now, it'll be dry before everyone else is back at work."

They fetched several cans between them, donned respirators, and fastened aprons. They opened the skylights, letting in the cold January air. Persephone took one corner furthest from the paternoster, and Rieko took the other. Together they worked quickly and neatly, creating arcs of mist on the floor below.

"We can't do much more now till we have more hands on deck," Persephone commented.

"No," Rieko said. "We should wait for the others to arrive."

"I was just thinking," Persephone said. "I could guide you in some doll-making today. If you'd like a lesson."

"I could instruct you in furniture-making, as an exchange. What type of doll should we make?"

"Porcelain dolls," Persephone said. "Have you done that before?"

Rieko shook her head. "I've only used wood. I know how to whittle, because I use that in furnishings; and I've tried whittling dolls in my free time. I've picked up basic points about jointing dolls just from watching Alastair work at home."

"You probably know more than you think."

"Did you know that it's highly prestigious, in Japan, to be a ceramicist?"

"No."

"I thought that might have informed your interest, if your mother had told you."

"She didn't. My mother's more British than Japanese." And they spoke infrequently. The sacrifice had finally paid off; Persephone won her hex, and all the sorcery she could wish for, years after letting her mother leave alone. It might still be some time before Persephone knew if her decision was the right one. She hoped their relationship could still be mended.

"Do you think the collectors should hear that things are changing around here?" Rieko asked. "*Everyone* at Kendricks could make a doll – and lay an enchantment upon it for sale. And we'll advertise it to our customers as a new collection. Except – I don't know if I can make something good enough for sale."

"Make something that says exactly what you want it

to," Persephone responded. "That tells the collectors you're *here*. Don't worry about making them like it."

Rieko laughed. "That's no way to succeed in business, Seph."

So they heated the kiln. They chose plaster moulds from the Sorcerers' shelves. Each mould split in half, and contained the impression of a limb or a head. Most had been cast from the Sorcerers' own clay figurines. A few used Lucy Kendrick's china dolls as a model, which allowed the Sorcerers to make sculptural replicas of her work, and modify them as they wished through the choice of glazes or wigs. It was one of Lucy's designs that Persephone and Rieko settled upon.

As Persephone arranged the heavy plaster cubes across the workbench, she judged herself to be a hypocrite because she had told Rieko to ignore other people's expectations of her work, and to focus solely on what she wanted to say. But for the past several months Persephone had been driven by a desire to be as good, as skilled, as Larkin, and to have him tell her so.

She forced herself to speak, because Rieko was awaiting her instructions.

"Notice the size of these moulds," Persephone said. "They need to be larger than the finished doll, because there will be shrinkage from firing and sanding. Now let's prepare the slip."

She opened the mixture of water, minerals, and white kaolin that made up the porcelain paste, and explained it must be watered down to form a slippery liquid.

"Keep adding water, and keep stirring it, to get rid of the

bubbles," Persephone said. Rieko did so, while Persephone found a square of nylon for straining the mixture. When it was the right consistency, without any lumps of paste remaining, Persephone held the moulds while Rieko tipped the slip into them. It would take fifteen minutes for the slip layer to thicken. Accordingly, Persephone and Rieko swapped roles; they discussed Persephone learning to make her own, diminutive furnishings.

"I'd like to get you working on chairs, first of all," Rieko was saying. "Maybe some nice modernist designs, with clean lines, would be a good learning project."

"That sounds good." How odd it would be, to be taught by a new person. Would she fall in love with Rieko too, given enough lessons? For Rieko excelled in her field as Larkin did in his. Persephone couldn't imagine falling in love again at all. Perhaps that was for the best; rather than follow her heart, which was self-evidently flawed in its inclinations, she should dispassionately choose a partner on objective merit, then lick the hex for Love upon their skin, just as she had upon her own.

Rieko talked about Arne Jacobsen and Ray Eames, Eero Aarnio and Hans Wegner; Persephone took mental notes until the slip layer was ready. They removed the pieces from the moulds so Persephone could show Rieko the seams that had been left in the clay. She demonstrated the scraping smooth of the legs and arms and head using a knife. Where parts must be adhered, she did so with slip, and kept them hydrated all the time, so they wouldn't crack.

They could hear voices on the floor below. People were finally arriving to start the new year of work.

"The doll will be in the kiln for hours," Persephone said. "If you have the time – I'd love to learn how to make that chair."

"I'm glad we're sharing," Rieko said. "We *will* make something good here, won't we?"

She moved forward to embrace Persephone, and Persephone flinched to evade her touch, lest Rieko feel the enchantment upon her. Rieko leant back immediately. Persephone feared she had caused offence. She regretted doing so, when their support for each other's work was so new. But Rieko wasn't offended. She was looking at Persephone with concern – and yes; love. For why shouldn't she care about Persephone? She had known her a long time; since Persephone was a little girl, the same age that Sara, Rieko's daughter, was now. Rieko had been there when Persephone received her hex. She had heard Persephone announce, the same day, that she would be a Sorcerer – and now they both had any number of enchantments at their fingertips. If the eyot had been different, less rigid and paranoid, Persephone might have noticed before now there were people who worried about her. Among the possible consequences of disturbing the order at Kendricks, Persephone had not anticipated that it would be easier to offer, and accept, friendship.

"We'll make something good," Persephone agreed. "We've already started."

55

Persephone waited, on the Iffley Road, for the taxi to pull over. It stopped on the opposite side of the street from her, and a door opened, revealing a man in his sixties, freshly shaven, in a threadbare coat. Her father. He waved at the driver when he'd shut the door.

"Sorry I'm late," he called to her.

She was merely relieved that he was sober, having half feared the reason for his lateness was a celebratory trip to the pub.

Briar looked both ways and half walked, half ran across the road. He inclined in her direction, a gesture towards embracing, but she kept her distance.

"The journey was OK?" Persephone checked.

He nodded.

"Good." She walked to the footbridge, with him falling in line behind her.

"There's something I need to tell you," he said.

Her heart beat faster. She needed to tell him something as

well. Ideally she would have told him away from the eyot, perhaps even before he was released, but things had moved faster than she had imagined after Conrad withdrew his identification of the doll.

"I'm still drinking," he said. "But only because it's dangerous to withdraw everything at once. I've been having just enough to prevent the DTs. But there's a rehab programme I'm going to start in two weeks. They didn't have a place till then."

The development might have pleased Persephone, but she saw it as a fragile statement of intent, easily broken in the wrong circumstances – which she may be about to create.

"That's good, Dad." She paused. "Listen. It would be good if you worked on getting better in your own space. You need a fresh start. And so do I. We shouldn't be living in the same house any more."

A flake of snow fell on her eyelash. She brushed it away, watching the path ahead rather than Dad's reaction.

"Where should I go?" he asked. He sounded sad; not angry – and in some ways that was worse.

"For now, your old place on the terrace. But – if we can find you somewhere else near the eyot—"

"I think it's a good idea," he said suddenly.

"You do?"

"I don't want to live on the eyot. Not after... everything. They all see me the same way, Sephy. They think I'm a drunk, and a failed son, and a failed father. A criminal."

He wouldn't believe her if she contradicted him. She pointed out: "Everyone here has failed at something. They can fuck off, with their opinions."

"Maybe I'll fail less, elsewhere."

Persephone changed the subject. "I've been making new dolls. All with enchantments."

She felt it was safe to look at him, for his reaction. His eyes crinkled with amusement.

"I bet you're better than any of the Sorcerers," he said.

"I *am* a Sorcerer," she said. "Conrad says so."

"And only a fool would argue with *him*."

She laughed. "*Sorcerer* doesn't mean the same thing any more. They're not keepers of secrets. I promised all the other members of staff I'd teach them every hex I have, no matter what Alastair does. Soon they'll all know what I know. Every day, everything changes more."

"Good."

"Dad. Do you want to come to the workshop? Other people will be there. But you could see what I've been working on—"

"I'd love to," he said.

So instead of stopping at the terrace of cottages, they went on to Kendricks. Neither of them spoke as they walked up the steps. In the foyer, Dennis was altering the lists of descendants on the wall. He had sanded Larkin's name away, leaving Jemima Ramsay's plaque blank again. A pale halo, where the wood had been revarnished, was visible if you knew where to look for it. She wondered where Larkin was now.

"Look," Briar said, pointing. Dennis had stencilled, in black outline, a word next to Persephone's name. He was about to fill the letters in gold. The word was *Sorcerer*. "Someone still thinks the title matters."

It did make her happy to see it there – for wasn't that what she'd always wanted?

"Here, Dennis," Briar said. "Let me have that brush."

A little perplexed, but willing to oblige, Dennis stepped down from the ladder and allowed Briar to go up in his place. Briar gilded each stem and serif, as Persephone held her breath, waiting for his hand to shake. But it did not. His poise held.

"Daddy?" she asked, as he finished.

"What? Don't you like it?"

"I love it. Can you add *Sorcerer* to everyone's name?"

"Steady on," said Dennis, and Persephone laughed. Briar did as she asked; he stencilled the word *Sorcerer* next to every living resident, and when he was done, he filled the letters with gold. Persephone watched the bright lacquer spread across the surface, thinking of the women just a few yards away, making dolls and rooms and houses to put them in, finally permitted to feel as they wished; to wield fear and anger and hope and love in whichever way they chose. Yes, they had all made changes. And there would be more to come.